BEAUTIFULLY MADE

ERIC ADOLPH

ADOLPH LITERARY

How we live is all that matters, not who made us, or out of what parts! Free will is what we make of it.

—Yukito Kishiro

A BAD DAY

Cara hung from her seatbelt, upside-down in the passenger seat of the overturned car. Painful spasms lanced through her neck as she turned towards the driver's seat. Adam's face looked red and bruised from the airbag, but he was breathing.

"Adam? Adam, are you okay?"

He moaned. Cara reached over to feel his neck with her fingertips. His pulse was strong and regular. She grabbed his dangling arm and squeezed. He groaned and blinked his eyes.

"Wha …?"

"How do you feel?"

"My head hurts. And my chest. Where are we? What happened?"

Suddenly he gasped. "Linnea?"

"Here," his younger sister said from the back seat, her voice weak. "My arm is killing me and there's an awful lot of blood. I feel sleepy."

Cara shouted, "Stay awake, Linnea. It's important."

Cara struggled to exit the vehicle, but a tree blocked her escape. Her heart raced as she broke out in a sweat.

Adam pushed against his door and opened it part-way. There was a sharp report, then the whine of a bullet ricocheting off the door, slamming it shut. "What the heck? Seriously? Someone's shooting at us."

"That's what caused us to crash," replied Cara. "Linnea needs medical care."

With trembling hands, she grabbed her cellphone from her pocket and dialed 911.

"Nine one one, what is your emergency?"

"We need help," she told the dispatcher. "We're on County Road 400 North, about two miles west of town. Our car crashed. Someone's shooting at us. A tree is blocking my door. There's three of us here, and we can't get out. Our little sister is bleeding. Send police and an ambulance."

Cara listened for a moment. Then she clenched her jaw and shook her head before responding. "Of course, I sound young. I *am* young. The three of us were on our way to school when we crashed."

She listened again. "Look, this is no prank. It sounded like gunshots. Then we lost control of our car and rolled." She paused. "We can't get out of the car. The shooter is still there and my door won't open. Yes, I'll stay on the line. Hurry, please."

Another gunshot hit the overturned car.

"Adam, I'm worried they'll hit the gas tank. That would be it for us. I hate like hell to do this, but I'm going to let Her help us. I don't see how we have a choice."

Adam nodded. "Linnea, close your eyes till you hear Her leave the car, but don't let yourself fall asleep."

Sirens, faint in the distance, rapidly grew louder. Minutes later, two police cars, two ambulances, and a firetruck stopped on the road above the now-burning husk of Adam's Toyota. Four officers approached the wreckage, weapons drawn.

The three young people rested on the embankment at a safe distance from the ruined vehicle. Linnea lay beside Adam as he held pressure on her right upper arm. Blood covered his hand and spattered the front of his shirt, but Linnea's active bleeding had slowed considerably.

White smoke emanated from the front end of the over-turned vehicle. Both driver's side doors were open; the front passenger door, mangled like a crushed soda can, hung limply from the remnants of a hinge. An uprooted tree lay beside the car.

A female police officer spoke to the teens as she scanned the surroundings for danger.

"I'm Officer Bright. Are you three okay?"

"My name is Cara Ferris. I'm the one who called for help."

She moved as though to climb to her feet, but Officer Bright motioned for her to stay down.

"Your report mentioned gunshots."

"From down the road that way," Cara said as she pointed in the direction the car had been heading. "But the shooting stopped about five minutes ago. My sister needs help. They hit her in the arm, and she's lost a lot of blood."

"Got it. By the way, the dispatcher sends her apology. We've had several prank calls recently."

"What convinced her I was for real?"

"You kept the line open as she asked. She heard more gunshots."

An officer checked the overturned car, pronounced it clear, then joined the other two officers proceeding in the direction Cara had pointed, guns still drawn.

The paramedics examined Linnea, stabilized her neck, and transferred her to a cot. One gave her oxygen, started an IV and hung a bag of fluid, while the other applied a field dressing to her arm.

Adam protested he felt okay except for facial and chest discomfort, but the medics convinced him to allow them to place him on a cot as well. Cara denied any pain other than facial tenderness.

Officer Bright surveyed the wreckage. "How did you three escape from the car?"

"Once the shooting stopped, I could climb out and carry Linnea up here to safety," Adam said.

"What happened to that tree by the passenger side of the car?"

"I don't know, officer. I guess the car knocked it over?"

"That's not how it works. When a car hits a tree, the car usually loses." Officer Bright looked speculatively at Cara. "You were riding in the passenger seat, correct?"

"Yes, ma'am."

"The dispatcher's report said that a tree was blocking your door and you couldn't get out. This one looks like it was ripped out by the roots. And what happened to the passenger-side door of the car?"

Cara shrugged.

By the time the ambulances arrived at the ER, Adam's adrenaline had worn off, and he felt drowsy. The background sounds of a busy emergency room seemed far away, like on TV.

"Linnea Samuelson, thirteen-year-old female, rollover MVA, presumed gunshot to right upper extremity. Blood pressure 90 over 40, heart rate 134. GCS 15. Sat 98 on 5 liters O2, and we hung a bag of LR."

"Shock Room Two. I'll meet you there."

"Yes, doctor."

Their mom and dad met them in the ER. From his examination room, Adam heard the emergency room physician speaking with them.

"I'm Doctor Sally Thomas. Your kids say you're both in the medical field. A physician and a nurse, correct?"

Katie Samuelson nodded. "I'm an ICU nurse at University Hospital, and Stephen is a physician on staff there."

"Let's talk about Linnea first. She was alert and fully oriented on arrival here. She has a superficial right upper arm injury consistent with a rifle bullet. Another centimeter and the cavitation effect would have shattered her humerus and severed her brachial artery. Her x-rays are …"

The doctor's voice faded as she and his parents moved away. A few minutes later, they returned close enough for Adam to hear the rest of their conversation.

"They'll be moving her to the surgery floor shortly for observation. The ward clerk will know the room number."

"That's good news," Katie replied.

"Adam and Cara have facial contusions from the airbags. Adam's chest may have struck the steering wheel, but I didn't see any rib fractures on x-ray. Their neck films are both clear. Adam broke his nose, again probably from the airbag, but it's not displaced and should heal fine."

"Thank you, doctor."

THAT AFTERNOON, the family was in Linnea's hospital room. The door opened, and a balding man in a rumpled suit entered.

"Detective Anders," Stephen Samuelson said. "I want to say it's good to see you again, but we only seem to meet when something violent happens."

The two men shook hands, and Detective Anders nodded to the rest of the family.

"I'm glad there were no serious injuries, but we need to talk. Is it okay for us to discuss this here so Linnea can participate?"

Stephen looked at his wife. "Honey?"

Katie nodded. "That's fine."

"I read the report from the officers on the scene, and I looked through the photos. You may not be aware, but we found the shooter."

"Thank God," Cara said. "Who was he? Why us?"

Anders shook his head slowly, lips pressed together. "We found the remains of him and his spotter by their car several hundred yards down the road from where your vehicle rolled over. They were on a hill, so they would have had a good view as you three approached."

Cara raised an eyebrow. "Their remains?"

"We'll need DNA and dental records to ID them. How much do you remember?"

Cara shrugged. "We were on our way to school. Adam was driving, as usual. I heard gunshots. The windshield starred. Linnea screamed ..."

"Then I suddenly lost c-control," Adam continued. "My car pulled strongly to the right. It felt like I lost a tire. There wasn't much of a shoulder along that part of the road. We rolled off the embankment. I felt dazed for a short t-time when the airbag went off, but I don't think I lost consciousness. When I opened my door, there were more gunshots. We had no way to escape the car."

"Cara, you told the dispatcher there was a tree blocking your door, correct?"

She hesitated, pursing her lips and rubbing her temples as she gathered her thoughts. "I saw a tree there. Maybe it wasn't blocking the door. Maybe the door was just stuck. Someone was shooting at us, and it scared me."

"Cara, remember what I told you the last time I spoke with you and your family," Anders said. "I promised you I'll do whatever I can to help you. But I can't afford to make assumptions. I don't know for sure what happened to the shooter and his colleague, though of course I have a suspicion.

"You were stuck in an overturned car, your sister injured and bleeding out, and someone was shooting at you with a high-powered rifle. Under those conditions, I won't judge you for allowing your … um … Her to help."

Cara intently studied the detective's face. Her eyes narrowed, and she frowned. Finally, she nodded. "Okay, detective," she said in a soft voice. "I asked Her to make the shooting stop."

Anders tented his fingers. "I've also been on the phone with Special Agent Tanaka. We believe this attack on you young people is related to the incident with Mikhail Sokolov."

"He's dead," Adam said.

"That's true, but his son, Pyotr Sokolov, is very alive."

"I don't understand," Stephen said.

"Pyotr Sokolov arrived at his parents' mansion a short while after the FBI got there," Anders said. "He was quite angry at the devastation in his home, as you can imagine. He swore revenge."

"No, I don't buy that," Cara said, shaking her head. "Someone broke into his house, so he decided to kill three teenagers on their way to school? Doesn't make sense."

Detective Anders rubbed his chin and pursed his lips. "Cara, you were *in* Mikhail Sokolov's office at the end. Do you not remember who else was there?"

She shook her head, brow furrowed.

He turned to Linnea. "Do you remember what happened in Sokolov's office?"

"No, detective," Linnea said. "Like I told you when you asked me after my rescue, I just remember he was trying to kill me, and I must have hit my head. Then Cara and Adam arrived and found him dead."

"Linnea, I understand you want to protect Cara and so you're limiting what you say. That's admirable, but this isn't the time."

Linnea stared at Detective Anders and shrugged, her lips set, her face impassive.

Anders paced the length of the room in silence, then returned to the Samuelsons and Cara. "Fine. The FBI found Sokolov's wife lying dead in the office close to him."

"What am I m-missing?" Adam asked. "What's this have to do with us?"

"Special Agent Tanaka said Pyotr and his mother were very close. When Pyotr saw his mom lying dead in the office, he swore he would find whoever was responsible and make them pay."

Cara leaped suddenly to her feet. Her chair flew backward and toppled to the carpet with a dull thud.

"Enough!" she shouted. "I'm done with the damn Sokolovs trying to kill my family and me. Detective, take care of this or so help me God …"

Cara caught her breath, and her voice broke. "*She* will."

Anders stood as well. "Is this a threat, Cara?"

"Detective, you know I have minimal control over Her. If you can't or won't protect us from this Pyotr Sokolov, I'm afraid She will decide to handle the problem. And heaven help any innocent people nearby."

MY FATHER'S CHAIR

*P*yotr Sokolov scanned the row of large brick warehouses. The sun was setting. Long shadows gave the warehouses a sinister look. The buildings were new eighty years ago and hadn't aged well. This area, near the waterfront, was bustling with activity during the workday. Now, all was quiet.

He maneuvered his red Ducati Monster 1200 R into the parking area behind the second warehouse from the left. He turned off his engine. Silence replaced the low growl of the Monster. He removed his riding goggles then placed them carefully in a soft case in the pocket of his leather jacket.

The warehouse loomed before him. A weathered sign that was missing several letters advertised that this building was home to a fruit and vegetable seller. Below the sign was a rusty service door. Pyotr approached and knocked once. The door opened, and he stepped into a small room with a scuffed linoleum floor. A stack of metal bins covered one wall. Behind a weather-beaten wooden table, an extremely large, bald man rose from a chair to face the newcomer.

"Remove your weapons. Put them on the table," the guard said in a deep voice.

Pyotr nodded and slowly removed a semiautomatic pistol from a waist holster. The man stared at him. Pyotr shrugged and pulled up his right pants leg to reveal an ankle holster with a small derringer. He removed that as well and placed it on the table beside his larger handgun. Then he held out his arms. The guard patted him down and grunted affirmatively. He pulled a numbered tab from one of the empty metal bins and handed the tab to Pyotr, who pocketed it without a word. The large man placed the two handguns in the bin and closed it.

"Downstairs."

"Thank you."

Pyotr walked through the anteroom to the doorway on the far side. He descended the concrete steps to the lower level. Another metal door blocked his progress. He noted an armored video camera high on the wall to one side. He smiled at the camera and pressed the button by the door. A guard on the other side opened it, revealing an ornate conference room. Men in business suits occupied most of the velvet-cushioned chairs around a massive teak table; only a couple of women sat at the table.

As Pyotr entered, the conversation suddenly ceased. Several men frowned at Pyotr's casual attire. He ignored them.

Anton Kuznetsov, balding and overweight, was seated near the door. He half-rose from his chair and nodded. "Pyotr, what a pleasure to see you here. So sorry about your parents."

"I can imagine you're devastated, Anton," Pyotr said. His face was blank.

"Ordinarily I would love to visit with you, Pyotr, but as you can see, there are important people here having a meeting. This is no place for children." He sat back down and turned to a colleague to continue their conversation.

Pyotr didn't move. "How long, Anton?" he said. "How long after my father's murder did you wait before you claimed my father's chair? Was his body still warm?"

"I don't know what you're talking about."

"Ah, but I think you do." Pyotr walked closer to the man, still speaking in a conversational tone. "You met with him that afternoon before he died. And now here you are. In. His. Chair."

Anton wiped sweat from his brow. His voice rose, indignant. "We had a business meeting over lunch. Then I left. And that's what you need to do now. Leave."

"I came home to chaos. Someone shut down our security systems and committed extreme violence in my father's house. All our people were dead or unconscious. My parents were lying dead in his office. I was holding my mother's head in my lap when the FBI came."

"Yes. We all grieve for your loss."

"Do you, now? This must have been an inside job, my friend. Someone who knew my father well." Pyotr rested his hand on the man's shoulder familiarly, as though they were buddies. He leaned even closer. "Someone my father trusted."

Anton could sense his colleagues watching him; he felt the weight of their gaze. *One must not show weakness.* "I told you. We spoke, then my men and I left. I heard what happened the next day, like everyone else.

"Now what exactly do you hope to accomplish here, Petya?" Pyotr frowned at the insulting diminutive of his name. "Your father is dead. His men that survived are in prison. His business is gone. And I mean no offense, little boy, but you don't have half the balls of your father. Now go play somewhere. We have business to attend."

He tried to turn away from Pyotr as he had done earlier,

but Pyotr's hand was still on his shoulder. His grip was stronger than Anton had expected, and he could not turn his chair.

"Antosha," Pyotr said with a silky voice. "You swore loyalty to my father. You should have stayed." In a smooth move with his free hand, keeping it low so that the others at the table could not see until he accomplished the deed, he pulled a knife that the cursory examination by the guard upstairs had missed. He plunged the thin blade under Anton's ribs, through his spleen and part of his stomach, and up through his diaphragm toward his heart. Anton moaned and slumped forward. Pyotr patted his right shoulder in a friendly way. He withdrew his blade, casually wiped it on Anton's jacket, and returned it to its sheath. Then he stared around the table at the people seated there.

"I will find whoever murdered my parents. I will kill them. I will kill their family, and I will burn their house to the ground. But for now, I will start by claiming my father's chair. Does anyone have any objections?" He waited. One after another, the other crime lords shook their heads. "Excellent. Then I need this trash removed from *my* seat." The host snapped his fingers, and two guards jumped up and carried the dead man off.

Pyotr Sokolov sat down in his father's chair. Finally. Within hours, his father's suppliers and various other business interests would learn of the change at the helm. *The man once known as Anton Kuznetsov made the mistake of underestimating him. They'll see now. They'll all see.*

The host, a stocky man with beefy shoulders and a nose flattened from many fights, hair just turning gray at the temples, turned, and addressed Pyotr. "Now you have taken over for your father. What do you request of us?"

Pyotr considered the question before answering. "I need men I can trust, guns, and a few other things." He pulled a small notebook from his pocket and read from the list he'd made.

"Very well," the host said. "It shall be as you request. We will bill your account." He motioned with his arm in a wide gesture to encompass everyone seated at the massive table. "What is the next order of business?"

LATER THAT NIGHT, Pyotr returned to his father's mansion for the second time since his parents' death. The first time, of course, was when the FBI wanted to speak with him soon after the incident. Agents swarmed his parents' estate and took with them anything they thought might be evidence. This included the security camera data and his father's office computer. But he thought perhaps the FBI didn't find everything.

Pyotr headed for his father's office. He smiled when he found the hidden camera high on a bookshelf. This camera was not wired nor on the home Wi-Fi network; it recorded, without transmitting, to its own local SD memory card. From his satchel, Pyotr produced a thin laptop and an adapter. He booted his computer, inserted the SD card into the adapter, and played the video.

A vent in the office ceiling opens and a young girl drops to the floor. After locking the door, she walks to the computer on Pyotr's father's desk and works for a few minutes. She attaches a plastic dry cleaning bag to the bottom of the office door, using duct tape, then she places a bucket and two bottles inside the plastic. She finds some items in the bathroom between the office and the indoor pool, and arranges them on the desk beside an ashtray.

Loud banging on the door. The girl pours chemicals from the bottles into the bucket, and yellow-green gas flows under the door.

Loud crash of a shotgun. The office door flies open, and his father storms in. As he enters, he trips on the dry cleaning bag and falls. The little girl pours a mixture of chemicals from the ashtray onto his chest and face as he lies on the ground. The brew clings to his clothing and flesh, smokes for several seconds, then spontaneously bursts into flames. He tries to brush it off, then rushes the girl. She somehow is holding the handgun Pyotr's father kept hidden in his desk. He grabs her and throws her against a wall. She swings the gun at his face and tries to escape, but even as his clothing burns, he leaps, grabs the girl, and attacks her with his bare hands.

Pyotr's mother, still in a wet swimsuit, enters the office from the pool. Simultaneously, a beautiful woman darts in the door, moving inhumanly fast. She heads towards his father and the girl. His mother tries to protect her husband, but the beautiful woman backhands his mother once, sending her flying across the office. She lands against a large potted plant and lies unmoving. The unknown woman grabs Pyotr's father and brutalizes him, using only her hands. He dies almost instantly from horrific injuries, still burning. The mysterious and deadly woman changes, becoming a teen girl with a prominent facial scar. She and the little girl hug each other and cry. A tall young man with a shock of dark hair enters the office, picks up the younger girl, and the three leave the office.

Pyotr Sokolov reversed the video and paused it on his mother lying motionless on the ground. He winced when he noticed the unnatural position of her head indicative of a broken neck. Her eyes were open but unseeing. She was clearly dead. His fingers trembled on the keyboard. He took a deep, shuddery breath.

"Mama!" He buried his face in his hands, and he sobbed.

AS YOU LOVE ME

Two days after the crash, the doctor released Linnea to home with a sling and a dressing on her upper arm. Due to blood loss from her wound, she didn't have her usual energy. Katie settled Linnea in a chair in the backyard so she could get some fresh air. Cara and Adam sat with her to keep her company.

"Linnea, I need to talk to you," Cara said in a strained voice.

"What's going on?" Linnea asked.

Cara stood and paced back and forth, her hands clenched. She was breathing rapidly, eyes wide. Suddenly, she stopped and turned to Linnea. "I need you to be honest with me."

"Of course. You're my sister, for all intents and purposes. What would you like me to tell you?"

"Linnea, what happened in Sokolov's office?"

"You know what happened. Sokolov was about to kill me. You came just in time and saved my life. I owe you more than I can ever tell you."

"Did I kill Sokolov?"

Linnea looked at the older girl. "Yes, you … I mean, Her

… She saw him attack me and She was so angry … like a force of nature … like the wrath of God. She spoke some words in a language I've never heard, like She did in the home invasion last winter … and She destroyed him. I'm sure he was dead in seconds. Nobody could fight Her.

"I fell to the ground and lay there till it was over. Then you were hugging me and we were crying. Adam found us there."

"Was there anyone else in the office before Adam came?"

Linnea was silent, staring at the ground.

Cara gave an anguished cry. "You must tell me. Was there anybody else in the office?"

Linnea sobbed. Still looking at the ground, she said in a soft voice, "It wasn't your fault."

Cara grabbed Linnea's good arm and screamed. "Tell me!"

Linnea just shook her head without speaking. Her cheeks were wet with tears, eyes clenched shut.

"If you care about me at all, Linnea, you'll tell me. Who else was there? Please."

Adam's little sister spoke to her feet, so softly Cara could hardly make out the words. "When I searched his office, I saw the indoor pool on the other side of his bathroom. But I didn't go in there, and I didn't notice anyone swimming."

"Go on."

"She must have heard the commotion. A lady in a swimsuit came through the door just as you entered the office. I yelled at her to stay back, but she ran to Sokolov. She tried to protect him, I think, but your … I don't know what to call it."

"My demon."

"No. But She backhanded the lady once. Sent her flying across the desk and she collapsed. She didn't move after that and you … I mean your … She didn't pay any further attention to her. It wasn't your fault."

Cara's face was a mask of pain. Linnea hugged her

fiercely, still crying. "It wasn't your fault. You couldn't help it. It wasn't your fault. You saved my life."

"I killed an innocent person. I really am a monster."

"No, Cara," Adam said. "You're b-brave and kind and smart." He tried to hold her, but she pulled away from him.

"I killed a lady I didn't even know. A lady who did nothing to me, who did nothing to you. She didn't deserve to die." She raised her voice. "My monster didn't care, but I do."

"Cara, p-please …"

"No, I can't. I can't allow this monster inside me to live, to keep on killing. It's time to put an end to it." She fell to her knees, hands clasped in front of her.

Adam knelt beside her, resting his hand gently on her shoulder.

"Cara? How can I help?"

"There's only one way to stop it," she said in a dull voice. "I'm so sorry, Adam. I'm sorry I wasn't strong enough to control this … this thing."

"I love you, Cara."

She shook her head. Then she stared at her hands. "My hands … they're so dirty. So much blood, so much pain."

Linnea was watching Cara and her brother, her eyes red and watery.

"It's g-getting dark. Let's go back to the house." The girls let him lead them up to their back door. Cara continued up to her room, silent. Adam held Linnea back.

"Linnea?" She looked up at him. "Please don't leave Cara alone tonight. I'm worried about what she might do. We can't lose her." Linnea nodded, gave him a quick hug, and followed Cara upstairs.

Linnea brushed her teeth and changed into her pajamas. She quietly opened Cara's bedroom door and looked inside. Cara was under the covers in her bed, sobbing. Linnea crossed the room and slid into the bed. She snuggled up to

Cara and gently placed her injured arm on her, then she placed a leg over one of Cara's, trying to get as close as possible. They lay there together without talking and, finally, slept.

THE NEXT MORNING, Cara was much more quiet and solemn than usual. She ate breakfast without speaking, without eye contact.

"Cara," Adam said, "w-would you walk with me?"

She responded in a dull voice. "If you like."

They walked in silence through the backyard towards the creek. Adam took Cara's hand.

"Cara, I'm familiar with each … uh … incident you've had since the b-beginning of the school year, right?"

"I suppose so."

"And I've heard, I mean, from someone other than you, about the man in the park in Boston."

She said nothing.

"Each incident was in response to a personal attack, or in response to deadly force on someone you love. In no instance did your … did She pop out and attack people for no reason."

"Your point?"

"If She's a demon, She's a p-pretty pathetic demon. Do you think She sits there on her little flame and waits till an innocent person needs saving? What the hell kind of demon is that?"

"Adam, I need a friend. I don't need someone else to mock me."

He stopped walking, turned to her, and stroked her hand. "I'm your friend. I love you more than life itself. I love your heart. I love that it hurts you to take a life. I love that you're so sweet, so kind. But now I need you to engage that phenomenal brain you have. *Think* about it. I'm no Bible scholar, but I've seen dozens of horror movies, and I've never heard of a demon who only comes out to s-save people who are about to be killed. And I've never seen a demon as beautiful as Her."

"Succubus."

"No dice. I read too. Succubi are demons that take the form of women to seduce men, usually while the men are asleep. They don't do what She does."

"Maybe I need a stupider boyfriend."

Adam took her in his arms and gently kissed her hair. Cara raised her face to him, and he kissed her lips. She sighed. "Sorry," he said, "this is the one you got."

"Okay." She laid her head on his chest and hugged him.

"I have some ideas, Cara. I'll help you figure this out. Please do nothing rash before I can help you."

She nodded. "I promise."

Linnea was in the kitchen when they returned home. Cara strode to her. "Linnea? I'm sorry."

The two girls hugged each other. "Cara, I'm so sorry I told you something that hurt you. I never meant to hurt you."

"I know. I … needed a friend last night. Thank you for being there for me."

"Cara, you saved my life in the home invasion, on the bus, and yet again when Sokolov kidnapped me. I could never thank you enough. I could never do enough for you. I'll always be your friend." Then, much softer, she said, "I love you."

At this, Cara hugged Linnea again.

"But Adam, Linnea, hear me when I say this: I will never again allow that thing out of me."

"Cara," Adam said, taking her hand in his. "You're making a promise you're unlikely to keep successfully."

"What do you mean?"

"I'm thinking you're pretty much just a vessel for Her. A vessel I love, but still … I mean, I like to think God cares about your feelings, but I wouldn't put money on it."

"You're saying you think She would come out if She felt I was in danger?"

He nodded. "I believe so. I'm coming to see that God has a plan for your life, not in the metaphysical way that most people mean when they say God has a plan for their life, but in a very literal way. That's why Boston happened. That's why you ended up in Indiana."

"I'm just a pawn?"

Adam shook his head. "You're a queen, love. Definitely a queen. The most valuable piece on the board." He kissed her forehead.

"Your queen needs a better kiss than that."

He smiled and drew her close. Their lips touched.

"Princess Linnea will leave the two royal lovebirds in peace," Linnea said.

THE OFFICE OF SPECIAL ASSETS

The sun had long since set, leaving the Potomac River dark. Most of the sixteen thousand employees had left the massive six-story headquarters of the Defense Intelligence Agency for the day. But on the fourth floor of the south wing of DIA headquarters, behind a dull-gray door marked Housekeeping, an analyst was hard at work.

Olivia Cabrera studied the data on two of her large monitors, then typed her report on a third monitor. Something extraordinary had happened in central Indiana.

Her focus was so intense that she jumped when she felt a gentle hand on her shoulder. "Olivia, go home now. You can pick this up again in the morning."

She was not surprised that her boss, Colonel Regina Taylor, was working late too, and that she would express concern for her team.

Olivia shook her head. "Colonel, I found one. A seventeen-year-old girl."

"Really? What's her talent?"

"I'm not sure, ma'am, but she's different from anyone we've found yet."

"Different in what way? The director is not looking for another subtle talent."

"Yes, I understand. But listen to this. I found this story about a hijacking of a school bus in Indiana back in March. Some guys shot the bus driver and drove the bus to a regional airport to transfer to a business jet that was waiting for them. Fortunately, a herd of police and SWAT team members met them at the airport. There was a standoff. The criminals were threatening to kill everyone on the bus with a grenade."

Colonel Taylor wrinkled her brow. "That was all over the news a few weeks ago, wasn't it?"

Olivia nodded. "It gets crazier. This young person I'm talking about somehow crossed the police line, approached the hijackers, and offered herself as a hostage if they would release the bus full of kids. For whatever reason, they agreed and brought her on the plane, then it took off. After a few minutes, from what I read, the jet appeared to be flying oddly. It circled back and crash-landed at the same airfield. The girl was the only survivor, though she was severely injured and spent some time in the hospital."

"What else did you find?"

"Well, I was watching the television coverage of the story. Ellen DeGeneres interviewed our young lady on her talk show. They referenced a home invasion several months earlier. I pulled the stories on that. Seems that she and a younger girl, who was also on the bus, were home alone when two armed men burst in on them. I can't find an account of how this happened, but the men were violently killed. The two girls were uninjured."

"That is interesting," the older lady agreed. "What did you learn about the teenager?"

"Her name is Cara Ferris. As I said, seventeen years old. She lived under the radar, alone on the street, for some time. I haven't been able to learn how long she was homeless or where she lived before last summer. But she turned up in a small town outside Indianapolis in time for this school year. She registered as a senior."

"Did you check her school records?"

"Yes, ma'am. She's running close to a 4.0 average in school, taking all the AP courses the high school offers. She registered using the McKinney-Vento Act, the federal law that allows public school education for homeless kids with no documentation."

"Where is she living now?"

"A local family took her in. Their name is Samuelson. The husband, Stephen, is a physician; his wife Katheryn is a nurse. They have two kids. Adam is seventeen and also a senior in high school, Linnea is thirteen and in eighth grade. They both do very well academically. Adam takes all AP courses.

"But Colonel, I learned something much more interesting. I wanted to know what caused the jet to crash, so I hacked into the NTSB to examine the data from the cockpit voice recorder and flight data recorder."

"And?"

"They build those so-called black boxes, that are actually orange, sturdily nowadays. They rarely fail in a crash. I accessed the NTSB investigation log. There's no mention that either of the black boxes malfunctioned, or that the data was not present when the NTSB retrieved them.

"However, the cockpit voice recorder has been erased. I've not yet been able to figure out who wiped the data."

"Unless I'm mistaken," Colonel Taylor said, "it violates federal law to delete flight recorder data before the investigation has concluded. And I doubt they'd have wrapped this up so quickly. Am I right?"

Olivia nodded. "You're correct."

"Were you able to access the flight data recorder?"

"Yes. It's odd, though. The jet was working fine, but then stalled, the pilots lost control, and crashed. There were two pilots, both with many years' experience with that type of jet. Either of them could have landed it safely if the other was disabled. But for the final few minutes before the crash, it's as though the pilots did not know what they were doing."

"Damn. And the only survivor of the crash was Cara?"

"That's correct."

"What's your next step? You told me some men hijacked a school bus, shot the bus driver, and threatened the kids on the bus with death."

Olivia nodded. "Yes."

"And then the hijackers broke into an airport, killed a guard, and escaped, however briefly, in a jet."

"All true."

"Local police matter?" Colonel Taylor asked.

"They violated several federal laws. This would involve the FBI."

"Bingo."

"Surely you're not suggesting the FBI deleted the cockpit voice recorder data?"

"I'm not sure that they did," Colonel Taylor said. "But remember that the FBI is a part of U.S. Intelligence, just like us and the CIA. If we can access the data, don't you suppose they can as well?"

Olivia nodded. "You're right, of course. The other possibility would be someone high in the NTSB itself. Though I don't see why anyone would go to the trouble to delete the cockpit voice recorder data, but leave the flight data recorder information intact ... Holy crap! Cara Ferris was the only one to survive the crash. There's no telling how the other people in the plane died because of the violence of the crash and explosion. But in the end, someone with no experience as a pilot flew the plane. What the hell happened on that plane? Anyone who listened to the voice recorder would know. And someone wants to keep it secret."

"So, what's your next move?"

"The most direct approach would be to speak with the FBI special agent of record for that case. It would probably be too much to hope that he or she would admit to illegally deleting FAA records, but I bet we could learn something more about this mysterious young lady … something that would make her worth violating federal law to protect."

GAMES PEOPLE PLAY

In a high school library, soon after the school day ended, a dozen young people and one of the math teachers clustered around a small table which held a chessboard. The two players, a dark-haired man and a young blonde girl whose right arm was in a sling, were focused on the board. Mid-game, there had been some pieces lost from both sides.

The girl moved her rook to c8, capturing the bishop. She tapped the timer.

Grandmaster Sandeep Pai had little choice here. He took her rook with his and tapped the timer. Something about the girl bothered him. *She doesn't fidget like a normal preteen. Completely focused. How odd.*

Calm, the girl countered with bishop to d7, taking his knight. Tap.

He moved his rook down the c file to c5. Tap.

Her bishop captured his rook at f5. Tap.

He replaced her bishop with his rook. Tap.

The girl studied the board for a moment, then moved her rook to d1. Tap.

Implacable. She's going for the kill. He moved his king to g8 and tapped.

The little blonde girl bit her lower lip as she assessed possibilities. She moved her queen to g2.

Tapped.

Only then did she look up at her opponent. Her large blue eyes were filled with intelligence and, Sandeep thought, a bit of amusement.

Sandeep was sweating profusely. This should not happen. From a preteen girl in a little town in Indiana, no less. How embarrassing.

The chessboard, usually his friend, seemed foreign. He considered his position for a moment, but saw no way out of his predicament. Carefully, he set his king on its side. He pushed his chair back then stood, offering the little girl his hand.

She shook it solemnly, then smiled as a thought occurred to her. "Thank you, sir. It was an excellent game. And it works out well that you're left-handed, since the usual hand I shake with," glancing at her right arm in a sling, "is indisposed at the moment."

The small audience of middle school and high school kids clustered around the board applauded.

"Thank you, Miss …," He scanned his notes and wrinkled his forehead. "Linn-ee-uh?"

"Linnea. Rhymes with 'okay.' You play very well, sir."

"I'm supposed to play well." He clenched his jaw and shook his head. "I'm the national champion. Or I was."

"I'm sorry, Mr. Sandeep."

He looked at her then, really looked at her. He saw a cute blonde girl, slight and not quite five feet tall. Her brow furrowed with concern.

"Never apologize for being smart, Linnea. My poor little

male ego will survive. I just expected nothing like this from a middle school student. Where did you learn to play?"

"My older brother and sister taught me."

"They must be very good. Have I heard of them?"

"I doubt it. They've never taken the trouble to get official Elo ratings by playing in FIDE-sanctioned live tournaments. But my brother, Adam, and my sister, Cara, both do well against our home computer. They taught me to play because they wanted more of a challenge.

"I'm lucky. I remember everything I read, with good recall, and I find patterns easily. When I play chess, it's as though I have all my chess books with me. For example, just now I was thinking of one of my heroes, Hungarian Grandmaster Judit Polgár."

"What about her?"

"A game she played when she was pretty young, before she earned the rank of grandmaster. She beat the great Indian player, Viswanathan Anand. Our match just now reminded me of theirs."

"How do you do that? I mean, pull things out of the air."

Linnea shrugged. "I have an excellent memory. And I suppose I'm reasonably intelligent."

"How do you fare against your siblings?"

She gave him a shy smile. "I do pretty well, but that's because I got the best from both of them. Adam plays from a position of knowledge. He's studied and memorized many hundreds of famous games and countless openings and their variations. Cara doesn't have nearly that breadth of chess knowledge, so she plays from a position of creativity and instinct. She's a mathematics whiz."

"And when they play against each other?"

"Cara more than holds her own," Linnea said with a little laugh. "Adam gets exasperated when Cara pulls something out of her hat he's never seen before."

"You don't talk like a preteen," Sandeep said. "How old are you?"

Linnea stood as straight as she could. "I am thirteen, which means I'm no longer a preteen. I'll be fourteen next month."

"My apologies. My younger sister is also thirteen and is a talented student, but she doesn't use words like 'exasperated' and 'breadth' in conversation."

Linnea smiled. "I get that a lot. My mom says I'm thirteen going on forty."

"I'd love to meet your brother and sister. Are they here?"

Linnea nodded. She indicated two of the older students with a gesture. The rest of the audience moved to let the two teens come closer.

Sandeep nodded at them. "You two are responsible for this young lady?"

The boy was tall and thin, with wavy black hair that wouldn't quite stay in place, and dark eyes. The girl was half a head shorter than him, with long, thick brown hair and gray eyes. Sandeep noted a thin scar on her left cheek, reminiscent of a Prussian dueling scar, extending from just below her eye nearly to her upper lip, and several smaller wounds that also were still healing. She and the young man smiled and nodded.

Sandeep held out his hand. "It is a pleasure to meet you."

Adam froze.

"Cara Ferris," Cara said as she shook his hand.

"Adam Samuelson," Adam said as he followed Cara's lead.

"You two are siblings?" Sandeep asked.

"It's c-complicated," Adam said. "No, Cara and I are not blood relatives, but she lives with Linnea and me and our f-folks. It's a long story. Cara and Linnea sort of unofficially adopted each other as sisters."

"I've never met a chess grandmaster," Cara added. "This is an honor."

Sandeep chuckled. "You two live with a world-class chess player, as I just now discovered."

Adam nodded. "We enjoy p-playing each other, though Linnea wins her fair share of our games."

Sandeep looked at Adam curiously, his brow furrowed. "The three of you should compete in sanctioned tournaments so you can earn official ratings."

"Yeah, we'll see. I just play for fun."

"Chess is fun for me as well," Sandeep said. "But there are prizes at this level of play. Sometimes a lot of money, if it's a major tournament."

"Is chess your full-time job?" Cara asked.

"No. My day job is at MIT. I run an artificial intelligence lab there."

"That's interesting stuff," Linnea said. "I have some ideas about how we might take AI further. I believe it's possible to build a truly intelligent machine—one that could pass a prolonged Turing test, could pass for a human if you couldn't see that it's a mechanism and not a person—and we could do it in a much faster time frame than the experts have been saying."

Sandeep cocked his head at her and smirked. "And you, a girl in middle school, think you can leapfrog over men who've been working in the field for years? I see."

Linnea met his gaze. "Perhaps I should stick to ... what? Home economics? Elementary education? Because girls can't understand computer science, right?"

"I don't mean to sound politically incorrect, but I have a doctorate in computer science, so I'm in a better position to judge what is possible and what is not."

He looked down for a moment. "Say, Miss Linnea, do you ever play online?"

Linnea nodded.

"This may be out of left field, but there is a player on Chess.com who goes by the handle of LilBlondeGirl. Whoever it is, they play remarkably well. I assumed it was actually some forty-year-old guy. I don't suppose there's any chance …?" He raised an eyebrow.

Cara turned to Linnea. "You're playing chess online?"

It was Linnea's turn to look sheepish. "I'm sorry, I should have told you. Sometimes at night, when I'm having trouble sleeping, I go to Chess.com. A few of the grandmasters give classes. Sometimes I play against them."

Sandeep asked again, "*You* are the mysterious LilBlonde-Girl? I thought your play felt familiar. May we all take a photo? My colleagues would not believe me otherwise."

"It would be my honor." Cara handed her cellphone to Mr. Harris, the head of the high school math department and the chess club who had arranged the visit and exhibition match. Cara, Adam, and Linnea posed with Grandmaster Sandeep Pai.

"It has been a delight to meet the three of you, despite my ignominious fall from the pinnacle of chess," Sandeep said with a smile. "If there is anything I can do for you, please don't hesitate to reach out." He handed each of them a card.

Then Mr. Harris thanked Grandmaster Pai for his visit. The audience briefly clapped one last time, and everyone dispersed.

I DON'T KNOW WHAT I AM

While Cara worked one afternoon at the Old World Bakery, the bell over the door jingled. Cara looked up and smiled.

"Good afternoon, detective. Are you here for business or pleasure?"

Anders smiled. "The first time I came here, I was trying to learn more about a certain mysterious young lady."

Cara arched an eyebrow, playing along. "I see. And what did you find?"

"That she's brave and kind, and she carries a burden that no one should have to bear. And that I love German pastries."

"I don't know what to tell you about the young lady, but I could help you find something tasty to eat."

"When I came the first time, the lady who owns this bakery gave me something she called, I think, *Buchteln*? It was some kind of sweet bun. Delicious."

"I love those. Mrs. Hamerschmidt showed me how to make them. I fill each *Buchtel* with plum jam and sprinkle a little powdered sugar on top." She looked through the display case and pulled out a tray of golden, caramelized confections that vaguely resembled cinnamon rolls. "Here, detective! Have you ever tried *Franzbrötchen*? They're made with butter and cinnamon. Slightly crisp on the outside, soft and flaky inside. You need to know about them. They're so good, they should be illegal." She smiled as she handed one to him on a napkin. "Imagine starting your day with a cup of excellent coffee and one of these. Go ahead, enjoy this one, and decide if you'd like to buy some."

"I'll buy half a dozen of these before I leave, but the real reason I came here is there's something I'd like to discuss with you. Can we take a short walk, please?"

"Just a minute." Cara turned and called softly into the back room. A rotund lady with a round, smiling face followed her out to the display case.

"Detective Anders." The lady had a slight German accent. "It is nice to see you again."

"And you, Mrs. Hamerschmidt. Would it be possible for me to borrow your helper for a few minutes? Just a short walk and we'll be right back. Then I absolutely must get half a dozen of these … what did you call them, Miss Cara?"

"*Franzbrötchen.*"

"Yes, these are to die for. And in my business, I don't say that lightly."

Mrs. Hamerschmidt laughed. "I suppose not. Go ahead. I'll watch the counter and let you two talk. See you in a few minutes."

"Thank you, ma'am."

DETECTIVE ANDERS and Cara headed off down the street together. As they walked, they passed several other small shops and restaurants before the street became more residential.

"Detective, I want to apologize for how I spoke to you in the hospital last week."

"It's fine, Cara. Your point was well taken. Let's move on. I told you and your family about my sister, Isabella."

"Yes, sir. I remember."

"I needed help to understand what was happening. I don't remember if I mentioned this at your house, but there was a witness to … what happened in Boston."

Cara's eyes widened in alarm. Her body tensed.

"Please don't be afraid, Cara. As I said a couple of weeks ago, I'm your friend and I will do everything I can to help you. But there was a man in the park in Boston who was, by his own admission, very drunk. He offered an accurate description of you sleeping on the bench. It must have been you; I'd imagine there are not too many young ladies with your particular features."

"My scar." Cara looked at the ground, unwilling to meet his eyes.

"Yes. I'm sorry. The drunk told the police that a man with a knife stood over you as you slept, about to stab you, then all the drunk would say is that he saw what he called an 'avenging angel' who struck the man down, in her anger almost ripping his head from his body."

"*Her* anger?"

"He was adamant the angel, or whatever it was, was female. As I told you and the Samuelsons, that man was wanted for other knife assaults in the Boston area and likely was responsible for my sister's murder many years ago."

"How can you say that?"

"This is what I came to discuss with you. I was walking my dog one evening, and a man who my dog and I could see, but who was invisible to a young couple nearby, called me by name and gave me a letter. The note was written in Isabella's handwriting as a haiku poem, which was our private way to communicate. Nobody, not our parents nor our friends, knew that we wrote notes to each other in haiku." He stopped walking and turned to Cara. "My sister has been dead for over twenty-five years, but *she* wrote that letter."

"What did she say?"

"She wrote, 'FATHER saw me die. The man paid the penalty. There is balance now.' That was the haiku part. Then she added 'Boston, June 20, 2016' and signed it 'Issa.'"

"Issa?"

"When I was very young, I couldn't pronounce 'Isabella,' so I called my sister 'Issa.' I was the only person she allowed to call her that."

"Wait. Did Isabella say that your father saw her die?"

"No, I'm the one who found my sister dead. My dad was at work, proven by numerous colleagues, phone records, and his key card. Isabella wrote the word FATHER in all caps. The only explanation that makes sense to me is that she was referring to God. You know, as in 'God the Father.'"

Cara nodded. "I can see that. Wasn't June 20, 2016, the day that …"

"Yes, that was when the drunk man in that park claimed to have seen an avenging angel."

"Wow! That's hard to believe."

"A lot of things recently have been hard to believe. Anyway, I consulted a theology professor at the university, hoping he could help me make sense of the letter and what happened in Boston.

"We spoke for quite a while in his office that first time, and by phone a couple times since. I've never mentioned you by name, nor any details about your life. Cara, I would like your permission for me to share with the professor some details of what happened with you many years ago in that alley. Perhaps he can help you understand.

"If it's okay with you, I can talk with him and then later I can set up an appointment for you, me, and ideally someone from your family who you trust, to meet the professor and talk."

"This theology professor can tell me what I am?"

Anders nodded. "He explained some things about my sister, and her letter, that I hadn't considered because to me it was the stuff of B-grade movies. I did not know that serious academics have been writing about these things for almost a thousand years. Have you heard of Saint Thomas Aquinas?"

"I've read a translation of his *Summa Theologica*."

"Did you study it in school?"

"No. Detective, when I was homeless, I spent a lot of time in public libraries. Reading, for me, was a way to escape my harsh reality for a while. I read Thomas Aquinas, and others, to help me make sense of what seemed to me to be a senseless world."

"Cara, do you have any idea how special you are?"

"Special as in strange? I've been told that once or twice."

"No, I mean special as in rare and priceless. How many American teenagers do you suppose have read Aquinas' *Summa Theologica*? And of that brief list, how many teens do you suppose sought out Thomas Aquinas *on their own* to help them understand how the world works?"

Cara shrugged. "I wouldn't know, Detective Anders."

"You are unique, and I am honored to help you. So, may I proceed with the professor?"

"Yes, sir. I'll ask Adam if he'll come with me."

"That young man would follow you into the pit of hell," Anders said.

"True," Cara replied. "That's what scares me most."

SHE

Detective Anders motioned Cara and Adam through the open office door, then followed them into the large office. Hundreds of leather-bound volumes, many of which looked quite old, lined the walls. An older but vital-looking man with red hair, a bushy mustache, and alert green eyes glanced up from his desk, then smiled and rose to greet them.

"Doctor McNair, I'd like you to meet Cara Ferris and her friend, Adam Samuelson. People, this is Doctor Finn McNair, Chair of Religious Studies here at the university."

"I'm pleased to meet you, professor," Cara said.

"The pleasure is mine, Miss Cara. Please take a chair, if you would." They sat. The professor pulled his chair around in front of his desk so he could sit with them.

Cara studied the room in silence, then turned to McNair. A slight smile played on her lips. "Detective Anders told me you're a professor of theology. You look different than I'd pictured in my mind."

McNair chuckled. "Yes, miss. I've been told that more

than once. A few years ago, a hapless undergrad mistook me for a construction worker when he first saw me."

"Wh-Whatever happened to him?" Adam asked.

McNair shrugged. "I heard he became a Mass Communications major."

"Professor," Cara said, "Detective Anders said you might be able to help me … to help me understand. Can you?"

"I may have some insight for you. Detective Anders came to me a month ago, before the incident with the bus and the plane crash that was all over the news. He told me about the letter that appeared to be from his long-dead sister. He told me about Boston and what the drunken eyewitness claimed to have seen, and he told me about the home invasion that led to him first meeting you. Most recently, and so far as I understand with your permission, the detective told me some things about your early life … what happened when you were ten, and in the alley … and about your life since then."

"I see," Cara said in a quiet voice.

Professor McNair regarded Cara with a thoughtful expression. "I cannot imagine what your childhood must have been like. I … I feel for you, and I hope I can help answer your questions."

"I appreciate that."

"Miss Cara," the professor asked, "what happens when you, uh, change?"

"I'm not sure, sir. Until recently I've never remembered the incident, only that someone was about to hurt me, and then the people around me are dead, and their deaths are invariably violent. In the last few months, I've developed some control while changed, so that in two cases, I stopped whatever I become from killing Adam or Linnea."

"Adam, do you have anything to add?"

"Yes, sir. M-My younger sister Linnea and I have had some experience with Her, as Cara mentioned."

"With whom?"

"I don't know what to call the … whatever is inside Cara. To myself, I think of Her as the female pronoun, capitalized."

"You've seen Her?"

Adam nodded. "Linnea has seen Her as well. We've compared notes."

"Would you describe what your sister and you saw? What is She like?"

"P-Professor, the change happens within just a few seconds. Something … different is inside Cara's clothes. She's larger than Cara, maybe twenty p-pounds heavier. Cara's clothes are small on Her. She's beautiful, but not in the way that Cara is attractive to me. I mean, I love Cara and I want to spend my life with her, and to me, she's the most gorgeous, wonderful girl. Things that someone else might see, looking at Cara, are insignificant in my eyes. But She … She is not a woman but a Being who is supernaturally beautiful. She has no blemishes or scars. Her limbs and her b-body are muscular but somehow feminine. She is supremely confident. Her body exudes power."

"Does She carry or use weapons?"

"No, sir, not that we've ever seen. Maybe if She had to fight an army."

"May I ask, have you heard Her speak?"

"Linnea heard Her speak. Just a few words in a language we didn't recognize. They were sharp like a command." Adam tried to mimic the sounds that to his ears were guttural, foreign.

He could see that he had Professor McNair's rapt attention. The professor repeated Adam's words to himself several times as though trying to make sense of them, then his eyes widened. He sucked in a breath and shook his head slowly.

Then, he spoke several words aloud, though enunciating them differently than Adam had.

Adam frowned, then nodded. "She never addressed me directly, but that sounds like what Linnea said she heard," Adam said.

McNair smiled and leaned forward. "You three have given me a gift. We joked earlier that I've been told I look like a construction worker. And I've thought for years that construction workers build things, they build things that are real, that make a difference in people's lives. After many decades in academic theology, sometimes I wondered to myself if what I was studying and teaching was in fact valid. You just proved to me that my life's work is real."

"I don't understand, Finn," Detective Anders said.

"Adam, your pronunciation needs work, but what Cara's … what She was saying was on whose authority She was there. She was speaking Biblical Hebrew, which was probably the last language She'd spoken in the presence of a human." He looked each of them in the eyes. "She spoke of the Sword of God."

"What kind of name is that?" Detective Anders asked. Cara and Adam sat wide-eyed.

"I can't be sure it's Her name per se, David. You know there are several angels in the Old and New Testament with specific names. I'm wondering if it's more like a job description, like when you introduce yourself as a detective."

"Angel?" Cara blurted.

"Miss Cara," the professor began, "what can you tell me about angels?"

"Angels? I don't know. They have wings, I guess. They supposedly protect people, though they didn't protect me from my mom's boyfriend. I'm not sure they're real."

"Okay, and demons? What about them?"

"Malformed minions of Satan, according to popular culture. Again, I don't know that they're real."

"Cara, do you believe in God?"

Cara nodded. "Despite everything I've experienced, I do. Not the thunderbolt-throwing flavor, though, but the One who loves me and grieves when I hurt. I can't prove God's existence, but I feel better with Him in my life. Still, bad things happen. Life is rough."

"I asked those questions so that I know how to continue our conversation. You've read the Bible, yes?"

"Yes, sir."

"And you, Adam?"

"Yes, sir," he said.

"The day I first spoke with David … Detective Anders, we discussed this passage." He thumbed open a Bible on his desk, found a passage, and handed it to Adam. "This is from Isaiah 37. Would you read verse 36 out loud, please?"

Adam took the book and found the verse. "Then the angel of the Lord went out and p-put to death a hundred and eighty-five thousand in the Assyrian camp. When the people got up the next morning—there were all the dead bodies."

The professor looked at each of them. "What do you make of this?"

Cara grabbed Adam's hand and squeezed it. "That's a lot of violence," he finally said.

"One angel slaughtered one hundred and eighty-five thousand armed soldiers over one night. Even if you allow for some exaggeration of the number of men killed, that gives you an idea of the incredible power of a biblical angel."

They were silent, considering his words based on their experiences.

"What do you suppose it would be like to confront an angel face to face?"

"A retribution angel would be pretty t-terrifying," Adam

said. "But there are other kinds of angels, too, right? Lots of people swear angels protected them from something bad."

"Turn to Numbers 22. Read the story of Balaam and his donkey."

Adam scooted his chair even closer to Cara and together they read the story. Cara looked up. "So the donkey, but not the man, could see the angel standing in their path."

"L-Like the guard dogs at ..." Cara touched Adam's shoulder to silence him, but she nodded.

"Yes."

"Cara," the professor began, "are you familiar with the concept of possession?"

"Like when a demon takes over someone's body? I've seen a few horror movies, but they did nothing for me. For much of my life, reality was tough enough that I did not need to look for more excitement."

"What you said about possession was sort of correct. Do you know the difference between demonic and angelic possession?"

"I've never heard of angelic possession."

"Basically, the theory is that if an angel has a person's permission, the angel may take over a person's body. Demons do not require permission. Otherwise, the idea is the same."

"So, you're saying that years ago in the alley, when I was a ten-year-old girl who was about to die, and when I prayed to God for help ..." Cara stared up at the professor and said in a quiet voice, "an angel understood my prayer as permission to take over my body?"

"We've ventured into territory where I have no direct experience, and it's admittedly a wild theory. But one that explains what's happened since then."

BEAUTIFUL INSIDE

When they returned home from the visit with the theology professor, Cara and Adam walked together, hand-in-hand, around their neighborhood.

"What do you think about all that, Adam?"

"I'm still processing it. The concept that you have an actual angel living inside you, it's fantastic. I mean, in the sense of relating to fantasy rather than reality, n-not fantastic meaning wonderful."

"No, it's definitely not wonderful. I live in fear that I'll kill people who don't deserve to die. Most people … even if they're mean or stupid … they don't deserve to be killed. Especially the way She does it. If it were possible to use just enough force to handle a situation, that wouldn't be so bad."

"B-But you're getting better at controlling Her, aren't you? That's what you said last winter. And then the day we rescued Linnea, when Special Agent Tanaka wanted to take you into custody, you changed and disappeared from our house without killing anyone."

"That was extremely difficult for me, Adam. It could have gone wrong. Terribly, terribly wrong. She is not a creature who runs away from a fight. And She's also not at my beck and call. I cannot make Her appear on my command. That day, I feared for my life, but more importantly, I feared for Linnea. I love her. So I ..." Cara stopped. Her face clouded over.

"Yes, babe?"

"I did something I'm really not proud of. It scares me when I think about it."

Adam gently pulled Cara to him. They hugged. Cara spoke softly into his chest, without meeting his eyes. "I used Her to escape our house, but in return I promised ..."

Cara spoke haltingly. Adam could hear the self-loathing in her voice. "Adam, I promised Her that when we reached Sokolov's mansion, where he was holding Linnea, that She could do as She liked."

"Oh my God."

"And as you saw, She killed almost everyone in the mansion. Everyone she encountered. I'm so sorry, Adam. I'm ugly inside and out."

"No! Cara, you're kind, you're brilliant, you're resource-ful. You're my closest friend. I love you more than anything in the world. I've told you this before, and I've backed up my words with action. You are beautiful to me; you always have been. I admired you even before we were officially together. There's nothing about you that's ugly."

"Have you been listening, Adam? Sokolov's men, who I didn't even know, I sentenced them all to death."

"They weren't Boy Scouts, Cara. They worked for an evil man, but Sokolov didn't kidnap our little sister by himself. These people helped him. And they stood between us and Linnea when Sokolov was about to kill her.

"Cara, She only kills violent, bad people. She doesn't pop up in school or in church. She doesn't kill random people on the street. She's never gone wild in the bakery where you work, nor in the library where we study. Don't you see? She answers to a different authority than you. I've thought a lot about what's happened to us. When Linnea texted you that some guys hijacked her bus on the way to school? It just *happened* that none of the police noticed us cross a field to reach the airport. There just *happened* to be a defect in the perimeter fence large enough for us to walk through. Neither the snipers nor SWAT members *happened* to see us as we crept close enough to the police line that we could hear the radio negotiations with the criminals. And you were able to cross the police line without them stopping you. And then the criminals *happened* to agree to take you instead of the kids. That's a lot of coincidences, don't you think?"

"When you list them all like that, it sounds unbelievable."

"Exactly what part of our life since you and I met would you say is believable?"

"Hmm. I guess I have some thinking to do." She looked up at him then. "Are you saying that my angel, or whatever, helped me elude the FBI, and then killed so many of Sokolov's men, and that it had nothing to do with my promise?"

"You don't actually converse with Her as though you were two different individuals, do you?"

"No, not like that. It's not like She's in my head. When I walked into our kitchen after talking with Special Agent Tanaka, I was certain I would leave the house. I guess I made that devil's bargain in my head, but I didn't literally have a conversation with Her."

"All this time you were f-feeling guilty because you thought you had more control over your angel than you really have. Again, I'm pretty sure She doesn't answer directly to you. Detective Anders is right that you're here for a reason. And I'll s-say it over and over till you believe it: You are beautiful inside and out."

REVENGE

*L*ater that day, Cara and Adam were home alone watching a video. They lay on the living room couch, spooning with her back to his chest and Adam's free hand on her hip. Cara slowly and deliberately took his hand in hers and moved it to her breast. Her hand remained on his.

"Cara?" Adam said.

"Yes?"

"What are you doing?"

"There's something I need to tell you."

"Uh, okay. So for future reference, when you place my hand on your boob, it means you're in the mood for conversation?"

Cara chuckled. "I love how you see the world. I feel comfortable with you."

"You float my boat, too."

"If I were crude, I'd say I feel the mast against my hip, but I'm a lady."

"That's what impresses Mom about you the most: that

you grew up in such a rough environment, but you always act like a lady."

"You can thank Frances Hodgson Burnett."

"The author?"

"Yeah. When I was younger, I discovered her novel, *A Little Princess*. The story is about a little rich girl in England who loses everything and has to live like a pauper. But through all adversity, she pretends that she's really a princess and acts the part. The story made a huge impression on me and my worldview."

"I read that. In the end, she found a home and people to love her," Adam said. "Just like you."

"I had no way to see how my story would play out, but yeah, life is pretty good right now. But there's something else on my mind.

"The thing is," she paused, "I want to talk to you about revenge. I've been thinking about it."

"You put my hand on your breast as a prelude to discussing revenge. Okay. Who would you like me to kill?"

"Not that kind of revenge, silly. You know what that man … Mom's boyfriend … did to me when I was ten."

"Yes." Quiet.

Cara turned on her back so she could look directly at Adam. "The best revenge would be for me to have a committed, loving relationship with a man who adores and respects me."

"Sign me up for that, Cara." He pecked her lightly on the lips.

Cara leaned in toward Adam for a better kiss. Her lips were warm and soft, her breath was fresh. She moaned into his mouth as her tongue touched his. She pressed her body close against his side. With an effort, he nudged her away. Cara pouted.

"Cara, love, we talked about this when you moved in with my family. I gave you my word I wouldn't—"

"You're right, Adam. I know we need to wait. I don't mean to tease you, but I want you to understand that when the time is right, I will enthusiastically give you everything."

"Can we get married today?"

Cara laughed. "I appreciate your enthusiasm. You make me feel beautiful and desirable."

"I always said you were beautiful."

"We need to get through engineering school. Be able to support ourselves. We're not living in your parents' basement. But I think about it a lot."

"About …"

"About what it will be like when we no longer have to hold back."

Adam chuckled. "You won't have the time or energy to do anything else."

"Men. It won't be me with no energy. I'm no expert, but from what I've read, the man's … uh … ability is the limiting factor. And I plan to wear you out, my guy."

"I love how you threaten me," Adam said. Then he nuzzled her thick brown hair.

"Cara," Adam asked, "there's something I wonder about. It's sensitive, and you don't have to tell me if you don't want to."

"I won't hide anything from you."

"The man who hurt you …"

"Mom's boyfriend, Les. What about him?"

"Did you ever see him again?"

Cara closed her eyes and swallowed, as though taking a bitter medicine. "I had fantasies for a while about killing him. But I already felt like I'd become a monster. I felt disgusted and horrified by what I did to the two men in the alley. I just … couldn't.

"The professor says I have an angel inside me. Not a warm, fuzzy cherub, but an angel from scripture, a biblical angel who kills as easily as you and I breathe, and who seems to care about it as little as we would care if we step on an ant. I may be damned already for what I've done, but I refuse to turn into judge, jury, and executioner. I'm not God."

"So Les is still alive?"

"I have no idea. I believe that in this world or the next, he will pay for what he did to me. But I never returned to Mom's apartment, and I haven't seen either of them since I left."

"You're a better person than me. I would have killed him."

TELL ME ABOUT THE LADY

"Tell me about this lady," Linnea asked, not for the first time.

Cara, Adam, and Linnea were walking down by the creek behind their house. Linnea had heard the broad outlines of her rescue from the Russian crime boss, Mikhail Sokolov, as Cara and Adam reported it to FBI Special Agent Vincent Tanaka and to Detective David Anders. The two teens had left out some details ... actually, they left out many of the details when they gave their official debriefing. They did not mention to law enforcement anything about Lelia Fortune or their special equipment, though Linnea picked up on something that Detective Anders said in passing, something about a lady who Linnea may get to meet. Adam had never been a good liar. His little sister was unusually perceptive, so when he slipped and said something about a lady who'd helped them when they needed it most, Linnea would not let the matter drop.

"Okay," Cara said with a sigh, "here's the story. Adam, please add whatever you like."

He nodded. "Linnea d-deserves to know. This all happened because of her."

Cara shook her head. "No, this all happened because of me. Sokolov kidnapped Linnea so he could control me."

"You're right, Cara," he said. "Though I'll bet at the end, he was wishing he'd never touched this p-particular little girl."

Linnea cleared her throat theatrically. "Focus. Tell me about the lady."

Cara laughed, then she pulled Linnea into a hug. "As you wish, though I warn you in advance, this is stranger than fiction."

"Nothing surprises me anymore."

"Oh, you haven't heard this story," Cara said. "Takes crazy to a whole new level. When the FBI agent, Tanaka, saw the video Sokolov forced you to make, he was afraid I actually might kill him. He tried to take me into custody. I disappeared off the grid so I could be free to help you. Your crazy brother stayed with me, even if that meant he was defying the FBI." She looked at Adam and smiled.

"You two are cute together," Linnea remarked.

"Thanks. Anyway, after Special Agent Tanaka left our house, Adam called Detective Anders. He had a feeling that Anders would help us, and he was right. Anders gave Adam a gold medallion and a name: Lelia Fortune. He wouldn't tell Adam anything about her, just that he should find her and give her the medallion."

"What happened then?"

Adam picked up the story. "I met up with Cara and we d-drove to Chicago. We went to the address listed for Ms. Fortune. She turns out to be the sweetest old lady. The public knows her as a reclusive mega-wealthy lady who donates vast sums to charity. Less well known is that she made her millions as an arms dealer and information broker."

Linnea snorted. "You've got to be kidding."

"You'd think. But it gets weirder. She invited us into her home … sort of forced us, really. She served us tea and made us tell our story, and she asked for the medallion. Then she took us through a hidden elevator down to her … Cara, do I call it a basement? Do I call it a lair?

"This lady has an arms warehouse and command center deep under her house. It's hard to describe, Linnea. You really need to meet her."

"This is the lady that Detective Anders mentioned?"

"Yeah," Cara said. "This lady has enough weapons to supply a small country. And she's somehow tied deeply into the internet. She found the house where you were being kept by tracking the packets of information you were sending to the FBI."

Here, Linnea raised her hand as though she were in class. "Sorry, Cara, but I'm familiar with the technology. You cannot backtrack individual IP packets, especially not the new IPv6 packets. It's mathematically impossible."

"That's fine, little sister, but Adam and I saw her do it. Again, that's how we found you. She told us where the mansion was located, based on the enormous amount of information going from there to the FBI."

"It's possible she already had Sokolov's address," Linnea stated.

"You may be right. But remember what Adam and I were wearing when we found you?"

"Yeah, I was wondering about that."

"Ms. Fortune measured us and fitted us with these special suits. They gave us a definite advantage. And she gave Adam a couple of special toys. You saw him use that little pistol on our way out of Sokolov's mansion. It somehow disables people without killing them. She also gave Adam a device that senses cameras and recording devices, and turns them off. Without those tools, we could never have reached you in time." Then, quieter, "We almost didn't reach you in time, anyway."

They were silent for a bit, each of them with their own thoughts.

"Thank you," Linnea murmured. "I thought he would kill me."

GOING TO CHICAGO

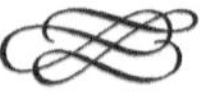

"**Y**es, ma'am. I'll take care of it. We'll see you when you get home. Bye."

Cara looked up from her iPhone. "Your mom is running late in the ICU. She asked us to start dinner. I need a couple of sous-chefs," she said to Adam and Linnea, smiling.

"Sure," Adam said. "How can we help?"

Cara set Linnea to preparing a rice pilaf while she worked on salmon *en papillote*. Adam set five eggs to boil, then busied himself cutting up vegetables for a salad. Mid-slice, he wrinkled his forehead and paused. "Cara, how d-did you get so comfortable in the kitchen while living ... um ..."

"On the street. You can say it. I won't be offended."

"I'm trying to be sensitive."

Cara moved to hug Adam, remembered she had raw fish on her hands, and settled for a quick kiss on his cheek.

"It's not much of a story. Until this past fall, I couldn't get a proper job because I had no identification or address. So, like lots of undocumented workers, I worked in the restaurant industry. Mopping floors and washing dishes for cash, stuff like that."

Linnea stopped working. She fixed her eyes on Cara. "Okay, but how did you learn to cook so well?"

"The usual way you move up in an organization. I worked hard, came early, stayed late, and asked questions of the kitchen staff. Meal prep in a top restaurant starts many hours before they open for business. I was reliable and willing to help, and I learn pretty quickly."

Linnea nodded. "That makes sense."

"Over time, I took on more responsibility and got paid for it … though I don't doubt I was still much cheaper than a W-2 employee."

"You just keep amazing me," Adam said. "Living alone on the street for seven years, changing cities when you felt the authorities were suspicious, you learned to cook and to play guitar, all the while maintaining close to a 4.0 GPA.

"If I didn't know you and someone told me your story, I'd think it was fiction."

"I'd call it a fairy tale," Linnea added with a sly grin, "complete with a peasant girl who's really a princess, and a knight who saves her."

"No," Adam said. "I'm no hero, and Cara never needed rescuing."

Cara chuckled. "I'm always up for a bit of rescuing. And you're my hero. If not for you, I'd still be on the street." She smiled fondly at Adam.

As they sat at dinner that evening, Stephen had a surprise for the family.

"The Friday after next, I have to go to Chicago for a drug study meeting. Would you all like to come with me and make a weekend out of it? You could go to the Museum of Science and Industry, or wherever, while I'm tied up in the meeting. We could stay in an upscale hotel. See a show. Whatever you like. Does that sound good?"

"Dad, that sounds awesome," Linnea said.

Katie pursed her lips, then she nodded. "I can find coverage at work. Will you kids be okay missing a day of school?"

"Mom …"

"Yes, Linnea?"

"All three of us are ahead of the curve. It'll give the other students a chance to catch up."

Katie smiled and shook her head. "I think you and I need to have a talk about humility."

"My humility is the quality about which I'm proudest," Linnea said with a smirk. They all laughed.

Stephen chuckled. "Okay, we'll do it."

LATER THAT EVENING, alone in his room, Adam pulled a business card from a hidden compartment in his desk. Just a name and a phone number. He stared at the card, reliving the memories of the day he received it from a remarkable lady. She had said she wanted to meet Linnea. This trip to Chicago might be an excellent opportunity to make it happen.

He closed his eyes for a minute to steady himself, then he dialed the number.

"G-Good evening, Ms. Fortune? This is Adam Samuelson."

"Hello, young man. You have a unique voice."

"Sorry, ma'am. I've talked like this as long as I can remember."

"Nothing to apologize for. I was hoping to hear from you. What can I do for you?"

"When we left your house, you said you wanted to meet my younger sister. Dad told us tonight at dinner that we're spending the weekend after next in Chicago. My parents don't know about you, but I hoped that if I told you we will be in the area, you could help me think of a way for us to get together."

"Hmm, I have an idea. Does your family like classical music?"

"We love classical."

"I'm a major donor to the Chicago Symphony. That weekend, we have a Saturday evening concert with Hilary Hahn as our guest artist."

"The violinist? Oh, my gosh. She's awesome! My parents have all her CDs, and I love watching her videos online."

"Would you like to meet her?"

"That would be incredible. Can you do that?"

"There's a meet-and-greet for a small circle of donors after the concert. They'll have finger foods and such. Not a proper dinner. But you can meet Ms. Hahn, and I can meet your family. Obviously, I can't talk business with your parents there."

"Makes sense."

"How many tickets will you need?"

"Just my mom and dad, Cara, Linnea, and me."

"Excellent. I'll send you five tickets to the concert and an invitation to the casual gathering afterwards. Tell your folks that you and Cara met me when you came to Chicago to find Linnea."

"How and why did we meet you? I want us to have the same story."

"Don't you remember? Even though you two were in such a hurry to find someone, you stopped to help when my car veered suddenly off the road. I blew a front tire. Thank goodness I wasn't hurt. We talked while you helped my driver change my tire. I just wanted to do a little something to thank you."

"How did you c-come up with that off the top of your head?"

Adam's new friend laughed. "Years of practice, Grasshopper. There is much for you to learn."

"I think you're right. Cara and Linnea and I need to spend more time with you."

"I would enjoy that very much. I'll get the tickets and invitation off to you tomorrow morning, and I'll look forward to seeing you in a couple of weeks."

NICHOLAS FRY

Olivia Cabrera reviewed her notes one last time. Today she would present her data to Lieutenant General Nicholas Fry, Director of the Defense Intelligence Agency, a first for her as a junior analyst.

"Come on, it's time," Colonel Taylor said. "This is your work, this is your find, so you should be the one to get credit for it."

"Thanks, I guess."

"You'll be fine. I'll be there with you, but you'll do the presentation."

"Are you sure? I mean, it's fine if …"

Colonel Taylor shook her head, smiling. "Olivia, you're good. Outstandingly good. It will be just the three of us in the room, and General Fry needs to meet you."

"But you talked me through so much of the investigative work."

"I talked you through very little. You are the one who hacked into the hospital, you are the one who hacked into the local police. It was you who found the FBI special agent.

You're the most talented hacker I've ever met, which is why we hired you. And again, it was *you* who discovered this asset."

"But ..."

"Olivia, for me, it's the difference between being a player and being a coach. When I was doing fieldwork, I pushed to be the first to report new intel. Now that I'm a mentor, I want the spotlight to shine on one of my people more than I want it on me. This is your time. You're a damn good analyst and I want the director to see what you've accomplished."

"Okay. I hope I don't let you down."

"You won't."

GENERAL FRY GLANCED AGAIN at his watch. He still had a few minutes before the monthly briefing from the Office of Special Assets. Their briefings never took long because in the year that he'd been director of the DIA, there had been little new to report. Nothing that would be of military or intelligence use. He almost didn't believe the OSA was worth his time and money, but then he thought of Colonel Regina Taylor. He reread her file as he waited. She had such a subtle gift. It was amazing to him that Admiral Decker—the legendary DIA director two decades previously—had spotted her. And it was more incredible that the CIA had allowed her to leave. They didn't know what they had. And Decker had pulled some very long strings. He had offered Taylor a commission in the U.S. Army and had arranged for her family to "win" a large sum of money, enough to repay all the educational loans for her and her sibling and to set them and their parents up for life. In return, the newly minted Captain Taylor became one of the greatest assets the DIA had ever seen. All over the world, in numerous languages, this ordinary-looking lady sat in top-secret meetings, or in cafés, or wherever people with something to hide would meet. She was there but somehow could remain unnoticed. Later, she would dictate entire conversations word-for-word when it was not feasible for her to wear a wire.

Over time, the DIA found a handful of other uniquely talented people. They found Olivia Cabrera three years ago. She didn't fit the stereotype of a hacker, being a clean-cut Latina in her early twenties. Ms. Cabrera could access any computer, seemingly effortlessly, no matter how well protected. What do you do with someone found looking around inside the ultra-secure, ultra-secret National Security Agency servers? Nobody could break those codes, but she did. So the previous director of the DIA hired her.

Now it was his turn. From what he'd heard preliminarily, they had a line on yet another young female. But this one could do serious violence. No more of that subtle shit that the OSA had found to date. *This* girl could potentially change the balance of power in the world. She *needed* to work for the United States.

The intercom beeped, announcing a message. "General Fry, Colonel Regina Taylor is here to see you."

He glanced again at his watch. 16:58 on the dot. He lived by his schedule and liked meetings to begin and end on time, and he believed that if one wasn't two minutes early, they were late. Colonel Taylor was a professional.

"Show her in."

"Colonel Taylor reporting, General. This is one of my analysts, Olivia Cabrera."

The ladies stood at attention, faces serious. General Fry extended his hand, and Colonel Taylor grasped it in both of hers, squeezed it firmly for a second, then released it.

General Fry nodded. "Colonel Taylor. Miss Cabrera. Please sit."

He observed that Colonel Taylor had an unremarkable yet

ageless face. Her hair was short and gray. Her uniform, as always, was immaculate. Beside her he saw a much-younger caramel-skinned woman, dark hair in a tight bun, wearing a conservative pantsuit, expression serious. She carried a laptop, which she set up on his desk so the three of them could see the screen. He knew this was her first presentation to him, but her hands were steady and sure as she brought up the PowerPoint. She impressed him; he respected competence and confidence.

"General, we've identified a new asset." Olivia continued her presentation as she had practiced. Once she began, she forgot the stress of presenting to the director of the DIA. She just told the story with which she'd become so familiar over the past two weeks.

When she'd concluded her presentation, General Fry leaned back in his chair. "Just to clarify: The FBI found both Mikhail Sokolov and his wife murdered in his office, and they both died violently?"

"That's correct, General. The FBI report stated that both Sokolov and his wife were dead, and their injuries were extreme."

"Do we have any idea why this potential new asset would have killed Sokolov's wife?"

"The official FBI position is that a competitor of Sokolov invaded his estate, killing him and his guards. They say the violence was over when the teens arrived to save their younger sister."

"But you're not convinced?"

"Sir, Sokolov's son Pyotr arrived at the mansion shortly after the FBI. They questioned him and released him at the scene, but his parents' deaths, especially his mother's, clearly shook him. From what I understand, Pyotr was very close to his mother. Neither of his parents were shot or stabbed or poisoned, as one would expect from an underworld competitor; they sustained brutal injuries. Apparently, it was quite an ugly scene."

"I see. Tell me, do you know exactly how this girl, Cara, can fight so superhumanly well?"

Olivia met his gaze. "There is no video of the girl's encounters. Just that she's been present in each case that I told you about. Injuries that even strong, trained men could not cause. I presume she has enhanced strength and speed, but I do not have direct proof."

He stroked his chin as he considered his options. A teenage girl was suboptimal for many reasons. She likely would be unreliable. Emotional. Easily swayed by her opponents. Schools and the media taught kids today to mistrust government and especially the military.

But that power! He could not allow her to fall into enemy hands. What could the Russians or the Chinese do with her? He hated to think of how that could end.

General Fry decided, and having decided, it was time to move. "We need more information about the girl's abilities. I'll have our special ops unit set up a test. We'll make it real for her, so that she sees it as an actual attack. The girl must be alone except for a person or people she cares about, in a place where we can control the environment. We'll have high-definition audio and video."

"Yes, sir. What do you need the Office of Special Assets to do?"

"Nothing at the moment. We'll talk again after her test."

"Sir?" Olivia asked. General Fry stared at her without speaking. "The people who would attack Cara? She will kill them."

General Fry snorted. "Our special ops agents are highly trained and seasoned warriors, mostly former Navy SEALS or Army Rangers, and they are experts in hand-to-hand and armed combat. I cannot envision a teen girl posing a threat to them."

Olivia nodded. "Sir."

He stood. "Dismissed."

The two women nodded, gathered their materials, and left his office.

MUSEUM OF SCIENCE AND INDUSTRY

For people like Cara or Adam or Linnea, all three of whom were planning on a career in engineering, the Museum of Science and Industry in Chicago was pretty much geek heaven. There were over four hundred thousand square feet of awesomeness. They spent a day there, wandering from one exhibit to another, but couldn't see everything.

At one point they were marveling at a forty-foot "tornado" of swirling, illuminated water vapor when a little girl asked her mom, loudly, in the innocent way children have, "Mommy, why does that girl have a scar on her face?" She pointed at Cara.

Nobody had a ready response. The girl's mom froze, her mouth open but with no sound. Cara smiled and, in her gentle voice, asked the mother, "May I?" The lady nodded.

Cara crouched down to the little girl's eye level and said, "A bad person hurt me when I was younger."

"Does it still hurt now?" the girl asked.

"No, it doesn't hurt."

"Okay. Do you like my shoes? They light up when I walk. See?" She demonstrated by walking back and forth.

"I love your shoes," Cara said. "Do you know how this tornado works?" She explained to her new friend, in simple words, how tornadoes form.

When the girl's mom could finally find her voice, she apologized for her daughter's question.

Adam shrugged. "I d-don't really notice my girlfriend's scar anymore. She's beautiful to me."

"Yes, I can see that. I don't think I could have handled that question so well. Anyway, it was nice to meet you."

The mom smiled at her daughter. "We need to go, peanut," she said.

Cara knelt and embraced the child. "I like you, you're nice," she whispered into Cara's shoulder as they hugged. The girl took her mom's hand and headed away. Before she left the area, though, she turned and waved at Cara and the Samuelsons.

ADAM FELT COMPELLED to read all the information around an exhibit which slowed his progress. Cara, Linnea, and Katie shared his interest, or at least put up with him. They were there until the museum closed, then they drove downtown to a Mexican restaurant a friend of Katie's had recommended.

By the time they headed back to the car, it was dark. The occasional utility lights did a poor job of illuminating the parking garage. The four of them entered the elevator laughing.

Adam gently hip-checked Linnea. "I can't believe you asked the waiter for a chocolate milkshake, extra spicy. You're a nut!"

"And the waiter was on his game," Cara added. "What'd he

say? 'We don't have spicy chocolate milkshakes on the menu, but I can make yours extra chocolatey.' Classic."

Katie shook her head, smiling. "I can't take you guys anywhere. Y'all are embarrassing."

"You love us. We keep you young," Linnea said.

"True enough," Katie replied as the elevator doors opened.

The fourth floor was mostly empty. Their car was at the far end of the garage. They made it halfway there when, off to one side, they heard the soft *snikt* of blades being quietly opened. Three young men in hoodies appeared around a corner, stopping about thirty feet from the Samuelsons. The ruffians all carried knives. As though choreographed, they spread apart so they could come at the family from three different angles. Adam's first thought was that he wished he'd been wearing his marauding suit, but then, his parents didn't know about it.

He motioned his mom and Linnea behind him and stepped forward. "We have n-no quarrel with you. Leave us be. Go in peace."

The middle thug laughed harshly. "You're gonna go in pieces!" He approached closer, and his two buddies followed suit.

"Leave now!" Cara called. She set her jaw, planted her feet in a wider stance, and balled her hands into fists. Adam knew from experience what would happen if the situation escalated.

She continued, "If you drop your weapons and leave immediately, you can live. You will lose if we fight. You three will die. Just drop your weapons and run. Now! Go!"

"I don't think so, girl. I think I'm gonna add scars to your ugly face. Teach you some respect." He laughed again, tossing his knife from hand to hand. He came forward faster now, his eyes hard.

Cara quickly spoke to her group. "Head back toward the elevators. Please don't look. I'm so sorry."

Linnea and Katie stayed by Adam's side. "M-Mom, please look this way. Focus on the elevators. You don't want to see what's going to happen. Please trust me," Adam said, his voice urgent. "Don't turn, no matter what you hear. Please."

Adam held his mom and Linnea against his chest until the screams and the crack of breaking bones and the dull smack of flesh against concrete stopped. He estimated only fifteen or twenty seconds until the parking garage was quiet once more. "S-Stay like this till she comes back," he whispered.

Soon they heard Cara's gentle voice beside them. "Let's return to the elevator, go down a level, then walk up the ramp to the car from the other way. Please don't look back."

Adam nodded, and they headed to the elevator, pushed the door-close button, and began descending. Cara was still breathing heavily from whatever she had done moments earlier. "I'm so sorry, Ms. Katie," she said again. "I never wanted you to see that."

THE SMARTEST PERSON IN
THE ROOM

"Colonel, you've seen the video, right?"

Colonel Regina Taylor nodded. "Yes, I have."

"We need to talk. Can we go for lunch? Ideally, somewhere far enough from here that we won't meet any colleagues from the DIA."

"Do you have a place in mind?"

"Are you good with Chinese?"

"Sure, though with traffic and construction, getting there and back will kill the rest of the afternoon."

"You're the boss and can do what you want, Colonel. Besides, we'll be working."

Colonel Taylor chuckled.

At the restaurant, it surprised Olivia to hear her supervisor speak to the hostess fluently in a language that Olivia did not recognize. The hostess was wide-eyed at first, but then smiled and bowed to Colonel Taylor. The two ladies conversed in the foreign language, then the hostess led her guests to a table against the back wall facing the dining area. This gave them privacy and protected their back.

"You speak Chinese?"

"That was Mandarin. I also speak Cantonese."

"Uh, you're American. But you sounded fluent."

"Thank you," Colonel Taylor said with a smile.

"I mean no offense, but you don't look as though you would speak Chinese?"

"It gets worse. I'm also fluent in Russian and Arabic, and about a dozen other languages."

"I did not know. How did you … I mean, why …?" Olivia coughed and shook her head. "I'm sorry. I never heard your story. Would you tell me some of it, please?"

"I'm not that interesting. I grew up in a suburb of Houston. Pretty nice middle-class life. Dad was a master plumber. Owned his own business. Mom was an elementary school teacher. My brother and I …" She laughed and shook her head. "We didn't really fit in well in high school."

"What do you mean?"

"We didn't … how should I put it … to some people, my brother Mark and I didn't *look* as though we would be strong academically, but we were. Mark was very good at science and math classes and became a chemical engineer. My thing was languages. I loved my English classes, and when I had the opportunity to learn Spanish and German, I signed up. I quickly became fluent. One summer in high school, I taught myself French.

"Mark and I didn't fit into any of the standard social groups. We both had some Black friends and some white friends, but nobody was very close. School friends. I had few sleepovers for whatever reason. Despite my facility with languages, I didn't have the words, the self-esteem, or the wisdom to discuss race relations with my white girlfriends. Some Black students gave Mark and me a hard time for placing so much importance on academics. They had a name for it: acting white. I never understood why someone would equate my success in school with turning my back on people who look like me."

"But ma'am …"

"Please call me Gina in private."

"Okay, but Gina, it sounds like your parents stressed education."

"They did. They wanted us to do better than them. 'The American Dream,' they called it. They did pretty well, and they provided a wonderful home for us."

Olivia nodded. "Same for me. My family emigrated from Colombia, though I was born here in the U.S. So how did you end up in intelligence?"

"I went to the University of Chicago, where I majored in Asian and African Studies, with minors in several unrelated languages. Lots of credit hours, as you can imagine."

"Impressive!"

"Thanks, but as a teenager, I felt that nobody noticed me. For years I thought it was 'Black girl in a white world' syndrome … and I don't doubt there was some of that. It was as though I was invisible, but I'd look down and see my hands, my body. Of course, I wasn't literally invisible, but I might as well have been."

"So it was like *Invisible Man* by Ralph Ellison rather than *The Invisible Man* by H. G. Wells, right?"

"Precisely. Same thing happened at the University of Chicago, and again in graduate school at Columbia. And not just in school. I could sit at a table in a coffee shop, and people around me would talk about private things … sometimes in English, sometimes not … and they were oblivious to my presence. The chip I carried on my shoulder was not something I was proud of. I was sure it was because I was a Black woman." She paused.

"And then …" Olivia prompted.

Colonel Taylor leaned forward conspiratorially. "My life

changed one evening at a party. I was in graduate school. Everybody at the party was Black. I was nursing a drink, thinking about how I might as well be invisible. And nobody noticed me. Nobody. Noticed. Me.

"You see, it wasn't a 'Black girl' thing, it was a 'Regina Taylor' thing. So I studied it. I practiced it. Ultimately, I perfected it. Of course, people can see me, but if I don't want them to notice me, they won't register in their mind that I'm there. Well, what could I do with fluency in multiple languages and the ability to avoid notice? I just *had* to work in intelligence. I won't say it's been easy, but it sure as hell has been fun.

"I started in the State Department. The CIA drafted me after a few years. Then the director of the DIA made me an offer I couldn't refuse. It's strange; I've sat in probably thousands of meetings all over the world, held in languages that a lot of Americans do not expect Black people to speak, for some reason. Nobody paid attention to me. I could have been wearing a cloak of invisibility."

"And in reality, you were the smartest person in the room."

"Thank you. But yeah, I suppose often that was true. I was extremely productive as a spy."

"Did you do much of that James Bond stuff?"

Colonel Taylor chuckled and shook her head. "No, that's not what most agents actually do. I suppose there's occasionally a place for that, but that's not where the money is, as they say."

"On another topic, Gina, we should discuss the video of Cara's test. The one from the garage in Chicago. What did we see? That wasn't CGI. That was real life. Cara was in the parking garage with her family, then she was gone and ... who or what the hell was that in her place? Nobody can move that fast. Nobody's that strong.

"I grew up Catholic, like most people from Colombia, and maybe that's coloring my interpretation, but that lady who replaced Cara made me think of the Angel of Death. Perhaps it was the way she killed. She didn't look angry so much as efficient and dispassionate, like she was doing a job she'd done many times before. She tore those men apart the way I might squash a bug. Then she stared directly at one of the video cameras before she disappeared, and Cara was there. It was as though she was challenging us."

"For the Angel of Death spread his wings on the blast / And breathed in the face of the foe as he passed; / And the eyes of the sleepers waxed deadly and chill / And their hearts but once heaved, and for ever grew still!"

"What's that from, Gina?"

"Lord Byron. A poem called 'The Destruction of Sennacherib.'"

"Lovely words, but this was a woman … or looked like one. An ultra-violent woman. Is that an oxymoron? And she did more than 'breathe in the face of the foe.'" Olivia grimaced and shook her head. "Did you notice how the family avoided looking at … whatever she was?"

"Like they were afraid something bad would happen if they saw her. Reminds me of the biblical story of Lot's wife, as they fled from the destruction of Sodom and Gomorrah. Lot warned her not to look back. She looked anyway and died. Pillar of salt."

"How about us? We saw the video. Will that beautiful monster come for us?"

"You said it yourself, Olivia. That Angel of Death lady looked bored, like it wasn't worth her trouble to show up and rip those guys apart."

"I'd hate to see her when she's angry!"

"The bigger question is what the director will decide to

do with her. That's an awful lot of power with which to trust a teenager ... or anyone."

A NIGHT AT THE SYMPHONY

Stephen arranged for his family to stay the weekend in two connected rooms at The Peninsula Chicago. This was the kids' first stay in a five-star hotel. They all agreed that this place set the bar very high. Adam got his own bed, sharing a room with his parents. Linnea and Cara had a room to themselves.

Their room overlooked Michigan Avenue and featured a fabric art wall filled with hand-stitched chrysanthemums, a huge television with sound bar, and a tablet in a cradle on the bedside table. The device, accessible in eleven languages, controlled room environment, offered hotel amenities, showed local attractions, and provided access to many newspapers. Their beds were luxurious. The bathroom was marble and featured a soaking tub in which one could lay and watch TV. Adam couldn't help but wonder why anyone would want to watch TV while bathing.

Ms. Fortune outdid herself. Their tickets were for box seats near the center. Just perfect! Adam was glad he wore a jacket, because most of the men seated near them wore suits or tuxedos. His dad wore his usual tweed jacket with a vest. Adam felt his mom, Cara, and Linnea were as elegant as anybody there.

Beethoven's "Violin Concerto in D" was one of Adam's favorite pieces. Hilary Hahn played her part impeccably, all from memory. After a rousing ovation, she gave the audience a masterful rendition of a solo Bach partita, then ended with the whirlwind craziness of Heinrich Wilhelm Ernst's "Erlkönig."

When the crowds thinned after the performance, they made their way upstairs to the club room on the ninth floor. Tables were scattered about, each with four chairs and white linen tablecloths. Servers wandered through the room with trays of various canapés. Ms. Hahn found herself surrounded by elderly donors who wanted their turn to congratulate her. The Samuelsons could see that she was not likely to get any food soon. Linnea made up a little plate of hors d'oeuvres and brought it to the beleaguered violinist, who accepted it with a gracious smile and thanks.

It was while Adam was watching the exchange between his younger sister and Ms. Hahn that the architect of their evening at the Chicago Symphony approached.

"Adam, Cara, it's a pleasure to see you again."

"Ms. Fortune. Th-Thank you so much for this delightful evening. I'd love for you to meet my parents." He turned and presented them. "Mom, Dad, this is Ms. Lelia Fortune. Cara and I met her several weeks ago when we were driving through Chicago."

The Samuelsons looked up to see a short elderly lady with a full head of white hair. She walked haltingly, as though it took effort to remain upright. Her blue eyes, though, were alert and bright.

Both parents smiled. "Stephen Samuelson. My wife, Katie."

"It's a pleasure to meet you, Ms. Fortune," Katie started. "The kids told us about you. I'd like to echo Adam's thanks for this wonderful evening."

"Lelia Fortune. Pronounced like 'cartoon.' The pleasure is mine. Cara and Adam are two remarkable young people. They may have saved my life." Her voice quavered.

"They didn't tell me about that. Just that they helped you change a tire."

"If they won't brag about themselves, allow an old lady to brag on them. The two were driving through Chicago. They were hurrying to pick up Adam's younger sister somewhere. My car was ahead of theirs. A front tire blew at highway speed. My driver lost control, and the car spun off the road. They pulled over, made sure I was okay, and helped him change the tire. He had a bad shoulder and appreciated their help.

"Is the little one here? I'd like to meet her, if I may. I remember they were worried about her."

"Of course," Katie said. She waved at Linnea and motioned her back. "Linnea, this is Ms. Fortune."

Linnea smiled and extended a hand. "It's a pleasure to meet you, ma'am. Thank you for giving us tickets to this concert."

"I'm happy to do it for you," Ms. Fortune replied. Then softer, "Would you help me to my table, young lady?" To Adam's parents she said, "Excuse me, I need to sit down."

Linnea took the elderly lady's arm. Adam took her other arm and Cara walked with him. They headed for a table across the room from where his folks were standing.

"Thank you," she said, her voice miraculously stronger. "We don't have long. I wanted to meet you, Miss Linnea. You impressed me with how you handled yourself in Sokolov's estate."

Linnea's eyes widened, but she caught herself quickly.

"Cara and Adam told me about you, but I wasn't sure you were real. Thank you for your help. He would have killed me if they hadn't shown up when they did."

"I owed a debt to an old friend, so I did what I could to help you. But now, things are happening. We must help each other."

"W-What's going on?" Adam asked.

"No time to go into it now. But stay together as much as possible, be alert, and keep your suits and equipment handy. I'm not sure how to make it happen, but you need to visit me at my home … just you three … at the earliest chance you have."

"Yes, ma'am," Cara said. "We'll figure something out."

"No, wait. Let's not make this more difficult than it needs to be. Call your parents over here."

When Katie and Stephen arrived, Ms. Fortune turned to them. "If an old lady might impose … I'd like to have some quality time with your young people. Do you have plans for tomorrow?"

"I guess we were probably going to shop on Michigan Avenue during the day, have dinner somewhere, then head home tomorrow evening," Stephen said.

"If you don't mind, I'll send a car for the three kids tomorrow morning, say nine o'clock a.m. I'll have them back to the hotel by late afternoon. Where are you staying?"

"We're at the Peninsula."

"Excellent choice. Tomorrow morning, then."

"Thank you."

When his parents excused themselves to speak with Hilary Hahn, whose line of admirers was now much shorter, Katie said to Stephen, "It's strange. We only spoke briefly with Lelia Fortune tonight, but there's something about her. As crazy as it sounds, I feel I can trust her with the kids."

At the same time, Adam asked Ms. Fortune, "How do you do that, ma'am? You're hard to resist."

She smiled. "If you know what you want, you have a tremendous advantage over a person who isn't sure. In American slang, we call it 'balls.' The French say *qui ne risque rien n'a rien*. It sounds better in French, I think."

TO GRANDMOTHER'S HOUSE
WE GO

The next morning, precisely at nine o'clock a.m., a black Mercedes with dark-tinted windows pulled up in front of the Peninsula Hotel. The three teens were waiting in the lobby. Adam was glad that he and Cara had thought to bring in their day bags their equipment that Lelia Fortune had given them.

The driver, a swarthy man wearing a black t-shirt and khaki pants, stepped out of the car. "Good morning. My name is Nuri," he greeted them in accented English.

"Adam S-Samuelson," Adam said as he shook the man's hand. He had a firm grip. "This is Cara Ferris and my sister, Linnea Samuelson."

"Ladies," he nodded to them. "Please, everyone, get in. Adam, you may wish to sit up front. More room."

They drove in silence for a while. Adam studied Nuri. He looked extremely fit, with alert dark eyes and hair cut short, military style. Adam suspected he could do much more than drive.

Nuri was the first to speak. "I understand you have been to Ms. Fortune's house before."

"Yes, sir," Cara replied, offering no more information. "What do you do for Ms. Fortune?" Cara asked.

He glanced at her briefly; his eyes flashed with amusement. "Very interesting, Cara. You verbalized the thing that Adam was thinking."

"It's the obvious question, sir."

"Indeed. My name is Nuri Ben-David." He pronounced it ben-dah-VEED. "Ms. Fortune is my boss and my friend. We have worked together for years."

"Ben-David. That sounds Israeli," Cara said.

"Hmm." Nuri spoke no further until they arrived at the house Cara and Adam visited the day they rescued their younger sister. Linnea was quiet on the ride from the hotel, looking around the car and studying their driver. Adam was sure she missed nothing.

Out of interest, Adam tried again to check Google Maps as they exited the Mercedes. As before, he could not get a signal. Nuri opened the massive front door and ushered the teens inside.

"Please, come in," Ms. Fortune said to them, smiling as she rose from a sofa. "Welcome to my home."

Linnea looked around, as she'd not been there before. "You have a beautiful home, ma'am," she said.

"Thank you, Linnea." Ms. Fortune leaned forward and stage-whispered to her in a conspiratorial fashion, "It gets better."

She gestured to Nuri. "You've met my colleague, Nuri Ben-David, I assume."

"Yes, ma'am."

"Nuri and I have worked together for many years. He has earned my complete trust. Now, does anyone wish for something to eat or drink?"

"N-No, thank you, ma'am," Adam said. "The three of us just had an amazing breakfast at the hotel."

"I'm sure you did. The Peninsula Hotel is always a splendid choice. I have stayed at several of them around the world." She turned to Adam. "Did you and Cara bring your suits and things, by any chance?"

"Yes. I brought the other two items as well."

"Excellent. I have a few upgrades, and we need to fit Linnea with her own suit. Follow me downstairs, please."

Linnea's eyes widened when she saw Ms. Fortune manipulate several books, seemingly at random, on a large bookshelf. The wall of books slid in and to one side, revealing a metal door in a concrete wall. Ms. Fortune stared into a retinal scanner. The door opened with a soft hiss and the group stepped into an elevator.

Linnea had heard about the secret elevator behind the bookcase. When the five of them stepped out into the massive underground warehouse, rows of shelves stacked full of various military ordnance, Linnea could not help but gasp. "My gosh, I was sure my brother and sister were exaggerating!"

"You like it, then?"

"Oh, this is amazing! Would you show me, please?"

Ms. Fortune's face lit up with a smile. She had the energy, the enthusiasm of a much younger person: a female Willie Wonka with a much deadlier candy factory.

Nuri leaned towards her and spoke in a low voice, "Ma'am, I'll be in Logistics if you need me."

She nodded. "Very well."

Linnea, her eyes wide, scanned shelves of pistols, rifles, hand-held rocket launchers, and grenades.

Ms. Fortune gestured to them. "This area here is all conventional small arms, as well as ammunition, scopes, night vision gear and body armor."

"Do you manufacture these?" Linnea asked.

"Mostly, no. I'm an authorized reseller. There's no reason to reinvent the wheel."

"But the equipment you gave Adam and Cara ..."

"That's different. My design. I'm an armorer and artificer."

"Guild?" Linnea wondered aloud.

Ms. Fortune stopped walking and turned to Linnea. "What did you say?"

Linnea backed away, her mouth suddenly dry, her heart fluttering. "I'm sorry, ma'am. I didn't mean anything bad."

"I'm not angry, Linnea. Just surprised. Why did you ask that?"

"It's just ... I've been thinking a lot about what I'd like to do with my life, especially given all the excitement of the last few months. I was doing some research into how I might combine my interests in electronics and engineering and chemistry. There was a vague reference in a book, something they referred to as the Armorer's Guild. It sounded like something medieval, or like one might encounter in a role-playing game. It piqued my interest, so I researched more. That's how I am."

The older teens nodded. "That is definitely you, and I l-love you for it," Adam said.

"But I fell in love with the concept. I dream about it being real. It's what I want to do." She looked directly at her host. "Is it real, Ms. Fortune?"

She drew Linnea into a grandmotherly hug. "My dear, sweet child. I felt I needed to meet you, and I was correct. You've fallen down the rabbit hole. Welcome!"

THE ARMORER'S GUILD

"The Armorer's Guild? I don't know what you guys are t-talking about," Adam said. "Would someone please bring me up to speed?" Cara and he looked at Ms. Fortune, who turned and nodded at Linnea.

"Go ahead, Linnea. Why don't you start? Let's sit here while we talk." Ms. Fortune gestured to several cloth-covered chairs and a low table in an open area adjoining the warehouse. The warehouse floors were smooth concrete, but this area where they sat had a marble floor. Behind the chairs, several fierce-looking swords hung on display on a wall.

The young girl took a breath to collect her thoughts. "Okay. We all learned that in medieval Europe, groups of merchants and tradespeople banded together to form guilds to protect their common interests."

The older teens nodded.

"Young people would start with an apprenticeship where they lived with the master who provided room and board in exchange for usually seven years of work and study. Then they became a journeyman and got paid for their work. Sometimes, they actually had to make a journey to learn from other masters, then build a 'masterpiece' to show they were worthy of becoming a master in their own right and training new apprentices.

"As production became progressively more specialized, trade guilds divided and subdivided until large cities such as London and Paris had hundreds of guilds, each with their own laws, paperwork and such." Linnea looked around to be sure she had everyone's attention. "But the various guilds were not equal. Some played politics better than others, got in good with the powers that be. For the ruler who wished to stay in power, some skills were frankly more valuable than others."

"What do you mean by more valuable?" Cara asked.

"Compare, for instance, armorers and bakers. Not to disparage baking, but from the viewpoint of a king or nobleman who enjoys staying alive … well, you know what I'm saying."

"This is all common knowledge, Linnea," Adam said. "But in my class on Western civilization, I read that toward the end of the eighteenth century and b-beginning of the nineteenth century, the guild system faced huge criticism that it was stifling free trade and technological innovation. And here we are in the second decade of the twenty-first century. Guilds fell from grace well over a hundred years ago. Why are we talking about them?"

Linnea turned to their host. "Ma'am, would you pick up the story from here, please?"

"Fine. Everything you said about guilds is true, as far as it goes. One guild, the Armorers, had leaders who were more far-sighted than many of their contemporaries. Two hundred years ago, in London, there was a secret meeting of all the top Master Armorers of the day. You can't imagine what it took to bring these powerful, egotistical men together. Remember, at this point in history, the trade had already subdivided into helmet makers, mail armor or plate armor makers, sword makers or bow or crossbow makers, fletchers, and the list goes on. And of course, early firearms brought experts in this burgeoning technology as well.

"They met and discussed and argued for a long time, but at the end there was a new guild, the Armorers Guild, that encompassed all the many talents present at that table."

"Earlier you also mentioned artificers. Where do they come in?" Adam asked.

"Yes. A few of the master weaponsmiths had created specific weapons so deadly they were given names. Over the years, stories grew around some of these. I have replicas here to remind us of our lineage."

She stood and laid her hand on each of the displayed weapons in turn. "Excalibur, that you'll recognize from the King Arthur tales; the Wallace Sword that William Wallace used during the wars of Scottish independence from England; Tizona, the sword that El Cid carried in his battles against the Moors; Zulfiqar, the scimitar that Ali wielded to defend Medina; and the Honjo Masamune, crafted by one of the greatest metallurgists the world has ever known. There are others, of course. But these master weaponsmiths are known as artificers. Within the Armorers Guild, they are honored. My marauding suit and the other tools I gave Adam earned me the title of Artificer."

"Okay, but what did this newly named Armorers Guild accomplish?" Cara asked.

"We foresaw the rise of industrialization, the emerging manufacturing technologies, and standardization. We realized that public opinion was turning against the guild system, and that we could not trust the patronage of the various city-states or countries where we worked, so we became a secret society.

"Most guilds simply faded away, though many have reappeared in modern times as professional societies. Consider, for example, medicine, where licensing requires years of low-paid training under harsh working conditions they call internship and residency, then acceptance by the local medical board. Basically, it's a guild by another name. Engineering, architecture, nursing, and many more specialties are structured similarly.

"But back to us: Most of the top weapons designers in the world belong to the Armorers Guild."

"Defense contractors?" Linnea asked.

"No, not the companies, the men and women *in* the companies who have the actual knowledge."

Adam nodded. "So what do you do, exactly, ma'am?"

"Look around you," she gestured. "This underground complex cost many tens of millions of dollars to build and support. I pay for it by selling arms to elite field agents. As I told you weeks ago, I don't do field work myself anymore. Instead, I help make it possible for these highly trained individuals to do their jobs. They pay me very well and they, in turn, keep the world safe for democracy. Without them, there would be chaos. Rule by the masses means lack of rules."

"B-By field agents, do you mean assassins? Who tells these people who to kill?"

"Governments, usually. Though targeted hits are actually quite infrequent. Assassins also abide by rules. For example, world leaders can't hire Guild assassins to kill other world leaders. That keeps the world in balance, so we all don't descend into anarchy. More often, the people with whom I do business engage themselves with hostage rescues, human trafficking, and monitoring of the world drug trade. I do not sell my products to terrorists or criminals."

"How c-can you be sure of that?"

Ms. Fortune shrugged. "I admit to making value judgements. We all do; we can't help it. One man's freedom fighter is another man's terrorist. My colleagues and I do the best we can, in our own way, to help make the world a better place.

"You look at me, and what do you see? A sweet old lady? I am old, but I'm not very sweet. This is a hard business and one in which few people die of old age. I've learned to be tough and ruthless. I am not a nice lady."

Adam digested what she said. "Do assassins have a g-guild also? Do they start out as apprentices?"

"Slow down," Ms. Fortune said as she raised her palm. "I just make and sell the candy. I don't eat it. The system actually works very well. Good guys kill bad guys so that the bad guys don't kill innocent people ... or at least we try to attenuate the collateral damage."

"We're just a bit shocked, I guess. They don't teach this stuff in school."

"There's a lot they don't teach in school. Anyway, what I was saying earlier is that I use funds from these sales to develop new technologies. Your suits, for example, and Adam's other equipment resulted from my work."

"Wow!" Linnea exclaimed. "How did you learn how to do this?"

Ms. Fortune laughed. "Come on. Let me finish showing you guys around." She opened a door off the immense warehouse and ushered the teens inside with a flourish.

"Cara, Adam, you remember this room, right?"

"Yes, ma'am. This is where you fitted us with our suits."

"Exactly. While we're here, Linnea, let me measure you for yours."

They watched while Linnea held out her arms and experienced the same procedure as Cara and Adam had weeks earlier. While they waited, they returned their marauding suits and tools to Ms. Fortune for the upgrades she'd promised.

"There's so much I'd like to do with these suits, but those stupid laws of thermodynamics keep getting in the way."

Linnea snickered. "Yeah, that conservation of energy thing is so last week."

"I hope the next generation of researchers will find a way around it. Some kind of loophole. Till then, I can only do so much."

HOW TO GET THERE

$\mathcal{L}$innea's eyes sparkled, and she bounced from foot to foot. "May we see your research lab? Your manufacturing facilities?"

Ms. Fortune turned to the teens and smiled. "You'd like that, would you?"

"Oh, yes!"

"Follow me, then." She turned and led them down a corridor, pausing by a large window. Through the window, they saw an ultra-modern laboratory that would be the envy of any university engineering department. Lab benches stretched the length of the room. White boards, most of which were covered with equations and diagrams, dotted the walls. A man and a woman, probably in their twenties, were working on individual projects. The man, facing a state-of-the-art smart board, had scribbled a series of intricate overlapping curves that resembled loose knots. He stood there gazing at it, hand on his chin, lost in thought. The woman seated at the lab bench, wearing safety goggles and gloves, was soldering something on a circuit board. An assortment of electronic equipment lay on the benches and showed signs of active use. An appliance the size of a large refrigerator, a glass window in the center, dominated one end of the lab.

"What is that?" Adam asked, pointing at the appliance.

"An industrial 3D printer," Ms. Fortune said. "It can print in metal or carbon fiber or Kevlar®, to extremely fine tolerances."

Cara studied the diagrams on the smart board that had apparently stymied the young man. "I see what he's trying to do," she said. "May I show him?"

Ms. Fortune smiled. "This should be good. Follow me, please."

She led the group around a corner, through a secure door, and stopped at another door. "Here we are." She tapped a button on the wall, and the door slid open with a barely perceptible hiss. "Matteo, Petra, I have some people I'd like you to meet."

The young man walked over to them. Dark hair, dark eyes, slim but athletic build. *Dangerous*, Cara thought. Ms. Fortune made the introductions. "Matteo, I'd like you to meet my friends Cara, Adam, and Linnea."

"Matteo Lanza," he said in accented English. "It is a pleasure to meet you."

"We were in the hallway outside the window, and Cara mentioned to me she saw a solution to the problem you've written on the board."

"Indeed," Matteo said with a nod. "I should appreciate your help."

Cara and Matteo approached the board. "It works like this," he said. He raised a finger close to the board and wrote in the air. The design appeared on the board. Then he waved his hand side-to-side, and the design vanished.

Cara scribbled furiously on the board, as though her hands were struggling to keep up with her brain. Matteo watched intently, nodding in agreement. He asked her a question. She answered with a series of equations.

Matteo's face lit up. "Yes, I see. That could work. Thank you."

Linnea ambled over by Cara to see what she and Matteo were working on.

The young lady finished her soldering, removed her safety glasses and gloves, and smiled at the visitors. She was a thin girl, with short light-brown hair and pale skin. Her ears had several piercings, and she had a small ring in her left eyebrow and another in her nose. "I apologize. I did not mean to be rude. My name is Petra Layevska." When she shook Adam's hand, he noted tattoos on both of her arms.

"I'm Adam, and that little blonde girl over there is my sister, Linnea." He gestured to Cara and Matteo, who were still engaged in quiet conversation by the smart board. "The older one is Cara."

Petra nodded in Cara's direction. "Nobody comes here unless they have a special skill. Cara obviously has a gift for mathematics. I'm curious to learn what you and your little sister can do."

"I'm curious to learn about my g-gift as well," Adam agreed. "When I figure it out, I'll let you know."

The girl laughed. "You are modest. And your sister?"

"Do you like comics?" Adam asked.

"Of course. We're all nerds here."

"Reed Richards. Tony Stark. Bruce Banner. Hank Pym. All pretty smart, yes?"

"Yes, they are all brilliant."

"Okay, and Shuri?"

"The Black Panther's teenage younger sister? Head of the Wakanda Design Group? Arguably the smartest person in the Marvel Universe? That Shuri?"

Adam nodded. "Linnea Samuelson," he said, nodding at

his sister. "I d-don't know if I can claim credit for this phrase, but I think of Linnea as being 'comic book smart.'"

"What do you mean by that?"

"I would say I'm pretty bright, like my parents. My dad is a professor of medicine and my mom's an ICU nurse. But Linnea is on a whole different level. You look at her, and she's small and cute and seems like a normal fourteen-year-old middle school kid. Well, starting high school in the fall."

"But …?"

"But she turned her bedroom into a lab." Adam paused for effect. "I mean a real laboratory, not some chemistry set."

"What does a kid do with a home laboratory?"

"Um, she built a particle accelerator in our basement."

"It is not possible. She is so cute."

"Yeah, it was cute until she mentioned antimatter. That made Dad nervous."

Petra giggled and lowered her voice to simulate an adult male. "I'm putting my foot down, girl. There will be no anti-matter in this house."

"That's p-pretty much how the conversation went. It was surreal."

"The tribulations of parenting a genius, huh?"

Adam chuckled. "Most parents worry about sex, drugs, and alcohol. Those were never a problem in our house. My folks had to specify no energetic chemistry, no radioactivity, and especially no antimatter."

"Energetic chemistry?"

Adam shook his head. "It's a funny story now, but let's save it for another time."

"Okay. Adam, I understand what's involved with building the sort of devices Linnea plays with. Back in my country, I constructed a railgun."

"A railgun? Seriously? No way."

"Yes way. A working railgun. I accelerated a projectile to

almost three thousand meters per second. That is admittedly at the low end for a military railgun, but I used mostly repurposed and recycled parts and a shoestring budget, so I feel pretty good about it. But I had people to teach me how to work safely with high voltages, how to weld, how to machine metal, stuff like that. How did Linnea learn the techniques she needs?"

"Good question. One of Dad's friends is a professor of Electrical Engineering at Rose-Hulman Institute of Technology in Indiana. He tried to get Linnea to enroll at Rose-Hulman as a student, but she was adamant she wanted to stay in middle school and be a kid. She plays soccer as much for socializing as for love of the game. Most of her free time she spends in her lab or learning necessary techniques from the engineering professor, Doctor Cox, or one of his colleagues, or from me. I guess I'm mostly her lab assistant, chauffeur, and safety director. Some things require an extra pair of hands. Recently she's been talking about designing an autonomous robot, so I may be out of a job soon."

Adam looked across the lab at his sister, who was in conversation with Matteo and Cara. "Linnea?" She looked over. "When you get a chance, would you come here, please?" Linnea smiled and nodded.

A minute later, she appeared beside Adam. "You summoned me, o esteemed elder brother?" she said with mock formality, though her eyes were mirthful.

"Petra, this nut is my favorite sister, Linnea ..."

"Your only sister!" Linnea interjected.

"... and the smartest person I know in this universe and any other."

Petra turned to her and smiled. "I am pleased to meet you, Linnea. You are adorable."

"Thank you, miss," Linnea said. "My brother exaggerates.

I'm not all that." She put her arm around Adam's waist and looked up at him fondly.

"Who p-played chess with a grandmaster, the current U.S. champion, and won?"

"I had a good day."

"Who is a wizard with anything involving chemistry or physics or engineering?"

"I'm just playing. You're embarrassing me." Linnea turned to the young scientist. "Are you from Russia, Miss Petra? I've heard an accent like yours recently, and those people were Russian."

"Just Petra, please. No, I'm from Ukraine, near Kyiv. Matteo is from Italy."

Ms. Fortune interrupted their conversation. "Where is Ying Yue?"

"I believe she is in the gym, Doctor Fortune."

"Doctor?" Adam exclaimed.

"Yes, your host has a doctorate in materials physics," Petra said. "You were not aware of this?"

"You n-never said, Ms. … er … Doctor Fortune."

"Please, Ms. Fortune is fine. Or Lelia. We're all friends here. I have had the good fortune, over the years, to host many highly intelligent young people from all over the world here in my laboratory. As we talked about earlier, the other masters and I mentor young armorers. You've met Petra and Matteo. Ying Yue is from China. She is extremely knowledgeable in artificial intelligence, and that's saying a lot, given that China has placed such a high priority on AI."

Petra smirked. "And beautiful. Is that not true, Matteo?"

"I … uh …" Matteo looked uncomfortable.

"It is okay, Matteo. I am standard brown-haired girl. Ying Yue is exotic. I cannot compete." She smiled.

"No, Petra. You are beautiful too. It's just that I …" He looked around, trying to conjure up the correct words. Then he shrugged. "This is why I'm more comfortable around computers. I do not understand women."

Just then, the object of their discussion entered the lab. She was tiny, only five feet tall, with ebony hair and pale skin. She approached the group. "I heard we had visitors. I am Jiang Ying Yue."

Ms. Fortune introduced the group again. "Ying Yue, these are my friends Cara, Adam, and Linnea."

Ying Yue bowed but did not extend a hand. "It is a pleasure to meet you." Adam thought, as he saw her stare at Cara, that Ying Yue did not look pleased.

BACK IN THE HALLWAY, Adam posed a question. "Ms. Fortune, you have s-students from all over the world?"

"That's correct, Adam."

"So your t-technology ends up in Europe, but also in the former Soviet bloc and in China? Doesn't it bother you?"

"I'll admit that my technology may spread outside of the United States, though my people maintain strict oversight of everything I sell. Why should it bother me?"

"It can't be a good idea for us to share our state-of-the-art technology, especially military-related technology, with Russia and China."

"I don't take students who are spies or who were sent here by their government."

"How could you tell? By definition, you can't ask someone if they're a spy and expect to hear the truth."

"I would know, Adam."

He glanced at her, doubt in his eyes. "Okay, but even if your students were all from here in the United States, I don't see why you would want to share your technology—for instance, the suits you made for us—with everyone for free.

Shouldn't you patent it and protect it so you can profit from it?"

"Ah, I understand your question. You need to understand my position. Adam, I am wealthy beyond my wildest dreams and most likely beyond yours. I have an insane amount of money in banks and investments around the world. I don't need more money; I need a legacy. So I give back to my community through my various charitable foundations. And I give back to my profession, to my colleagues, to my guild, by mentoring promising young students. I give them access to world-class facilities, but of equal importance, here in my lab they can network with each other, and with me, and together we accomplish much more than any of us could individually."

"What sorts of things are you working on, apart from those marauding suits?" Linnea asked.

"We're on the cusp of some exciting developments in artificial intelligence and robotics. There are a few more hurdles we need to overcome—a few things we haven't found a way around yet—but I feel we're close to a breakthrough. I'm excited about the team we've put together. Petra is brilliant with microprocessors and robotics. Ying Yue is one of her country's top artificial intelligence experts, and Matteo has a doctorate in applied mathematics. And I know something about materials physics."

"Ms. Fortune, what do I need to do to work in a place like this?"

"You're serious, Linnea. Your face, your eyes … you really want this."

"I do, ma'am. I want to work at the point of the spear, if you understand what I'm trying to say. The newest, coolest, most state-of-the-art technology starts out as military tech. It's been that way throughout history. Learning how to temper steel, discovering the art of metallurgy; the idea at first was to make a better sword, to make sturdier armor. Afterwards, people applied that knowledge to other things."

"You're an unusual young lady. I mean that in a good way. We'll work well together."

"So how do I get from being a high school freshman this coming fall to a lab like yours? I'd be honored to study with you, Ms. Fortune. This is the most wonderful place I've ever seen."

"Here's what I recommend. Test out of high school as soon as possible. They have nothing to teach you. Go to a university and learn as much as you can about physics, math, engineering, computer science, and chemistry. Nobody will care exactly what your doctorates are in, just that you are comfortable with the material. When you're ready, I will sponsor you."

"But first I should earn at least one doctorate?"

"Most of the students I mentor are already experts in their chosen fields, and most of them have doctorates. Matteo and Ying Yue are graduates of prestigious universities in their home countries. Petra is an exception in that she is not college-educated. She is self-taught, but brilliant. Sadly, she didn't start out under ideal circumstances. Now she is where she needs to be."

"I understand living under less-than-ideal circumstances," Cara said. Adam squeezed her hand.

*L*elia Fortune walked her three guests to a small kitchen. They sat in comfortable chairs around a teak table and talked while Ms. Fortune prepared tea and brought out a tin of white chocolate macadamia cookies.

"Our chef baked these last night. Does anyone have a nut allergy?"

"No, ma'am. We're good with all cookies," Cara said.

Adam cleared his throat. "Ms. Fortune, last n-night at the reception you said that things were happening. What did you mean by that?"

"Yes, I need to talk with the three of you about that. Cara seems to have stirred things up."

Cara raised an eyebrow, questioning.

"Let me explain. You understand that as a part of my work, I have access to some very delicate information. Over the years, I've developed a network of informants. I also have advanced technology that helps me to keep abreast of developments that might affect my interests."

"That makes sense," Cara said.

"One issue we need to discuss concerns Mikhail Sokolov's crime syndicate."

"He's d-dead. Special Agent Tanaka said that the information Linnea sent from his office computer to the FBI will put away any of Sokolov's lieutenants who are still alive."

"That's an oversimplification. Sokolov's organization did billions of dollars' worth of business each year. Some of it was legal; much was not. It's like a hydra with many heads. You chop some off, but other heads grow back. It's not logical to expect this vast syndicate simply to disappear."

"B-But there's no leader now."

"Actually, there is. His son, Pyotr Sokolov, has apparently taken control of what's left of his father's organization. Mikhail Sokolov was primarily a businessman; amoral and cold, but at heart, he was a businessman. My sources tell me that Pyotr Sokolov travels a lot, usually to Europe and South America. It's not clear how he spends his time there. But from what I understand, he's quite the sociopath. I don't know what he will do now, but I doubt it will be good."

"Detective Anders and Special Agent Tanaka suspect Pyotr Sokolov was behind the shooting incident last month," Cara said.

Ms. Fortune wrinkled her brow. "Tell me about that."

"The three of us were on our way to school. We heard gunshots. Our windshield starred and Linnea screamed. Then the car pulled suddenly to the right. Adam lost control and we rolled. When we tried to crawl out of the car, there was more shooting."

"Then what happened?"

"She had to, um, make the shooting stop," Cara said in a soft voice.

"She?"

"You know, my uh … monster. Whatever."

Ms. Fortune nodded. "Yeah. Got it."

"One round got me in the arm," Linnea said, "but luckily the wound was superficial. I wore a sling for a while, but now I just have a small dressing."

"Pyotr Sokolov has focused on you three young people already," Ms. Fortune said. "Pardon a direct and possibly unpleasant question, but were you responsible for the death of his parents?"

"Yes, ma'am," Cara said. "I suppose he can see it that way. But I would remind you we came to his house only because his father, Mikhail Sokolov, kidnapped Linnea and threatened to kill her."

"I understand, and I'd be the last person to judge you. As we've discussed, I'm not the sweet old lady you originally took me for. For now, keep your marauding suits and gear close at hand, and try to stay together as much as possible."

"The police will protect us," Linnea said.

"When s-seconds count, the p-police are minutes away. Ms. Fortune is right. We need to take responsibility for our own protection, to the extent we can."

"What can we do against men with guns who want to kill us?" Linnea asked. "We're kids."

"Says the girl who outplayed a grandmaster in chess and who engineered a phenomenal escape from a drug lord's lair," Cara said as she ran her fingers through Linnea's hair.

"You s-said this was one issue, implying there's another issue."

"I believe there is something else going on, but I have limited data. Let me give you a little background. In the late 1970s, there was a secret government project to investigate the potential usefulness of psychic phenomena in military and domestic intelligence applications. The program was initially under the auspices of the Defense Intelligence Agency, or DIA, though it was transferred to the CIA in the mid-1990s. Soon after that, the so-called Stargate Project was found not to be useful and was terminated and declassified."

"What do you mean by psychic phenomena?"

"The primary focus of the project was what they termed 'remote viewing.' As you might guess, this refers to information that the viewer obtains through extrasensory perception, commonly called ESP, as opposed to using the five senses or technological methods of obtaining information. But they also evaluated telekinesis and other psychic phenomena. A CIA report stated the Stargate Project never generated any actionable information."

"Why did the DIA think this was a g-good idea in the first place?"

"Because our intelligence learned that the Soviet Union had a similar program. Remember that this began during the Cold War. It was a different time. Us versus Them. We couldn't risk that the Soviets might develop capabilities against which we would have no defense."

"I don't understand what this has to do with us," Cara said. "You just told us the government shut the program down several years before we were born."

"They did … officially," Ms. Fortune said. "They defunded the Stargate Project in 1995. But here's the thing: The project is still alive. The name is different; they call themselves the Office of Special Assets. Once again, it's part of the DIA. Their funding is secret, skimmed from the Intelligence budget."

"B-But why would our government decide not to let a useless program die?"

"Because it's not useless. The original Stargate Project took a wrong tack. They mistakenly gave credence to charlatans such as Uri Geller, the Israeli so-called mentalist. You can look him up on YouTube. He could supposedly bend spoons with his mind. Silly stuff like that. There are charlatans in any field, but it does not follow that everyone who works in that field is a fraud. The ones who are for real … you won't see them on YouTube."

"Are you sure that this Office of Special Assets really exists?"

Ms. Fortune nodded. "I'm certain that it does. A long time ago—probably twenty years—I had a friend. She was a unique lady with an unusual skill set and was an operative for the CIA. I know this because I supplied her with specialized equipment, much like I do now. We became … close. Two women in a man's world. One day, she confided in me that the DIA had approached her to work with them in the Office of Special Assets. She mentioned they were being very persuasive."

"And then?"

"And then she accepted their offer. We've not spoken since then."

"Again," Cara pressed, "what does this have to do with us?"

Ms. Fortune took a deep breath and exhaled slowly. Her face was solemn. Cara, Adam, and Linnea leaned forward to catch every word.

She gestured to Cara. "Over the last eight months, there have been several instances of extreme violence in central Indiana, and now in Chicago. Superhuman violence. In each instance, Cara was involved. After years of living under the radar, I worry that you have attracted their attention. Cara, I am not omniscient. I cannot be sure what's going on inside a secret agency that is itself inside a secret government agency. But this I know: The Office of Special Assets does exactly what its name says. It collects special assets. People who can do the impossible. There are similar programs in Russia, China, India, and Britain, and possibly other countries as well. This is real."

"Was your friend—the one you haven't heard from in twenty years—like me?" asked Cara. "You said she had an unusual skill set. Did she do what I do?"

"No, her gift was much more subtle. To be honest, I'm surprised someone at the DIA recognized it. But they did."

"How would they know about me? Special Agent Tanaka said he deleted the cockpit voice recorder data at the NTSB."

"Cara, the FBI is part of U.S. Intelligence, same as the CIA, the DIA, and the NSA. If the FBI can delete the data, don't you suppose another branch of U.S. Intelligence can see that it had been deleted? Don't you suppose they'll wonder why?"

"What would they do to recruit me? How could I tell it's them?"

"That's a good question, Cara. I do not know what you should look for, no idea what you should expect. I can't even guarantee that they're coming for you, though I'd be surprised if they don't."

Linnea gasped, suddenly tearful. "What does that mean? They can't take Cara. We can't let them take her away!"

Ms. Fortune laid a comforting hand on Linnea's leg. "I don't think they would kidnap her. Not in America. They would want Cara to work for them willingly. However, I do not know what they would do if she refused."

UNCLE SAM WANTS YOU

"Hey, may I talk to you guys?" Linnea asked.

The three teens sat at their kitchen island enjoying coffee and a pastry as an after-school snack.

"Sure. What's on your mind?" Cara asked.

"It's Dad. I think I'm confusing him."

"Your change of plans, huh?"

Linnea nodded. "I guess the sticking point is that for years I've been adamant about staying in my age-appropriate classes because I like my friends. Dad and Mom agreed, and that was our plan. Then we drove to Chicago, we met Ms. Fortune, and I saw all these possibilities that I never knew existed. Ms. Fortune told me basically that I've been punching well below my weight class, and she's right."

"Then you took the ACT and got a 34 of 36. And your SAT score was almost perfect. As an eighth-grader," Cara said.

"You also got a 34, Cara. Adam got a 33. You're both in the top two percent of all students who took the test. Our SAT scores were all similar."

"Yeah, but we're juniors. You're in the freaking eighth grade!"

"You make me feel like a weirdo. Anyway, I'm going into ninth grade."

"You kind of are a weirdo, sis. In a good way. Embrace your inner geek. Adam and I are proud of you."

Adam smiled at them. "And you girls impressed the heck out of Purdue University."

"You were there with us, Adam. I distinctly remember you there with us," Linnea said.

"Anyway," Adam said, "I'm looking forward to the three of us going to Purdue this fall. I've talked with Mom and Dad at some length. I promised them I'd take care of you. They'll rent us a house near campus. I have a car. The university gave us a waiver to not live in a dormitory during our freshman year. We're good to go."

"Do you feel like Dad's changing his mind?"

Linnea thought for a moment. "The truth is, they really are being cool about this. They're just freaking out a little. I'm their baby girl and all."

"Oh, for heaven's sake, we'll be an hour from home. It's not like we're headed off to find the New World. We can come home, or they can visit us every weekend if they want."

THE BELL AFFIXED to the bakery door jingled. Cara looked up from behind the counter.

"Welcome to the Old World Bakery," she said with a smile. "What may I help you find?"

A twenty-something woman removed her sunglasses,

looked around the bakery and approached the counter. "This shop smells heavenly," she said. "Are you Cara Ferris?"

"Yes, I am," Cara replied. She frowned. "Have we met?"

"No, I've not yet had the pleasure. My name is Olivia Cabrera. I'd like to talk with you if that's okay. Would you have a few minutes after you get off work today?"

"What is there for us to discuss?" Cara asked.

"I'm sorry, this is out of the blue. Nothing to worry about. May I buy you a coffee after work?"

"I suppose that would be okay. I get off at six today."

"Great! I'll see you then." The lady turned and left the bakery.

That was odd, Cara thought.

PROMPTLY AT SIX o'clock that evening, the woman returned. She and Cara walked to the coffee shop next door to the bakery, ordered their drinks, and sat at a small table away from others so they could talk privately.

"You said your name is Olivia?"

The lady nodded. "Olivia Cabrera."

"What can I do for you?"

"I'm with the federal government."

Cara nodded. "That covers a lot of ground. There are over two million federal employees, not counting postal service workers or active-duty military. What do you do, precisely?"

"I work for an agency that is a part of United States Intelligence."

"What does that have to do with me?"

"My job is to identify people who are, should I say, uniquely talented. People who love our country and what it stands for, and who are willing to help protect our freedom."

"I'm a loyal American, but I have no special talents. I'm

just a girl in high school. There is no reason for U.S. Intelligence to be interested in me."

"Cara, may I speak with you frankly?"

"I would appreciate that."

"What I do is take information from diverse sources, whether it's news media, databases, or files hidden in all sorts of places ..."

"You're a hacker?"

"Yes, that's a part of what I do. But I work for the United States. I'm one of the good guys."

Cara raised an eyebrow but remained silent.

"As I was saying, I take all this information and put it together meaningfully. From time to time, my colleagues and I identify people who can do things that ... that humans aren't supposed to be able to do."

"Again, I'm a high school student. What do you want from me?"

"I'd like you to agree to come to Washington, D.C. with me, to talk with my superiors. We believe you would be useful to our country."

"In what way?"

Olivia stood, taking her cinnamon cappuccino. "Let's walk. We need privacy for this."

Together, they left the coffee shop and walked along a side street.

"Cara, in the past eight months, there have been several violent deaths in central Indiana and, more recently, in Chicago."

"There have been violent deaths all over the world ever since there were humans. It's how we're wired, I guess. Read the news."

"Let me be more specific, then. I'm not referring to the epidemic of gun violence nor to gang activity. I'm talking about men who were themselves violent criminals, who died from injuries so extreme that they could not have been caused by any human."

"How does that relate to me?"

"In each of these cases I'm talking about, you were present."

Cara stopped walking. "I don't like where this is going. Look at me. I'm a teenage girl. Are you accusing me of a crime?"

"No, I'm not accusing you of anything. You're not in trouble, Cara."

"You talk to me about ultra-violence, and you say I was present each time. I don't understand what you think you know, but you have the wrong person."

Olivia nodded. "I'm like you, in a way. No, I never lived on the street." Cara's eyes went wide at this revelation. "But I'm … different from most people. My skill is that with a computer …" She paused. Cara looked into her eyes. "With a computer, I can access anything. I can find anything. I can go anywhere. I can't always explain, in words, how I know exactly what to do. It just seems obvious, though I've learned it's not at all obvious to other people."

"Like math is to me," Cara said.

"Yes, like that. Three years ago, I was a college student. Computer science and informatics, obviously. Outside of my schoolwork, I spent my time exercising my unique talent. I entered systems that were thought to be impenetrable, just because I could. I never sold information; I never threatened anyone or destroyed anything. I just went in and looked around. I loved the feeling of winning. It was like a rush of endorphins for me.

"Then one day, a colonel from the Defense Intelligence Agency came to me. We had a long talk. Now I work for her. She's my boss, but she's also my mentor, and she's become a dear friend. And like me, like you, she is unique. She has her own unusual skill set."

"You'll excuse me, but this all sounds very Marvel Comics. Secret government organization, huh? Superpowered meta-humans, huh? Do you have a code name and a skin-tight spandex cat suit?"

Olivia chuckled at this. "No, this isn't the Marvel Universe. I have no name other than Olivia Cabrera, which my parents gave me at birth. I wear normal clothes. But yes, there are secret government organizations, and yes, there are … rarely … people with unique abilities. There are similar secret government organizations in other countries as well, and not all of them are aligned with the United States. People like you and me can be found and recruited. I'm one of the good guys. We prefer people to work for us voluntarily. Not every, uh, recruiter will be so thoughtful. That's why it was important that we talk with you before someone else does."

"I have a life here, Olivia. You've apparently learned all about me, so you're aware I lived alone on the street for many years. Now I have a family who cares about me. Ms. Katie's been like a real mom to me. I have a little sister who I adore." Then softer, "And I have a boyfriend who loves me despite everything." She gestured at her facial scar. "And I love him back. And knowing all this, you expect me to go with you to Washington, D.C.? Because you believe I've committed acts of ultra-violence that, as a normal teenager, would have been impossible for me. That makes little sense.

"Come to think of it, why should I trust you at all? How can I be sure you're really from our government?"

"I understand, Cara. Your hesitation is reasonable. You don't have to decide right now. Here's my ID." She pulled a plastic-coated card from her pocket and allowed Cara to examine it. Her face on the ID was very serious, hair in a tight bun. *Nobody looks good on an ID*, Cara thought. Below the photo was the word "Analyst." The logo showed the earth surrounded by two orthogonal ellipses, reminding Cara of electrons orbiting an atomic nucleus. A torch and stars above, a wreath below. Surrounding it all: "Defense Intelligence Agency" and "United States of America."

"Cara, take a couple of days to think about this. You have an opportunity to make an enormous difference. Talk with your family to whatever degree you feel is appropriate. You will come up with more questions. I'll reach out to you again in two days. I would like to meet with you and your family, and we can proceed from there. Does that sound fair?"

"Uh, to be honest, you're scaring me. I don't understand what you want. I don't know in what way you think I would be useful to my country. I want this to go away."

Olivia Cabrera nodded. "I get it," she said. "I really understand. I felt scared too when they first spoke with me. I promise it gets better. Now try to relax. I'll talk to you in a couple of days." Olivia smiled at Cara and walked away.

Holy shit, Cara thought, *what am I supposed to do?*

MISSED OPPORTUNITIES

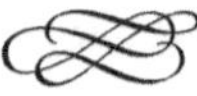

 ara returned home that evening just in time for dinner. She sat quietly, shoulders drooping, and picked at her food. Katie took her aside after the meal.

"Is something wrong, Cara?"

"No, I'm fine."

"I know how to translate a teenager's 'I'm fine.'"

Cara was silent, a faraway look in her eyes.

"You and Adam?"

"No, it's not Adam. We love each other very much. I'm sorry, I don't mean to be a downer. I just have a lot on my mind."

"I told you once before that family is a choice. It's much more than simply DNA. I see you as my child, and I love you like a daughter."

Cara moved closer. Katie drew her in and hugged her.

"Thank you, ma'am. That helps."

"If there's anything I can do for you, or if you just want someone to listen, I'm here."

"Thanks, I appreciate that."

Cara mounted the stairs to her room, closed her door,

and sat on the edge of her bed. She pulled out her iPhone and chose a playlist she'd titled Missed Opportunities, a collection of sad songs about despair, about life not going the way one had hoped. Cara didn't listen to this playlist often, but at the moment, it seemed appropriate. She started the music and lay down on top of her bed. An hour passed as she dozed.

A soft knock at the door. "Come in," she said.

Linnea stood there, hesitant.

"Come in, you. Sit with me." Cara sat up and patted the bed beside her.

Linnea sat down, and Cara put an arm around her. Linnea leaned her head against Cara's shoulder.

"There's something not right, Cara. I feel it."

"I'm okay. Just a lot on my mind."

"It's more than that. We have a bond."

"Sisters."

"You saved my life. Not once, not twice. Three times in the past few months, I would have died. I wonder if I was supposed to have died."

"Linnea! Don't say that."

"I'm serious. I don't know why I was targeted. I'm nobody important. But you protected me repeatedly."

"You're important to me. Your family loves you."

Cara moved to kiss her on the cheek, but Linnea turned her head so that their lips touched. Linnea smiled, licked her lips, and kissed Cara again, deliberately. "I'm just a fourteen-year-old kid and nobody takes a young person's feelings seriously, but I'm in love with you, Cara. You're everything in the world to me. I want you to know that."

"You're in love with me?"

Linnea nodded.

"Adam," Cara said.

"Yeah," Linnea replied, her voice forlorn. "Adam is the

best brother I could ever wish for. He always talks to me like I'm a real person, not just a kid. He's taught me most of what I know. He drives me where I need to go. He attends my games to cheer me on. And I'm in love with his girlfriend. Guess I'm not a very good person." She looked down at her feet.

Cara hugged her tighter. She stroked Linnea's hair with her free hand. "In a lot of ways, you're not a standard fourteen-year-old. You're struggling with concepts that most people don't have to worry about till they're older. Adam once told me that people are messy."

Linnea nodded. "That's a good word for this. Messy."

"But never be afraid to love. There's nothing wrong with loving."

"But ..."

Cara smiled. "We'll figure it out. Don't you change. There's nothing wrong with you. You're a breath of fresh air, a drop of golden sunshine, all the tacky, overused metaphors for 'delightful.'"

Linnea grinned at her. Cara kissed her forehead and hugged her again.

"You see, Linnea, you make me feel better. Thank you!"

AFTER LINNEA LEFT, Cara asked Adam to go with her back to the coffee shop where she'd spoken with the government agent. Adam bought them both a chai latte, then they sat to talk at a small table.

"Adam, I'm scared."

"What's g-going on?"

"After school today, I was working at the bakery next door, as usual."

"Yes?"

"A customer came in. I hadn't seen her before. She asked to talk to me after my shift ended. Wouldn't tell me what it was about."

"I thought s-something was on your mind this evening. What did she look like?"

"Maybe twenty-something with light-brown skin and dark hair. I would guess Latina by her name. Casual clothes. Anyway, we came here, and she bought me a coffee. She said she's with the government. Intelligence. She knew an awful lot about me: my years on the street, things that have happened in the past eight months since that night by the elementary school."

"Holy crap! How would she ... how is that p-possible? This sounds like what Ms. F ..."

Cara raised her forefinger to her lips. She shook her head.

"... what we were told might happen."

"That's what I'm thinking. The agent said she looks for people with unusual abilities. Said she's one herself. She told me her talent is that with a computer she can access anything, regardless of how secret or well-protected. She told me about the three guys who attacked you that night last fall, about the home invasion and the bus and the plane and Sokolov's mansion ... at least the information in the official reports. I suppose she must have hacked the police and the FBI files."

"I repeat, holy crap! What does she want from you?"

"She wants me to go with her to Washington, D.C., supposedly to talk to someone. But it wasn't clear what would happen to me after I 'talk.'" Cara made air quotes here. "I think they want me to stay in Washington and work for them. She said our country needs me, though she wouldn't say in exactly what way I could be of service."

"Does she know about … Her?"

"I don't think so. I don't think she knows exactly how all those people died. But the way she talked, my impression is she thinks I naturally have enhanced strength and speed."

"So she wants you as an assassin? Some kind of hit girl?"

Cara nodded. "That's my best guess. I mean, she mentioned nothing about my mad math skills."

"D-Do you think she's for real?"

"Hard to say for sure. She showed me her ID. She's from the Defense Intelligence Agency."

"Just like the story we were told. Hold on a minute. Let's see what Google says." Adam pulled out his iPhone and tapped for a few seconds. "Hmm. Look at this." He showed Cara what he found.

"See, they're involved with military intelligence. They can't … no, Adam, we can't let them weaponize Her."

"We have no reason to think She would go along with it. My understanding, especially after talking with the theology guy, is that She answers to a whole different authority. Which is probably a good thing. Cara, She could wipe out an entire army! She's done it before."

The two sat silent for a while, stunned.

"How did the government person say she'd follow up with you? Are you supposed to call her?"

"No, she said she'd get back with me in two days. She wanted me to think about it, and then she wanted to talk with your mom and dad."

Adam took her hands in his. "Does she really expect you to leave your life here in Indiana, to leave everyone who loves you?"

"I could never do it. I told you once before: The hardest thing about living alone on the street was that there was nobody I could trust. There was nobody who would have my back. Now that you're in my life, Adam, I will never leave you. Your mom, she's been the mother I wish I'd always had. Your dad's been so nice, so helpful to me.

"And Linnea … Adam, we need to talk about her. Are you aware she has a crush on me?"

He grinned. "My little sister has good taste. I have a crush on you, too."

"No, I'm serious. She told me she loves me."

"I don't doubt it. You two have said you're sisters."

"I mean, she's *in love* with me. Not just like sister, but like girlfriend."

"Oh." He paused. "I still can't find it in my heart to be upset with her."

"Good, I'm glad you understand. I told her we'd figure it all out. I told her you'd said people are messy."

"They sure are."

"But anyway, for all these reasons, I can't go to Washington. I can't do what they're going to ask me to do."

"I agree. When you see her again, just say 'no.'"

"I hope it's that easy."

THE NEXT AFTERNOON, Adam was at work in the library. A Black lady who he thought could have been fifty or sixty years old, with short gray hair, a conservative pantsuit, and a pleasant smile, approached him.

"Good afternoon, ma'am. May I help you find s-something?"

"Are you Adam Samuelson?"

"Yes, ma'am." He looked puzzled.

"No, we haven't met. My name is Regina Taylor. May I have a few minutes of your time?"

"Uh, sure, I guess. We can use one of the study rooms."

They sat facing each other across the table. The lady tented her fingers and smiled. "Should I call you Mr. Samuelson, or would you prefer Adam?"

"Adam is fine. What can I do for you?"

"I'd like to talk about your girlfriend, Cara."

Adam leaned back and crossed his arms. "There's nothing to discuss." His voice was wary.

"She's an unusual girl."

Adam looked at her for a minute without speaking. The lady waited him out, a benign expression on her face.

"Who are you?"

"As I told you, my name is Regina Taylor."

Adam sighed. "I mean, who do you work for?"

"Ah, yes." She pulled an ID from her pocket and handed it to Adam. "I'm with the United States government."

He carefully studied her ID. "Colonel Regina Taylor?"

She nodded.

"What's with you p-people in the Defense Intelligence Agency? You're the second one to show up here. Cara said another lady from your same agency spoke with her yesterday. Cara was quite upset."

"I can imagine this is a surprise for you, and I apologize. We do not mean to upset either of you. Tell me, Adam, are you aware of Cara's talent? Can you tell me how she does it?"

Adam cocked his head and stared at her, expressionless, meeting her eyes.

After a few minutes, the lady nodded. "I see. You want to protect her. That's commendable, Adam. So you pretend this isn't happening. Maybe if you ignore it, it'll go away. *La politique de l'autruche*. French for the politics of the ostrich. Hiding your head in the sand in the theory that if you can't see them, they can't see you." She leaned forward toward Adam. "In real life, Adam, ostriches don't actually do that. It's a myth. Just like the idea that if you ignore a problem, it will go away."

"What exactly d-do you expect me to say … Colonel?" He flung her title like a curse. "Of course I want to protect Cara. I love her! What does the military want with her?"

"Is that a rhetorical question? Have you really no idea?"

"You think you can use her like some kind of weapon?"

"The more I learn about her, the more I believe we must … or another country will. The Russians, the Chinese, they won't care about your cooperation. They won't care about Cara's cooperation. They'll make her do exactly what they want."

"Ah. You p-plan to weaponize my girlfriend for her own safety? And you want me to help?"

"For her safety and for that of our country. Cara can make a tremendous difference in the world, to be of service to the United States. Are you a loyal American, Adam? Think about your life here. America has given you so much. Now I'm asking you to give back. Help convince Cara to work with us."

"Colonel, Cara survived for s-seven years alone on the street, homeless and friendless. Do you have any idea what it was like for her? Damnit, she was just a kid! Where was this glorious country for her? What exactly does she owe you?" Adam stood, angry. "After seven years of hell, Cara has a family, friends, people who care about her. And I will always have her back. Good day, Colonel!"

Adam stalked from the room.

AN OFFER YOU CAN'T REFUSE

wo days after their initial encounter, Olivia
Cabrera returned to the Old World Bakery. The
bell jingled as the door opened. Cara looked up with a smile
that quickly vanished.

"You're back, I see."

"Yes, Cara. In retrospect, it was a mistake for me to have
spoken with you alone. I should have included Adam from
the beginning. No doubt he told you that my colleague talked
with him yesterday."

"He was quite angry."

"That's what I understand. I apologize, but this is too
important. It's unavoidable that we talk again. Would the two
of you be willing to meet with us this evening? I think your
home would be the most appropriate venue. We should
involve your family in this decision."

"I don't suppose there's any chance you would get lost if I
told you to, huh?"

Olivia shook her head. "No, I'm sorry. So … eight p.m.?
Will you have had dinner by then?"

"Fine. I'll tell my family to expect you."

. . .

DINNER CONVERSATION at the Samuelson's table that evening was more serious than usual.

"Tell me again about these people," Stephen said.

"They say they're from the g-government. The Defense Intelligence Agency. From a quick Google search, it appears the DIA provides intelligence to the military."

"Isn't that what the CIA does?"

"There's some overlap, yes. The CIA provides intelligence to the President and Cabinet."

"Why are they interested in you?"

"They're interested in me, sir," Cara said. "I'm not sure exactly what they want of me, though I have my suspicions. They seem to feel I have some special … uh … abilities that they say would be useful to the United States."

"Abilities?"

Cara nodded, her expression somber. "For seven years I lived below the radar, as you know. I was afraid of attracting attention to myself. I thought the authorities would send me back to my mom. Now I've been in the news, apparently all over the world. People have heard about the home invasion and the plane crash. Some people in the government think I can … do things. Violent, bad things. They want me to work for the U.S., I guess before the Russians or Chinese or whoever force me to work *against* the U.S."

"S-So they're coming here tonight to make their case with you and Mom."

"This was my fault, Cara. I'm sorry." Linnea looked forlorn.

"No, Linnea, don't talk like that!" Cara protested. "Nothing that happened in the past eight months was your fault. You didn't ask for the home invasion, or your school bus, or the kidnapping. And if they happened again, I'd save you again. We don't need to waste time assigning blame; we need to figure out what's best for our family."

Katie shook her head at this. "No, we need to figure out what's best for you, Cara. I remember Detective Anders telling us that Special Agent Tanaka destroyed all copies of the audio from the plane, because he did not believe this was something the government should have. Now the government is here, and I'm wondering what exactly they know and who we can trust."

"Tanaka is from the government," Adam said. "The FBI is a part of U.S. Intelligence, like the CIA and the DIA. And the NSA."

Cara nodded. "I feel like I trust Special Agent Tanaka. He could have sold me up the river at any point, even just by failing to delete that audio recorder data from the plane crash."

"Hmm," Linnea said. "He could have missed a copy somewhere. Or maybe the people from the Defense Intelligence Agency suspect things but aren't sure. Maybe they're being proactive. When we talk to them, try to determine what they know for sure. Is it only what's in the official reports, or are they aware of what actually happened?"

Adam smiled. "That's the sister I love. That's the girl who outplayed a grandmaster."

Linnea glanced up at Adam. Her eyes were bright, face flushed. "Stop it!" she said. "You're embarrassing me."

THE DOORBELL RANG. Adam glanced at his watch. "Eight o'clock. The g-government is right on time."

Stephen answered the door and invited the two women inside.

"Doctor Samuelson? I'm Colonel Regina Taylor." She

nodded at her colleague. "Olivia Cabrera is an analyst in my department." They shook hands.

"Come in. Let's sit and talk. Would you like anything to drink?"

"No, thank you."

Stephen made introductions around the table. Colonel Taylor and Olivia passed out business cards to each of the Samuelsons and Cara.

Colonel Taylor began. "Two days ago, Olivia spoke with Cara. I talked to Adam yesterday. In retrospect, I think we should have spoken with Cara and Adam at the same time. I have little experience interacting with teenagers; I have no children of my own. It must have felt intimidating."

Cara and Adam nodded in agreement. "It did."

"You ought to have spoken with their parents first. They're both in high school, Colonel," Katie said.

"Yes, Mrs. Samuelson, in almost every situation, you would be correct. The reason you would be correct is that as their parents, you would have the parental right to say no. However, my colleague and I are here on a matter of national security. I am hoping for your cooperation."

"Explain to us, Colonel Taylor, your interest in our children," Stephen said.

"No slight intended to your other children, Doctor Samuelson, but we are interested in Cara."

"I see. Why is that, pray tell?"

Colonel Taylor tented her fingers as she considered how to begin. "You're an educated man. How do you explain what happened during the home invasion here last winter? Two large, armed, violent, drug-crazed men versus a teenage girl and a preteen. How do you understand that?"

"The girls did what they could. Thank God it was enough."

"The two men suffered injuries so extreme, the coroner said no human could have caused them."

Silence as the adults regarded each other.

Colonel Taylor continued, "And then there was the incident with the school bus and the jet. The story made headlines all over the world. I have nothing to add except to wonder how you explain it to yourself." She looked around the table. "There have been other similar incidents as well. Each time, bad men died violently in ways that defy the limits of human strength and speed. And each time, Cara was present."

"What are you accusing her of, precisely?"

"We are not law enforcement, sir. We are here to recruit, not to punish."

"To recruit a teenage girl for what?"

"Our office looks for people with unique abilities. People who can do things that are impossible. There are such people, you know."

"Olivia C-Cabrera told Cara her special talent was with computers, that she is some sort of uber-hacker. Do you have a talent as well?"

Colonel Taylor nodded. "I do, in fact, though I'm afraid you may find the details upsetting."

Linnea cleared her throat. "In the past six months, I survived a violent home invasion. I watched as men shot my school bus driver to death, and a criminal kingpin kidnapped me and threatened to kill me. But you're afraid you might shock me? Really?"

"Very well. My talent is that if I wish not to be noticed, nobody will see me or remember that I was there."

"It's not one of those skills that would make for great TV," Adam said.

"Some of the most useful skills do not make for great TV. I can show you. This is the part you might find upsetting."

Colonel Taylor had everyone's attention. "Adam, last night, you and Cara had drinks at the coffee shop by Cara's bakery."

Adam shrugged.

"The two of you sat at one of the small, round tables in the back, against the wall to the left of the restrooms. I sat at the table next to you so I could listen to your conversation."

"No, you didn't, ma'am. The table next to us was empty the whole time we were there."

Colonel Taylor sighed, then recounted Cara and Adam's conversation word for word as she watched their faces. She saw disbelief turn into shock.

"So you can see why I work in Intelligence. My point, Doctor and Mrs. Samuelson, is that there are people who can do things that humans are not supposed to be able to do. By the way, Adam, who is Ms. F?"

Adam wrinkled his brow. "I have n-no idea. I d-don't know anyone with that name. You must have misunderstood."

Colonel Taylor pursed her lips and shrugged. "I see."

Olivia broke the awkward silence. "As I explained to Cara, we don't have code names and we don't wear spandex suits. Cara, think about this. You were featured in the news all over the world. Today, Colonel Taylor and I are here to recruit you, voluntarily, to serve your country. Tomorrow who? Russia? China? North Korea, heaven forbid? They won't care about recruiting you voluntarily. They will force you."

"Nobody can force me to do anything."

Olivia gestured to encompass everyone sitting at the table. "There are people you love. Think about it, Cara. They can find a weak spot somewhere."

Cara put down her cup and put her hands together as though in prayer. "I cannot do the thing I think you want me to do. Not only do I not *wish* to do it, but I physically cannot."

"You can, because you did."

"You don't actually know what happened. It wasn't me."

Colonel Taylor raised an eyebrow. "You were there each time. If it wasn't you who caused the devastation, please share with me what happened."

"No, Colonel Taylor," Cara said, growing visibly angry, "you tell us. You explain to us—if I'm truly some kind of bad-ass teenage devastation machine—why I spent two weeks in the hospital recently recovering from injuries. Look at the scars on my face! If you cut me, I bleed. If you shoot me or stab me, I die, just like everyone else. I am just a human."

Colonel Taylor and Cara stared at each other. "Come with us to Washington, Cara. You won't be alone; Olivia and I will stay with you. Our plan is for you to have a complete medical evaluation at Walter Reed Medical Center, including bloodwork, a full-body MRI and possibly some other scans, and a psychiatric assessment. We will cover all costs, including medical and room, board, and travel. Our director, Lieutenant General Nicholas Fry, may request some field exercises as well. The entire process should take less than two weeks, after which we will return you here."

"Return me here? I expected you to wish to keep me like you kept Olivia." She turned to Olivia. "You never graduated from university once they found you, correct?"

"Not completely correct. I chose to stay in Washington, D.C. and complete my coursework online. But you have to understand my situation differed from yours. I was twenty-one years old when Colonel Taylor found me, already living far from home, and I was single. And this was an opportunity to work with some of the greatest minds in my industry.

"You, on the other hand, are the first teenager we've worked with. After our initial discussions with Adam and you, we decided that if we agree to continue to work together after these two weeks of assessment, it would be best if you are free to live with your family when you're not actively on duty with us.

"Your plan is to attend Purdue University in the fall, correct?"

"Yes, the three of us have been accepted to their engineering school."

"All three of you? Very impressive," Colonel Taylor said. "Linnea, you just recently turned fourteen, isn't that right?"

Linnea smirked. "Yes, ma'am. It looks as though I'll miss my entire high school experience."

Colonel Taylor smiled and shook her head. "You won't be missing much. I enjoyed the academics, but socially … no. It was an awkward time for me. I don't remember high school as being the best years of my life. I didn't figure out where I fit in the world until graduate school. But we each have to follow our own path.

"Anyway, Cara, what do you think of our offer?"

"Doctor Samuelson, Ms. Katie? You're not legally my parents, but you're the closest thing to parents I've ever had. What's your opinion?"

"You know that Stephen and I met in the military. But this has to be your call. We will support whatever you choose."

Cara took Adam's hand in hers, and she gently stroked it. "What do you think, Adam?"

"Honestly? My heart wants you to stay here." He paused. "But my head says maybe through this you will learn something about … um, I mean something that will help you."

Cara sighed and nodded. "Fine, Colonel Taylor. Let's do this."

JUST A FEW TESTS

wo days after the family meeting, Cara, Colonel Regina Taylor, and Olivia Cabrera flew from Indianapolis International Airport by private jet.

"You ladies travel in style," Cara said. "I didn't expect this level of comfort."

Colonel Taylor nodded. "Given what we do, we prefer to avoid TSA and the facial recognition cameras inside major airports."

"That makes sense. I've heard a lot about TSA, none of it complimentary, but I've never flown commercial."

"You know, I suppose they do the best they can," the colonel said. "They handle millions of travelers and of those, only a few intend to disrupt a flight. But if they miss even one terrorist, we have a tragedy."

"Are there special procedures for people who must always travel armed, or government couriers who cannot be separated from their briefcase or whatever?"

"Yes, there are, but the rank-and-file TSA agent most likely has never encountered such a situation and sometimes overreacts. That's another reason I avoid commercial flights whenever possible."

They landed in a small airfield somewhere in Virginia. Cara noted several armed soldiers. One of them saluted Colonel Taylor as the three of them descended the airstair.

"Colonel. Your car is waiting. Follow me, please."

THE BLACK GOVERNMENT car left the base. Cara watched out the window on the short drive to a neighborhood full of colonial-style homes, red brick with white accents. She noted the many old trees, the immaculate lawns, and the neatly trimmed shrubbery.

The car pulled up to one home. The soldier who drove the ladies unloaded their luggage in the foyer, saluted Colonel Taylor once again, and left.

"Uh, wow, Colonel! This is nice," Cara said.

"We're going to be living together for the next two weeks," Colonel Taylor said. "While we're here in private, we can be less formal. You may call me Gina if you like."

"And I'm just Olivia."

Colonel Taylor made a gesture with her arm to indicate their surroundings. "We usually reserve this house for visiting officers. Before we explore it, let me discuss some rules. Well, only one, really. One of us, usually Olivia, will accompany you at all times other than when you're in your bedroom. You are not to leave here by yourself."

Cara's eyes grew hard.

"I don't know if you've considered the lengths to which we've gone, and the expense, to bring you here and keep you safe while we evaluate each other. I gave your parents my word as an officer that I would bring you home, in good condition, in two weeks."

"Yes, ma'am. I remember the conversation."

"There is more, Cara. Our government considers this critical for national security. Yes, most everyone in our neighborhood has an affiliation with the U.S. military, but very few of them—probably only Olivia and me—have sufficient security clearance to know about you. So I'm asking you not to engage in conversation with anyone unless you're being formally tested."

"I understand."

"I also have no desire to trick you. You have your iPhone, but you should know that while you're here, it is being monitored for the reasons I mentioned a moment ago."

"Then I deserve no privacy at all?"

"You do. There are no cameras inside this house."

"Cara?" Olivia said. "You know about me. I've told you what I can do. I can access any computer anywhere. It's perhaps not as cool of a skill as yours, but it's useful." Olivia paused and bit her lip.

"Look, Cara, you deserve to be treated with respect and to be allowed as much privacy as possible. We brought you here to learn how your unique skills work and under what circumstances you can activate them. That's all."

Cara sighed. "It sounds like we'll need to learn to trust each other."

Colonel Taylor added, "Yes, I want you to get to know Olivia and me as people, not as mindless government drones. If we decide to work together, I will be your direct supervisor. It would help if we build at least a baseline level of trust while we're together these next two weeks.

"You may go anywhere in this house. Why don't you pick your bedroom now. To limit our interactions with other people, we'll be eating most of our meals here. I arranged for the kitchen to be stocked. We can take turns cooking and cleaning up. Mrs. Samuelson mentioned you're quite comfortable in the kitchen. Meals should be fun. I'll take care of dinner tonight, though I might not be at your level of culinary skill."

Over a dinner of baked chicken quarters, roasted potatoes, and salad, the two government agents asked Cara in depth about her abilities and how she accomplished them.

Colonel Taylor shook her head. "I would find it easier to believe that you have innately enhanced strength and speed, which is more like what Olivia and I can do. The concept that you're really just a normal girl possessed by a supernatural creature … I'm sorry, but that is hard to swallow. What do you expect the Department of Defense to do with someone who claims they have an angel living somehow inside of them?"

"I never expected the government to '*do*' anything with me except to leave me alone and let me be a student. You are the ones who chased *me* down and brought me here. I never asked you to believe me.

"Over the next few days, when the various doctors question me, what should I tell them?"

"Tell them what you told us. Let them make of it what they will."

Ten days later, the three were at dinner again.

"Olivia, I appreciate you staying with me through all those tests. Army doctors are intimidating," Cara said.

"Not a problem. That's what I'm here for."

"The reports say you're a healthy young woman," Colonel Taylor said. "Your physical exam and your bloodwork are normal. You had a full-body CT scan, an MRI and a PET scan, and an EEG, all of which were within normal limits.

They found no evidence of any supernatural creatures hiding inside of you."

Cara grimaced. "I was fine with all those tests. I didn't complain when they took what felt like a gallon of blood. But that damn psychologist! It was all I could do to remain polite. Days of stupid tests with stupid questions, and hours of conversation where he tried to convince me that my real-life experiences did not and could not have happened, and after all that, he never gave me a diagnosis."

"The psychologist believes you have grandiose-type delusional disorder … you know, the 'possessed by an angel' bit."

"But then how did he explain, in his own mind, how all those people died from injuries a normal human could not have caused?"

"The usual way people parse stories they don't believe; they convince themselves that the stories didn't actually happen … at least not the way you remember them." Colonel Taylor's face darkened. "Sadly, even today it's way too common for a man to dismiss a woman's words as the ramblings of a silly girl. I know something of this.

"On a related topic, General Fry is not sure whether you're 'sandbagging' regarding your strength and speed or whether your powers manifest only when something threatens your life."

"Of course, my so-called 'powers' manifest only when my life or the life of someone I love is threatened. I've explained that to you all ad nauseam. Most of the time I'm just a normal human girl like my physical exam showed."

"And Fry is not sure what to make of the 'dog incident.'"

The dog incident. Cara and Olivia had gone out for a run. Three large pit bulls left their property and chased after them, barking furiously. Cara turned and faced the snarling dogs. They abruptly stopped, whined, and fled.

"I explained to you both what happened with the dogs.

I've seen that before. Animals and sometimes small children can see, or at least sense, what's inside me, and animals are smart enough to be afraid."

"Well, General Fry wants to evaluate, in the field, what it takes for you to manifest your gifts and what the limits of those gifts are."

"You're kidding, right? When She appears, people die. Always. And I have very little control over Her."

"I'm not kidding. The U.S. military has no sense of humor. They do, however, have a few hundred thousand acres of desert in Nevada to play in. Don't worry about it. Olivia and I will be with you to make sure things don't get out of hand."

"Is that supposed to make me feel better? Now that I know the two of you so well, how do you think I'll feel if She kills you? You still don't get it. My angel, or whatever, is not domesticated. When She appears, She does what She damn well pleases, and that usually involves lots of dead people." Cara sighed and bit her lip. "She's not like a dog that we can train to attack on command; she is more like a polar bear who is as likely to kill you as not. Colonel, it is too dangerous to play games with Her."

"I hear what you're saying, but Director Fry has decided, and he never second-guesses himself. The testing will proceed as planned. There's no way to avoid it."

THE SWORD OF GOD

uried in the Nevada desert, there is a control room built of reinforced concrete, accessible only by a hidden and heavily guarded door. Inside, giant monitors line one wall. They show, in all directions, a semi-arid desert.

Six computer terminals, each with their own smaller screens, face the wall of monitors. Technicians dressed in military uniform are seated at five of the workstations. Olivia Cabrera sits at the sixth workstation, typing rapidly. She alone wears civilian clothes. There is no extraneous conversation.

Behind the row of technicians, Lieutenant General Nicholas Fry, Director of the Defense Intelligence Agency, sits at a table, notebook open and ready. Beside him sits Colonel Regina Taylor. Their attention is fixed on the giant monitors.

Suddenly, the center monitor zooms in.

"The girl is awake, sir. Heart rate 64 and regular. Respirations and blood pressure are normal. Oxygenation 99%."

On the screen, Director Fry and the others in the control room could see that Cara was still lying on the ground where she'd been placed, but her eyes were open. Slowly, she sat up, looked around, then rose unsteadily to her feet. She paused a moment to regain her equilibrium, then she climbed up a low hill and shaded her eyes with a hand to better survey the surroundings. In this part of the American Southwest, there was nothing for hundreds of miles but scrub, rocks, and the occasional saguaro or other cactus. Many years of flash floods left arroyos scattered in low areas.

Director Fry cleared his throat. "Initiate small arms protocol."

"Yes, General."

A bullet whined as it ricocheted off the rocks near Cara's feet. She jumped in surprise but did not cry out. Quickly, she crouched behind a boulder, trying to figure out from which direction the bullet had come.

Crack! A second round stirred up dust close beside her. She scurried to the other side of the boulder, but the next round, seconds later, struck even closer to her. Silence, then another loud crack and chips flew off the top of the boulder close to her head.

Directional microphones picked up her voice, low and soft as she spoke to herself. "Damn, they're giving me no choice. I told them how dangerous She is, but of course they didn't believe me. I don't want this. I really don't want this."

"Subject heart rate 128 and regular. Respirations slightly elevated at 24. Other vital signs are stable."

A collective gasp filled the control room as Cara suddenly arched her back, her face contorted as though she was in pain. Her eyes were closed, but then they flew open. As Director Fry and the others in the control room watched in amazement, Cara changed. She still wore the same clothes, but they were noticeably tighter. Her hair was the same as before, but all facial scars had disappeared. Her face itself had changed so that it was perfect in every detail, a living Venus de Milo. She stood tall and calm, powerful and in control.

"She's beautiful," a technician said. "I've never seen anyone so stunning. But she's … different somehow."

"I imagine if angels are real, they'd look like her," Olivia added. "I was raised Catholic. Once when I was young, I asked a nun what angels looked like. She said they were too beautiful for words."

"It's hard to believe," Colonel Taylor said. "Even after seeing the parking garage video, I had trouble understanding She was real."

"There are no angels and there is no God," Director Fry said with a low growl. "This thing is a monster, not a person. We will refer to this creature as 'it.' Understood?"

"Yes, sir," the uniformed soldiers at the computer stations said. Olivia and Colonel Taylor were silent.

"Medical, what's on telemetry?"

"Heart rate … Director, it has no heart rate."

"Check the—"

"I did, sir. The telemetry remains perfectly functional."

"Then continue the protocol. We need to see what it can do. Shoot to kill."

"Sir?"

"Now, soldier."

The man's fingers flew over the keyboard. From the north and the west, teams of fully armored soldiers, automatic weapons in hand, approached their target.

First one, then all of them emptied their magazines into the beautiful being as it calmly surveyed them, arms resting loosely at its sides. Hundreds of bullets struck but were no inconvenience.

"Vitals?"

"Its vital signs are still zero, and oxygenation reads zero."

"Magnification, take us closer."

The center screen now showed a closeup of the mysterious creature. As bullets hit it, they deformed and fell as though they'd struck a Kevlar vest. Cara's clothes showed signs of damage, but there was no blood.

It spoke some words in a strange, harsh tongue in a voice that was no longer Cara's. Then it moved much quicker than was possible for a human, darting through the soldiers, ripping, tearing, bashing. Severed limbs lay strewn on the arid ground amid pools of blood. Three soldiers tried to run, whether to escape or simply to regroup was not clear. Their effort was futile. It chased them then slaughtered them as they ran. Like that, twenty elite soldiers were dead.

"My God," a technician said, then he vomited into a wastebasket by his workstation.

Director Fry coughed in dismissal. "Continue protocol escalation. Let's see how this thing likes a tank."

With a loud whine, an M1A2 Abrams tank climbed out of an arroyo several thousand yards away at full speed.

The M2 .50-caliber machine gun barked authoritatively and continuously as the creature dodged and weaved, again much faster than any human.

The tank's 120 mm cannon lowered and tracked the target. The soldier operating the machine gun disappeared inside the hatch. A loud boom, a cloud of dirt and rock, and a crater appeared where the creature had been moments before. It spoke a few more words in an alien tongue then rushed the tank at incredible speed, leaped atop, and grabbed the .50-cal machine gun with both hands. With hardly an effort, it wrenched the heavy gun from its base and threw it to the ground a hundred yards away.

"Oh, shit!" another technician in the control room said.

The creature stooped to grip the edges of the commander's hatch on the tank and ripped it open. It reached in and with one hand pulled out a soldier by his face, not even noticing his struggles, then broke him over a knee and tossed him over the side of the tank. The directional microphones picked up the sharp crack as his spine snapped and the dull thud when his lifeless body hit the ground. Next, it reached in for another soldier without pausing to look at the man it had killed. In less than a minute, the commander, the gunner, and the loader were dead. The tank continued to move, and the creature's gaze showed that it sensed the driver was in the forward part of the tank, his hatch obstructed by the position of the turret.

It stood erect atop the tank and reached into the air. A giant sword appeared in its hand, glowing white with an internal light of its own. It sliced through the front of the tank. There was a brief gush of red, and the tank stopped. The sword continued to glow.

"Damn it!" Fry said. "I need the Black Hawks. This ends now."

"Director, this is getting out of hand. If it is an actual angel, do we want to aggravate it further? We're more likely to make it angry than to kill it," Colonel Taylor said. "Cara told us she does not have very good control of her angel. So far as I know, it has never yet manifested that sword. I believe we should de-escalate."

Director Fry's eyes were cold, his mouth tight. He leaned forward in his chair, gripping the armrests. A vein jutted in his neck. His voice was low and precise as he tried, with little success, to control himself. "I said there are no angels. That monster, or whatever it is, killed my men. It destroyed my tank. Now it must pay."

"Respectfully, General, your men were trying to kill it. I gave Cara's parents my word I would bring her back safely. Cara did not agree to this test because, as she told us, she was afraid of exactly this."

"It's too much power for one person. We need to stop it."

He turned to one of the soldiers. "Black Hawks now. I want that *thing* dead!"

A minute later, the people in the control room heard the distant thrum of helicopter blades, gradually growing louder. Then they appeared, five heavily armed Black Hawk helicopters, each approximately a quarter of a mile distant from its neighbor. As they approached Cara's hill, where the creature in Cara's clothes still stood atop the ruined tank, casually holding the glowing sword as though it were a barbarian queen from the movies, the Black Hawks opened fire.

"You want God?" Director Fry said with a growl. "This is as close as you're going to get."

A volley of Hellfire missiles struck the crippled tank which shuddered from the massive explosions. Smoke and dust made it difficult to see if the creature was still there. Then the five Black Hawk helicopters opened fire with their twin .50-caliber machine guns and 70 mm rockets. After almost a minute of sustained fire that saturated the entire hill, the bombardment stopped, and the area was strangely silent.

The artillery fire had reduced the once-mighty M1A2 Abrams tank to a smoking husk. The creature with the sword was no longer standing on the tank, but beside it. It raised the sword with both hands and, even as the bullet and rocket attack recommenced, flew into the air. In flight, it moved much like on the ground, surprisingly fast. The battle was over quickly as the sword sliced through tails and rotors like a razor through silk. All five Black Hawk helicopters crashed and burned, with no apparent survivors. The creature then returned to the hill and stood as though waiting.

The control room was silent. Then Olivia muttered under her breath, "Now I am become Death, the destroyer of worlds. God help us all," and crossed herself. Though she whispered, everyone in the room heard.

"Enough," Colonel Taylor said as she stood. "I'm leaving this command bunker to try to de-escalate this battle that we cannot win and should never have started."

"Colonel, you do not have permission to leave," her commanding officer said.

Colonel Taylor replied evenly, "With all due respect, General Fry, you and your men won't remember I was ever here." Before she headed for the exit, she looked at Olivia and nodded. The hacker nodded back.

Colonel Taylor left the relative safety of the secret bunker, walked to within several hundred yards of the still-smoking hill, removed her service pistol and tossed it to one side, and sat down on the ground. She kept her hands visible in her lap, weaponless, and her eyes fixed on the strange creature who had once been Cara.

It darted in a distinctly alien way toward Colonel Taylor and stopped a few feet in front of her. The colonel stared at it impassively and did not move. The creature glanced at the sword it was holding as though forgetting it still held it, and the sword disappeared with a soft pop.

Then the creature was gone, and Cara collapsed in front of the colonel. Cara's clothes were ragged and bloody, and she was gasping for breath.

"How many … did I kill?"

"You killed nobody. But that … the angel—"

"Are you fucking kidding me? My monster is part of me. When She kills, it's because I lost control. Don't you try to sugarcoat this. You brought me here against my will. I deserve a straight answer."

Colonel Taylor thought for a moment, then she said in an even, expressionless voice, "I estimate twenty special forces, four soldiers in the tank, and if we assume a pilot and two crew per helicopter that would be an additional fifteen people." She took a deep breath, then looked Cara in the eyes. "And three in the parking garage in Chicago."

Cara clenched her hands in tight fists. The veins in her neck were engorged, her face reddened. "You're telling me the men in the parking garage were a set-up? A sick pre-test that I must have passed? You're telling me forty-two lives were lost for Director Fry's 'test'? Forty-two fathers or mothers, sons or daughters, dead for no reason?"

"They were soldiers following orders. This is what soldiers do."

Cara yelled, a raw scream of pain from deep inside her. "No!" She sobbed, wiping her face on her sleeve. "No. We have a volunteer army. Those soldiers wanted to serve and protect their country. They didn't sign up to die for some stupid, useless test that I already knew the answer to. They never had a chance. Can't you understand, Colonel? No armor, no weapons would have made a difference. Not artillery, not fighter jets, and probably not even nukes."

"I understand now," Colonel Taylor said. "You're preaching to the choir. But let me ask you this: Why didn't your angel kill me? Why did She stop in front of me and release you? Did She understand I'm an officer and I represent the most powerful army on earth?"

Cara scowled. "You know how if you see an ant crawling on your leg, you might brush it gently off?"

Colonel Taylor nodded.

"Or you might crush it first and then flick it off and pay it no further mind. To Her, you are that ant. It took every ounce of my willpower to convince Her not to crush you.

"Now I need to clean up, and I need to get home to my family. I am done with the tests, and I am done with General Fry. I assume now he understands I'm not a useful weapon."

"Cara, nobody just walks away from the director of the DIA," Colonel Taylor said, though even as she said it, she thought to herself, *technically, I walked away from him a few minutes ago.*

"You cannot run from him."

Cara's voice was steady, and her jaw was set. She looked directly into the colonel's eyes. "I am leaving. It would be a mistake for Director Fry to come after me. He won't be happy if he and I meet again."

"Is that a threat?"

"Colonel …" Cara took a breath. "Gina, I've enjoyed this past week and a half with you and Olivia more than I expected … other than today, of course. You understand duty and following orders, but I've come to know you enough that I'm sure you know what is 'right' in an ethical sense, and what is not.

"Tell me, how would you military people use a blunt instrument like my monster? Would you knock me out like you did today—which, by the way, I did not appreciate— smuggle me into an enemy country, alert them so that my life is in danger and my monster will appear, then let Her have at it? Knowing She'll kill men, women, children, soldiers and civilians, old people, sick and injured people, everyone?

"If international convention has outlawed poison gas and bioweapons, by what crazy logic is it okay to unleash a literally supernatural, unkillable, and uncontrollable creature? Further, I do not know whether She is the only such creature or if there are others. Imagine if Russia or China or whoever releases a monster like this in New York City or Washington, D.C. Because once the United States does this, we lose moral standing to object when others do the same thing.

"Think about it, Gina. Is this really what you want to do?"

Colonel Taylor stood silent for what seemed like a long time. Then she nodded and said, "Olivia and I will escort you home like we promised."

A JOB FOR YOU

General Nicholas Fry looked up from his desk. "Colonel Taylor. Please come in."

Colonel Taylor closed the office door and stood at attention.

"Proceed, Colonel."

"General. We spoke with the girl, Cara, and her family."

"And?"

Colonel Taylor shook her head. "It's a non-starter. They unanimously refused to work further with us."

"I see. That's a shame. Do you believe there's any way we can persuade Cara? Anything in her life that we can help or fix? Money?"

"Cara's a remarkably low-maintenance young lady. After seven years of being homeless, she feels as though she's already hit the jackpot. She has a home and a bed, a mother-figure, and a boyfriend, Adam. She's a very strong student; she and Adam are headed to Purdue University in the fall to study engineering. There is nothing more she needs or wants at the moment."

"What do you recommend?"

"Sir, Ms. Cabrera and I are uniquely qualified and positioned to keep a close eye on Cara and the Samuelsons. The girl will not work for a foreign power. I guarantee it."

"I'm aware of your ... talents, Colonel. But you cannot be everywhere at once. You can't protect that entire family twenty-four hours a day, seven days a week, forever. Especially with Cara and the Samuelson boy heading off to college in August. And you have other responsibilities here. How can you guarantee our enemies will not turn the girl against us?"

"I don't need to be personally by her side at all times. As you've said, that is not viable. Ms. Cabrera and I can monitor her status and that of her family remotely. If there should be any problem, we can quickly call in the appropriate assets and take care of it.

"And I still have hope that Cara will change her mind."

"Okay then, Colonel. Keep me informed of any changes."

"Yes, sir." She turned and left the DIA Director's office, closing the door behind her.

When he was again alone, General Nicholas Fry lifted the handset of the secure phone on his desk and dialed a number from memory.

"*U menya yest' rabota dlya vas.*" I have a job for you.

EVERYTHING WE HOLD DEAR

$\mathcal{A}$ week after Cara returned home, the three teens sat in Linnea's bedroom.

"I still have an awful feeling about this," Linnea said. "They threatened us, maybe not in so many words, but they implied bad things would happen if they couldn't have Cara."

"I agree. I s-suggest we wear our marauding suits instead of pajamas. We need to be very careful."

"Though our folks are unaware of our special equipment or what Ms. Fortune really does, and it would be very awkward to explain," Linnea pointed out.

"The g-government doesn't know about them either. That's an edge we don't want to lose."

"You never saw the original suits, Linnea," Cara said, "but these improved ones are easier to wear under street clothes. The camouflage functions so well, the armor looks like normal clothes. I say we wear them all the time."

"That m-makes sense."

"I wish I could wear the suit while I play soccer. I'd be unstoppable."

Cara laughed and ruffled Linnea's hair. "You're a nut!"

"I feel like I want to do something now," Linnea said as she jumped up. "Can we practice with our suits again tonight?"

"That's a good idea. Let's wait till Mom and Dad are asleep. Then we can go into the woods down by the creek and work on some stuff."

Soon after Stephen and Katie retired to their bedroom for the night, three dark figures crept soundlessly outside and down the backyard to the creek in the woods. They all wore their special sunglasses so they could see in the dark.

"It's amazing how easily I can jump across the creek," Linnea whispered.

Cara, Adam, and Linnea practiced climbing up and down trees as quickly as possible, sometimes using the power of their suits to jump from one branch to another.

"Remember, Ms. Fortune t-told us to run our marauding suits at night to use up the charge, so we feel the difference between powered and unpowered."

"Yeah," Linnea added, "the suits take longer to recharge through ambient energy at night, when it's dark and cooler outside."

"I feel like I'm there now," Cara said. "So you two are probably close as well."

Adam tried jumping, but didn't go very high. "I'm out. Linnea?"

"Me too."

"Okay, let's try some of those fighting drills we found on YouTube while we're under our own power."

The three laughed quietly as they took turns pairing up to practice holds and throws.

"Grapple-resistant suits make this really hard," Cara said. "If we ever have to use these moves, we need to remember that people with normal clothes will be a lot easier to grasp."

They fell together in a knot, panting from exertion and laughter. "I love you guys," Linnea said.

MEANWHILE, an old brown sedan pulled into the neighborhood and parked by the curb four blocks from the Samuelson's house. The driver opened the battered black leather briefcase that was lying on the front passenger seat. From it, he pulled a flip phone, a burner that he'd purchased earlier in the week under an assumed name. He opened the phone and touched speed dial one. A radio signal burst from the phone to the closest cell tower, which routed it through a computer network searching for a number, then back to the original tower, and from there through an antenna to another burner phone hidden inside a box in a basement. The electrical signal generated by the second phone did not ring the speaker; rather it set off a blasting cap, which detonated five pounds of C4 military-grade high explosive.

Three seconds after the man in the brown sedan pushed the speed dial button, a blinding flash lit the street, then a resounding blast shattered the cool evening. Moments later, flames burst from the ground-floor windows of the Samuelson's house. Smoke billowed as the wooden frame of the brick house caught fire.

The man drove carefully away, pulling to the side of the road to allow the firetrucks and ambulances to pass.

CARA, Adam, and Linnea looked up as they felt the ground vibrate. They heard a rumble as a dull red glow showed through the ground-floor windows of their house. Then, in slow motion, the walls swayed.

"Mom! Dad! No!" Linnea jumped up and dashed towards the house.

"No, Linnea. Come back!" Adam yelled, but Linnea didn't stop. She barely made it inside when a second explosion threw curtains of flame and smoke from the windows. The intense heat forced Cara and Adam back.

Cara fell to her knees. "Linnea! Oh God, no. Linnea."

Adam started towards the ruined house. Cara grabbed his legs and pulled him down.

"Adam, no! Our suits can't survive that. We'll die."

"I can't let Linnea—"

"Adam, think damnit," she screamed. "Use your brain like you told me. Someone wants us dead. We're the only two left to find out who did this. If we follow Linnea, we all die and they win."

Adam buried his head in his hands. "Then I d-don't know what to do. They killed Mom and Dad and Linnea. Damnit, she's only fourteen. She's just a kid."

"Did the government want you that badly?"

"I can't believe our government would do this. No, it makes no sense."

"You said that General Fry sounded threatening when you left."

"I agree. Still, I can't believe this would be in our government's playbook. Maybe they would kill me if they're really worried I might fall into enemy hands, but they wouldn't kill Linnea. Or any of the rest of you, for that matter."

"Cara, what do we do now? Mom and Dad are dead. Linnea is dead. If the firefighters don't find us inside as well, they'll think we did it."

"Nobody who knows us would think we'd kill our family. Not after everything that's happened in the past eight months. And maybe they're not dead."

"In that inferno? Are you kidding? That's not survivable."

"Yeah, unfortunately, you're probably right. But maybe Linnea's suit …" She looked at Adam. His face had gone slack, eyes vacant, lips trembling. "No, I guess not." Cara's eyes grew harder. Her nostrils flared. She clenched her fists as she glared at the destroyed house. Then she spoke in an icy voice. "Give me your phone."

Adam stood staring at his burning house. He did not seem to hear her.

"Your phone, Adam. Quick!"

He handed his iPhone to Cara. She removed the SIM card and crushed it beneath her heel, then she did the same with her own and tossed the cards into the blaze.

They heard sirens in the distance, growing slowly louder. "Come on, Adam. We need to get out of here."

The two of them vanished like ghosts into the dark forest.

WELCOME TO MY WORLD

hey ran silently through the woods until they came to a small river. Adam figured it was a tributary of the Wabash River that would eventually merge into the Ohio and then the Mississippi. Cara pulled up short.

She pulled their iPhones from her pocket and smashed them between two rocks until the screens crumbled and the insides were visible. When she was satisfied, she tossed them in the current, where they promptly sank.

"Cara, what the hell—"

"They think we're dead, at least until the authorities can search the ruins of our house. But if we text or call someone, then they will know we're alive. And they can track our location through our phones even if we don't text or call."

"Oh."

They ran on in silence, their special sunglasses allowing them to see well in the dark forest.

"Where are we going, Cara?"

"We need to reach another city. Somewhere where people don't know us. We need supplies, money, prepaid phones.

Eventually, we'll need new IDs, but we may have to go to a bigger city for that."

Adam stopped. "I have no money and no identification. My family is dead, I lost my home, somebody wants to kill me, and I don't know what to do." He stared at the ground and shook his head. "I don't know what to do now," he muttered.

Cara came close to Adam and hugged him gently. "Do you trust me, Adam?"

"Yes, I do. Completely."

"Then let me take care of you. I've lived like this for seven years." She kissed him, her lips soft on his. "Welcome to my world, Adam. We'll get some stuff together, then we'll make a plan. We can't think at our best right now, so let's take things one step at a time. Our priority is to get some supplies and a place to sleep, and obviously we should avoid attracting attention."

"How c-can you tell which direction to go?"

"The stars. My internal compass. I have an excellent sense of direction."

Adam nodded without talking. He followed when Cara took off running.

IT WASN'T long before they came to a state road. They followed it, staying as much as possible in the woods. A passing car wouldn't likely have seen them anyway, thanks to the active camouflage in their marauding suits. Several hours later, they reached another city.

"Let's stop here, Adam. I've been thinking as we ran. Who are our likely enemies? I suppose the Defense Intelligence Agency has to be on our list. Olivia Cabrera, their super-hacker, can only see the data that's available online. That's why she didn't know exactly what happens when bad people around me die. Similarly, Colonel Taylor could be anywhere, and we wouldn't see her if she didn't wish to be seen … but that's only a worry if she knows where we are. Maybe I can't make myself as invisible as she can, but I have extensive experience living under the radar. Other than the incident in Boston that, if you can believe it, Detective Anders' dead sister told him about, nobody's been able to track me over the past seven years."

"B-But as soon as we buy something, there's credit card data that a smart tracker could access."

"Correct you are. So welcome to the cash-only economy. Adam, there are whole swaths of our country who don't have access to credit. We can do fine using cash, which is untraceable."

"But where do we get cash? From an ATM?"

Cara shook her head. "You're not thinking deviously enough. ATM transactions are trackable. And we're supposed to be dead. Cash withdrawals from accounts whose owners are dead will surely be noticed."

"Then I'm out of ideas. I've got no money on me, and you say we can't access our funds in our bank accounts. So how do we get this marvelous untraceable cash that we need to buy our supplies?"

"Don't worry. I'll take care of it."

"What … I mean how …"

"No, Adam. I may need your help at times, but mostly I got this. I don't want you to see everything I learned to do to survive. I told you guys I wasn't proud of some things I did."

"Are you, um, considering earning us money through sex? I don't want you to do that, Cara."

"You're sweet, Adam. But no, now that I have you, nobody else will ever touch me."

"Then how? I don't understand."

"I steal it."

"Just like that?"

"Adam, when I'm in a civilized environment, I have the luxury of acting civilized. When it's me against the world, I'm just another animal. I am determined to survive. Somebody with significant resources wants us dead. At the moment, they believe all five of us perished in the explosion and fire.

"The only thing I know for sure is that you and I are still alive. Whoever did this, we owe it to your parents and to Linnea to find the scumbags and make them sorry they failed to kill us. I will do whatever is necessary for us to win. Yes, I will steal. I've done it many times. I'm not proud of this skill, but I'm good at it."

"Okay, I'm not judging you. I love you."

"I love you, too. For now, let's try to get some rest. The things I need to do are better done during the day."

They clicked the wrist buttons that activated the head and face protection of their marauding suits and curled up together on the softest ground they could find in the forest close to the town. Their camouflage was so good that a passerby would have had to trip over them to notice their bodies. Nonetheless, neither could sleep.

IN TOWN

"Adam, stay here and wait for me. I need to get us some supplies."

"I'll go with you."

"No, for this, I'll work better alone. Wait here and stay out of sight. I'll be back in an hour or two."

They embraced, then Cara headed into town. While he waited, Adam tried to think about anything but his loss. It didn't help; he kept replaying in his mind the rumble, the glow, the walls, his little sister running into the house … and the explosion and flames. He felt overwhelmed, lost, and did not know what his next move should be. *If Linnea were here, she would have a plan. She always played several moves ahead of her opponents.*

Adam was still thinking about his sister when a figure approached, wearing old jeans, an oversized sweatshirt, and a knit cap. The person stopped in front of him.

"Adam?"

"What the hell!" He jumped up, ready to fight.

"Relax, it's me. Cara."

"How the hell …"

She gave a quick, mirthless laugh. "There are security cameras all over. We don't think about them as we live our lives, but there are traffic cameras, security cameras inside and outside of stores. All over. So we must change our appearance. I rarely use makeup, but it helps to hide my scar. Here, put these on over your marauding suit."

Cara reached into a bag and handed him a pair of worn jeans, an old flannel shirt, and a baseball cap. After he dressed, she had him run his hands through the dirt so he would more resemble someone who'd been living rough.

"Just like that, you look less like Adam and more like a street person."

"Um, thanks, I guess."

"I got us some other things, too: personal care stuff, change of underwear. Oh, and a line on a cheap room. Let's go."

Cara continued to speak as they walked into town. "Walk like a loser, like someone beaten down by life. Slump your shoulders a bit. Look more at the ground, so the brim of your cap will hide your face better. Yes, you're doing great.

"My name will be Nikki Dunn. You are Tommy Carlin. We're both twenty-one years old, so do the math for your birthdate in case anyone asks."

"How do you come up with this?"

"I've had many names over seven years on the street. There was never anyone I could trust before you. My birth name is Cara Ferris, but it didn't seem like a good idea to tell people that when I was in a position that they could hurt me."

Adam squeezed her hand.

They ambled into town. A crumpled fast-food wrapper bounced through the street, tossed by an errant gust of wind. The wrapper stopped at Adam's feet. He kicked it halfheartedly, and it rolled away. A siren wailed in the distance. Here a place for quick payday loans, there a bar, a pool hall, another bar. A grizzled man sat on the sidewalk outside of the pool hall, smoking a cigarette and staring into the distance. From time to time, he took a drink from a container inside a brown paper bag.

Adam followed Cara into a narrow alley between two buildings. A stack of old crates and a couple of broken wooden pallets rested against the dirty red brick by a doorway, unmarked except for a No Loitering sign.

They were alone until a man stepped out from behind a rusty dumpster.

"Give me your wallets and phones. Now!"

Adam glared at him. "Fuck you."

The man pulled a butterfly knife from his pocket and flicked it open. The sharp metal blade glinted in the morning light.

"Fuck you," Adam said again. He ran at the man and punched him hard, over and over. The man swiped and stabbed with his knife without effect. His knife penetrated Adam's shirt but slid off the marauding suit underneath. Suddenly, the anguish of losing his family and his home overwhelmed Adam. He fought like a man possessed—striking, kicking, choking. Then the man was on the ground, Adam astride him, pounding the man's head into the pavement. Adam cried as he emptied his pain into the nameless man.

Cara pulled him off. "It's okay, Adam. It's over. He's dead."

Adam waited until his breathing slowed. He looked down at the motionless body. Bloodstains soiled the ground by the man's head.

"Oh, God. What did I do?" He fell to his knees. "I'm sorry, Cara. What happened to me?"

Cara helped Adam to his feet and hugged him. "I understand. More than you know." She tightened her mouth with resolve. "We need to get out of here now, before anyone finds us. Come on."

She rifled through the man's pockets and took his cash. Then she grabbed Adam's hand in hers and he followed her, numb and silent.

"We shouldn't stay in town here like I was planning. The local police will surely question us when they discover the body."

They ran for hours, mostly along country roads, without further conversation. The thick soles of their marauding suits muffled their footsteps. Eventually, they reached a town far enough away that Cara felt comfortable. She scouted around and found a cheap hotel.

The two exhausted teens lay on top of the lumpy mattress, still fully dressed. Cara curled as close to Adam as she could get, her head on his chest, legs intertwined, and they finally slept.

PRODIGY

They awoke several hours later. It took Adam a few seconds to get his bearings and to realize that Cara's head was still on his chest. He stroked her hair. He looked at the clock. It was getting on toward evening.

"You're awake, Adam." She didn't move away from him.

"I'm awake, I guess. I'm alive, but Mom and Dad and my sister …" He paused. "I still c-can't believe they're …" He couldn't say the word. His breath caught and his lip quivered as he fought back tears.

Cara held him. *He needs to talk about his sister to help him process what happened.*

"Adam, tell me something about Linnea. When did your parents and you realize she was gifted?"

"We saw she was unusual from the beginning. She potty-trained herself before she was a year old. By two, she spoke in complete sentences and was reading kid's books. At five, she was asking about things she read or heard in the news. That's when Dad had us begin the dinnertime conversations about what was happening in the world. We wanted to supplement Linnea and let her learn as fast as she could."

"I was curious why your folks left her in the public schools, as precocious as she is … was." Cara grimaced.

"She skipped a year. Mom and Dad talked about putting her in a school for accelerated learners, but unlike a lot of child prodigies, she was very social. Linnea had friends, mostly associated with soccer. She was only an average soccer player, but she loved the game." Adam smiled wanly. "She wanted to stay in school where she was … at least that's what she wanted until she met Ms. Fortune."

"That makes sense, I guess, though academically she was years ahead of her classmates. I would think that would grow annoying after a while."

"When we bought our house, it originally had five bedrooms. We hired a carpenter to remove a wall between two of the bedrooms so Linnea could have room for her science and engineering explorations. Trust me, there was little chance of her getting bored."

"Ah, that's why her bedroom was so large."

"Yes. Dad bought her whatever equipment she wanted … though I confess he paused for a moment the day she requested an oscilloscope."

"You're kidding. An oscilloscope?"

"Yeah. Apparently, a high-bandwidth multi-channel oscilloscope costs several thousand dollars. Linnea made a case for why she needed it. Doctor Cox at Rose-Hulman agreed and found her a used device that was a lot less expensive.

"I remember once when she was about eight, our TV stopped working. Not a big deal in our family because we mostly use it for streaming the occasional movie or TED Talk. Linnea asked if she could look at it. Dad and I brought the TV up to her room. She opened it and did some tests. She asked Dad to order a specific integrated circuit online. The chip was just a few dollars. She installed it and boom, our TV worked again."

"Did your parents get her tested? IQ or whatever they use now?"

"They tried."

"They tried?"

"Linnea was off the scale. Answered every question correctly as fast as the psychologist showed them to her."

"That's crazy." Cara caressed Adam's cheek. "You've always acted like you love her, but how did her intellect make you feel inside?"

"How did it make me feel? Proud. Linnea was the best thing that ever happened in my life, I mean until you. Linnea and I have always been very close. I like to think I'm smarter than average, like Dad and Mom. But Linnea was at a different level. She could have tested out of high school whenever she liked. Doctor Cox at Rose-Hulman wanted her in his classes. Hell, she was taking online classes through MIT at night, then going back to middle school by day. Linnea was a contradiction, an impossibility. Sweet and cute and beyond brilliant.

"Think about it. Any other thirteen-year-old kid who found herself tied to a chair in a locked room deep in the sanctuary of a sadistic criminal would have died there. But my sister escaped and used her knowledge of chemistry to bring pain to her captors."

Cara nodded. "Linnea was a force of nature, that's for sure. I loved her like a sister."

"It just d-doesn't make sense that she was so incredibly gifted, and suddenly she's gone. I can't get my mind around it."

"Adam, one of the many things I don't understand is why those government agents were interested in me rather than Linnea. Sure, my monster or angel or whatever can kick some ass, but Linnea? Think what she could have built for them! I can't even imagine what she might have created with sufficient motivation."

"I understand their interest in you. Your angel has been kicking ass, as you say, for over three thousand years."

"Yeah, I suppose. I still think they picked the wrong person. And another thing: They never realized the secret sauce that allowed Linnea and me to function at our best."

"Secret sauce?"

"Yes, silly. You. Without you, I'd still be homeless. Linnea and I often talked about what you meant to us. She told me you were the wind beneath her wings … you know, like the song. You always treated Linnea as an equal, a friend, and not like an annoying little sister. You were the one who taught her about computers and networking. You helped her in her lab and made sure her experiments were safe. You drove her to see the engineering professor. You were the one who introduced her to chess. You were always her biggest cheerleader. She loved you. And I love you."

END OF THE LINE

Cara came back to the room with some fast food and a newspaper. "Look at this, Adam," she said as she handed him the paper which she'd folded to their story:

FIVE PEOPLE DEAD IN HOUSE EXPLOSION

AP newswire.

A house fire and explosion in central Indiana resulted in the death of two adults and three children. Names are being withheld pending notification of relatives. The blast broke windows in several neighboring houses.

Police suspect a gas leak, though the investigation is ongoing.

"THAT'S IT? A few goddamned lines in the middle of the paper? That's all my family was worth?" Adam threw the paper to the ground in disgust.

"I'm sorry. I figured it would upset you, but you had to see it."

"Not your fault, Cara. I just don't understand a world where someone can murder my parents and my little sister in seconds, and nobody but us cares. I mean, a gas leak? Seriously?"

Cara sat beside him on the threadbare couch. "Adam, what did the newspaper mean about notification of relatives? I've never met any of your extended family members."

"There aren't any. There's nobody to notify. Mom and Dad both lost their parents. Dad was an only child, and Mom's older brother, my uncle Jesse, died years ago in an automobile accident."

"So we're …"

"The end of the line. No more Samuelsons."

Cara hugged him. "I'm so sorry, Adam."

"I wish we could see how the investigation of the explosion is going. I feel helpless, not knowing."

"What would you like to know?"

"I want confirmation that my family is or is not dead. I mean, I assume they're gone, but I'd like to see an official report. And I want someone to blame. I want answers. I want justice. Code of Hammurabi justice."

"You mean revenge."

"Yes. Guess I'm not as good of a person as you, Cara, but whoever k-killed my parents and my sister needs to die."

"You don't have to justify anything to me, Adam. My choices aren't right for everybody. I'm not judging you. I love you, Adam."

"Thank you, Cara. Love you too."

"Though I'm not sure how to get the information you want. I don't know how to hack the police or fire investigators."

"Me neither. T-Too bad we don't have Olivia Cabrera working with us, huh?"

"Yeah. I just hope she's not working against us."

"We're dead, remember?"

"What do you think about asking for help from Detective Anders? Or even Special Agent Tanaka?"

"A p-part of me wants to trust them, but a bigger part of me is hesitant. There's a big difference between asking for a bit of help and coming back from the dead with a desire for revenge. I'm not sure we can trust either of them not to tell someone we're alive. They may well think they're helping us, but our only advantage over whoever tried to kill us is that right now, our unknown enemy believes they succeeded."

"That makes sense. I just wish we had someone else on our side."

"I'm afraid, Cara, it's you and me against the world."

<<<<>>>>

CARA RETURNED from her next foraging expedition with a gigantic smile.

"Adam, check this out. I got us a used laptop and charger."

"Awesome! Where did you find one?"

"Don't ask. We needed it more. Be sure to wipe the previous user's information."

"I'm on it." Adam plugged it in and got to work. "Yes! Found s-someone's unprotected Wi-Fi. I'll download a few tools, then we'll see what I can find out."

Adam worked in silence for the rest of the afternoon, stopping only when Cara brought some more food.

"How's it coming, Adam?"

"Slowly, to be honest. It's hard to know where to start. Obviously, I c-can't log into anything as me."

"No, that would be difficult to explain."

"Here's something." Adam looked up from the laptop. "This Wednesday, there will be a memorial service for our family at our church."

"What time?"

"Wednesday at one p.m. Cara, we should go."

"How can we show up at our own funeral?"

"It's a memorial service, not a funeral. Maybe they didn't find enough of our bodies for a funeral, or maybe the police investigation wasn't complete. Regarding how we show up, I have some ideas. Haven't thought everything through yet, but I think it can work with no one seeing us. We should be there to say goodbye. Linnea, Mom, and Dad deserve that."

"So you think we should go *back* to the town where we supposedly died, then enter inside the church where everyone knew us so we can attend our own memorial? Adam, I loved Linnea and your parents, too. Differently than you, for sure, but it ripped my heart out when they died. They were the only proper family I ever had. But this sounds like a horrible idea."

"No, we can pull it off. We'll wear our marauding suits, of course. If we arrive at the church a couple hours before the service, we can get inside and hide somewhere so that nobody would see us."

"You're serious, Adam?"

"I really want this. Please, Cara. It's important."

She looked at Adam, saw the pleading on his face, and she nodded. "Okay, Adam. We'll do it."

Tuesday night found them back in the woods behind the ruins of the Samuelson's house. They'd activated the head and hand protection of their marauding suits to make themselves as invisible as possible. Prior experimentation showed that with the suit's invisibility mode activated, they were not totally invisible. Some backgrounds were easier to mimic than others, and there was always a faint shimmer when someone in a marauding suit moved. Despite the light-bending technology in their suits, bright lights would sometimes cause unusual shadows.

Not much of the original structure remained, just a couple of partial brick walls and a refuse-filled hole where the basement had been. Smoke and water-damaged building materials and furniture lay scattered in the yard near the house. Police tape hung limply from orange cones, but the investigation had long since ended.

"I wonder what the police found," Adam said. "I'm pretty g-good with computers, but God knows I'm no Olivia Cabrera. I do not know how to hack into their system."

"The original article mentioned something about a gas leak. Did you see anything else in the news since then?"

"Nothing. I mean n-nothing except for the notice of the memorial service."

"Could a gas leak cause this amount of devastation, do you think?"

"I think it would take a lot of natural gas to produce an explosion this strong. None of us smelled anything as we left the house that evening. B-Besides, it wasn't just an explosion. The flames were out of control. I'm not a trained fire investigator, but I'll bet whoever did this used an accelerant."

"You mean like gasoline? Something like that?"

Adam nodded. "The wooden structure of a modern house can burn, but that fire was insane. It's like they wanted to make sure nothing would survive."

"Then they were successful," Cara said. "Damn them to hell! This is the only house where I've ever felt safe."

Adam hugged her. "I know, Cara. They've hurt us both." He sighed. "Let's head to the church. It's about three miles. I'd like to get there before dawn. We can stay in the woods behind the church till mid-morning. The doors should be unlocked by then, so we can enter and find a hiding spot. Maybe the baptistery."

A voice behind them startled the two teens.

"Cara? Adam? I hear your voices. Are you here?"

They turned to see Detective Anders stride up from the woods.

"D-Detective? What are you doing here? We didn't expect to see anyone."

Anders shrugged. "I'm glad the two of you are alive. Interesting equipment you have, by the way. Makes you difficult to see. From Ms. Fortune's lab, I presume?"

Cara and Adam deactivated the invisibility feature of their marauding suits. Adam nodded. "Yes."

"We found … uh … we found your parents, but none of you young people. Special Agent Tanaka had the idea of arranging the memorial with your pastor. He thought maybe, if you'd survived, that you would return for the memorial service. And I thought if you did that, you would stop here first. So I waited in the woods. Is Linnea okay?"

"The three of us were outside, b-behind the house. When we first heard the blast, Linnea ran back inside the house yelling for our folks. Then there was a s-second explosion, not as loud as the first but with fire. Detective, it was like the gates of hell opened. It was an inferno. We tried, but it was too hot to go after her. We never saw her again."

"My God, I'm sorry." He rested his hand gently on Adam's shoulder. "We'll search the ruins one more time. But where have the two of you been for the past few—"

A sharp, loud crack split the night. Cara's head flew back, and she collapsed.

"No!" Adam yelled as he knelt by her side.

Detective Anders crouched, gun in hand, ready to return

fire. He scanned around them for a visible threat. Another sharp report and dirt flew up beside Adam's knee.

"Shit! Adam, get her in my car. I'll cover you."

Adam lifted Cara's limp body in his arms, and they ran to Anders' car, which he'd parked a few houses down the street. The moment the teens were in the back seat, Detective Anders peeled away. He was already on the radio, calling for backup as he drove.

In the car, Cara was unresponsive, but Adam was thrilled to see she was breathing. He scanned her body and head but found no blood or bullet wounds in her marauding suit.

Adam gently opened the head covering of Cara's suit until it retracted into her turtleneck. Immediately, he noticed a large bruise with blood matting the hair on the top of her head.

"Detective, she needs a doctor. Fast."

THREE MILLISECONDS

Olivia Cabrera leaned into Colonel Taylor's office.

"Colonel, we have a problem."

As an analyst, Olivia had earned a reputation for being calm no matter what the emergency. This morning, however, she was pale. Her hands trembled, and she wiped her palms repeatedly on her pants. She closed the office door and pulled up a chair by her supervisor's desk.

"What's going on?" Colonel Taylor asked.

Olivia swallowed and took a deep breath to collect herself. "You know how I am about security, right?"

Colonel Taylor nodded.

"In the course of my work here, I've hacked into some dangerous places, and I've tried to be careful to cover my tracks for fear that someone would try to backtrack me here, the way you guys did when you found me initially. I set some tells deep in our servers …"

"What do you mean by 'tells'?"

"You know how in spy novels someone might leave a hair placed just so on their doorknob or wherever, so they can see if there had been unscheduled visitors?"

"Yes. I've done that when I worked in the field."

"I built a little black box—some hardware, some software, my design—so that if there's been any untoward intrusion I'm alerted, and I can see where the intruder went."

"I'm surprised you could add a black box to our servers. I mean, with all our security, but I'm with you so far."

"Ma'am, somebody is after us. There was an intrusion last night."

"On an ultra-secure government server? A *secret* ultra-secure government server? Who the hell could break in here? It would be like hacking the NSA."

"I've hacked the NSA. That's what got me this job, remember?" Olivia shook her head. "No, we're apparently not so secure as we'd like to think. Someone was inside our system, looking around. Looking for us. You and me, specifically, by name. They've accessed our files. They know everything about us, everything that the government knows."

"That's not possible. How long were they inside our system?"

"This is what has me shaken. They entered, looked around, found our files, and left."

"How long ..."

"Three milliseconds."

Colonel Taylor laughed. "You had me going there for a minute. Olivia, relax. Nobody can break into a system, look around, find stuff, and leave all within three milliseconds. You can't type your name in three milliseconds, much less hack a secure server. We're talking three one-thousandths of a second."

Olivia pushed back her chair and stood, her voice now firm and clipped, lips tight. "Colonel. You've known me for three years. Do you seriously think I would bring this to you without having checked my work? I am certain what happened; I just don't see how it was possible. I stand by my words. Last night, somebody hacked into the DIA and found the two of us."

"Okay, then. Forget about *how* for a moment. Let's focus on *who*. Who would know both of our names and have an interest in us?"

"I want to say that teen girl Cara and her family, but they're all dead." She sat down and leaned her forehead into her hands. "It was my fault. A family wiped out, and it was my fault."

Colonel Taylor rested her hand on the younger woman's shoulder. "You didn't kill them. How do you figure it was your fault?"

"I killed them by proxy. I shouldn't have gone looking. Or at least I should have stopped researching after you found the cockpit voice recorder files wiped from the NTSB. Think about it. Someone was trying to protect her. She sure as hell couldn't have wiped the files herself. Somebody felt it was a bad idea for the government to get involved.

"And now somebody with incredible resources is looking for us. A part of me wants to let them find me. You remember when you first talked to me? I liked to look around in secure networks, but I did no damage. I didn't sign up to kill people. That girl, Cara, she clearly felt the same way. Why didn't I leave her alone?" Her eyes filled with tears. She sobbed quietly, shoulders shaking.

"Olivia, you didn't kill the Samuelsons, and you were not party to a government-sanctioned hit. I won't tell you our government has never, officially or not, sanctioned an assassination, but I give you my word that this was not that. You're welcome to research the matter for yourself. The reason we hired you is that you can uncover any secret; you're not a good person for me to lie to."

"But then who?"

"Heavens, the list of possibilities would be long. It did not thrill General Fry to recruit a teenage girl. An enemy state might decide it makes more sense to shut Cara Ferris down than attempt to recruit her. And our experience with Cara and her family confirms that line of thinking."

"You're sure it was nobody American then, ma'am?"

"I'm sure it was not the American government. I would have known if it was the DIA, and I don't believe any other agency knows about her."

"I respectfully disagree. It had to have been someone in U.S. Intelligence who erased the voice data recorder in the plane that crashed with Cara inside."

Colonel Taylor nodded. "You're correct, though it's odd they would try to protect her and then … oh. What if they weren't trying to protect her? What if the idea was to erase any trace of Cara's unique abilities and then erase Cara herself?"

"You're saying I discovered an asset that had already been sentenced to death?"

"I don't know, but we need to find out."

Olivia gave a curt nod. "I'll get right on it."

SAFE HOUSE

Thirty minutes of driving led Cara and Adam farther away from town.

"Detective, there's no hospital this way. There's nothing here but farms."

"No choice, Adam. I was just speaking with Special Agent Tanaka. He says hospitals aren't safe for you two. I don't know who's after you, but Tanaka doesn't scare easily. He is quite on edge."

The police car exited the paved road and turned into a gravel driveway. Ten minutes later, they parked beside a ranch-style farmhouse.

Adam saw nothing but fields in all directions.

"Where are we?"

"Special Agent Tanaka opened this for us. We're at an FBI safe house. There's a doctor here."

As he spoke, three men exited the building and approached the car. One man was carrying a backboard. The man in the lead spoke. "I'm Doctor Vicks. This is Agent Gordon and Agent Stone. Where's the girl?"

Detective Anders nodded toward the back seat of his vehicle.

Doctor Vicks leaned inside. "I assume you're Adam and this is Cara?"

"Yes, sir."

"Excellent. You two will be safe here. Let's get her inside."

Quickly, but gently, they placed Cara on the backboard and fastened the straps.

"Adam, you stabilize her head and neck while we move."

He nodded. They brought Cara inside and transferred her to a bed. Doctor Vicks examined her head and shined a flashlight in her eyes. "I'd love to get a CT scan of her head, but we can't do that here. You say this was a rifle bullet, detective?"

"That's my best guess, doctor. There was nobody within handgun range of us. Somebody besides me was waiting for these kids. If not for this suit, she would be dead."

The suit in question was frustrating the efforts of Agent Stone to cut it with medical shears.

"That won't work," Adam said. "I'll get it." Moving Cara as little as possible, Adam removed her marauding suit, leaving her in a sports bra, a thin t-shirt, and panties. He covered her with a blanket. "I have street clothes for her when you're done."

"Do you need us here, doctor?" Agent Gordon asked.

"No, I'm good, thanks."

The two agents left the room.

While the doctor completed his exam and cleaned and bandaged Cara's head wound, Adam folded Cara's suit into its little satchel and donned street clothes over his own suit. The two of them then dressed Cara.

Doctor Vicks turned to Adam. "She has a concussion, but I don't think she has bleeding in her brain."

"How l-long will she be out?"

"Hopefully, she'll wake up soon. If not, that would suggest there may in fact be something bad going on in her head. If we get to that point, we'll have some decisions to make regarding more advanced medical care."

The doctor turned and left. Before Detective Anders followed, he leaned toward Adam and whispered, "Special Agent Tanaka will be here within the hour. He and I have some questions. I think the fewer people who know about those special suits, the better. You may want to keep yours in reserve along with Cara's."

Adam nodded. "I understand. There are some questions I have as well. I expect the flow of information to go b-both ways."

"That's reasonable. I'll be in the living room waiting for Tanaka."

Adam changed out of his marauding suit, then sat beside Cara on the bed.

Cara's eyes fluttered, then opened. She focused on Adam.

He smiled at her. "Thank God you're okay."

Cara's eyes grew wide, and she shrank away from Adam. "Who are you?"

"I'm Adam. Your boyfriend."

"I don't know you."

He slid closer to her. Tried to take her hand. She pulled away, then retreated to a corner of the room. "Stay away from me!" Her pupils had dilated, and her breathing was rapid. She held her arms up in a defensive posture.

"Okay, I won't touch you." He sat down on the floor near the door, trying to look as unthreatening as possible. "Do you remember your name?"

Cara thought for a second, then shook her head. "I don't know who I am, and I don't know you."

"You're eighteen years old. Do you remember anything about your life?"

"No."

Adam sighed. "Okay. I'm Adam and I'm your friend. I will never hurt you."

"Okay," she said, but she didn't relax.

"How do you feel?"

"My head hurts." She gingerly touched the bandage.

"You're very lucky. S-Someone shot you in the head." She considered this, but didn't respond. "Would you like something to drink?"

"Water please."

"Okay, I'll get some. I'll be back in a few minutes."

Cara watched him suspiciously as he left the room.

"How's she doing?" Detective Anders asked when Adam entered the living room.

"Cara is awake and seems to move normally, but we have a complication."

Anders cocked his head. "Yes?"

"She's l-lost her memory. Cara doesn't recognize me and can't even think of her own name or anything about her life prior to being shot."

The men all stood as though to re-enter the bedroom.

"No, don't," Adam said. "She's already panicking. If she fears for her life ..." He shook his head. "If she changes, we're all dead. Her will was barely strong enough in the past to prevent ... you-know-who ... from killing Linnea and me."

"What are you talking about?" Doctor Vicks asked.

"You d-don't want to know, doctor. Just believe me, we don't want Cara to feel she's in danger. I promised her I'd bring her some water. Let me do that and go back in with her. I can keep her calm."

Agent Stone showed Adam to the kitchen and pointed at a cabinet. "The glasses are in there."

Adam stood in the doorway to the bedroom, a glass of

cold water in his hand. Cara remained crouched in the far corner of the room.

"Here, I brought you some water." He held it out to her.

She stood and reached for the glass. "Thank you." She quickly drank and handed the empty glass back to Adam. He set it down by the door.

"I'll put it away in a moment. May I get you anything else?"

"No, thank you. I think I'll lie down for a while."

"That's a g-good idea. If you need anything, I'll be here or just outside the door in the living room."

When Adam saw Cara was asleep, he left the room to put away the glass and to try talking with law enforcement.

DAMNED IF YOU DO ...

Adam and Detective Anders made small talk at the kitchen table while they waited for Special Agent Tanaka. They heard him enter the house and speak with the two agents in a low voice, then walk to the bedroom where Cara lay. After a few minutes, he joined them in the kitchen.

Tanaka's jacket was wrinkled, his tie was ajar and, Adam noted as the lawman entered the room, his shoes were scuffed. His face was lined and tired, and there was something new in his eyes that Adam didn't recognize. He thought back to the first time he met Special Agent Tanaka, when Cara was in the hospital recovering from the plane crash. The Tanaka he remembered dressed immaculately, perfectly coiffed, everything in place: a man in control of his environment.

"Detective Anders. Adam." They rose to greet him, but he motioned for them to sit. "We haven't much time."

"Wh-What's the plan?" Adam asked. "Who wants us dead?"

"Someone powerful. They want Cara, not you. Here's

what we need to do. I'll take Cara with me to someplace safe. You need to leave quickly, Adam. I can't protect you."

"Th-This is someplace safe. Detective Anders said you opened this safe house for us."

"They'll find you here. There's nothing I can do about it. There's a leak in the FBI. Someone knows every move I make."

"So ...," Detective Anders began.

Special Agent Tanaka shook his head at Anders, tight-lipped. "Cara goes with me. You worry about yourself, Adam. Hopefully, they'll leave you alone."

"Who?"

"Just get out of here, Adam. Go with Detective Anders and save yourself. We need to move now."

Adam looked into Special Agent Tanaka's eyes and he knew, viscerally, that if Cara left with Tanaka, she would not survive. He focused on his hands for a moment to compose himself, then looked up again and nodded.

"May I say goodbye to her?"

"You've got five minutes."

Adam got up and left the kitchen.

He entered the bedroom to find Cara lying on the bed. She was awake, staring at him. She watched him without speaking as he changed into his marauding suit and pulled hers out of the bag.

"We have to go or you'll die here. Get dressed."

"I don't know you. I'm not going anywhere with you. Get out or I'll call for help."

"I'm sorry, Cara," Adam said as he pulled out his little plastic gun, the one he once dismissed as a toy, and shot Cara point-blank in her chest. A lattice of energy hissed across her body, then disappeared. Cara collapsed soundlessly on the bed.

As quickly as he could, Adam changed her into her

marauding suit. It was more difficult to put it on an unresisting, floppy body than it was to take it off. He gathered their belongings into his day bag and strapped it on his back. He opened a bedroom window, saying a silent prayer of thanks that it was unlocked. Then, Adam grabbed Cara under her arms and raised her floppy body to the level of the window, slid her through and out onto the ground, then followed. He closed the window from the outside, though he didn't expect to fool the agents for long.

They were in the open and could be seen from the house. Adam knew that even with their marauding suits set to invisible mode, the camouflage was most effective if they were still. As they moved, the air would shimmer in the shape of their bodies. But there was no help for it. He lifted Cara under her knees and shoulders and jogged to Anders' dark blue police sedan. He strapped Cara into the passenger seat and himself in the driver's seat. The keys were in the ignition. The car started with a low rumble. *Better engine than I've ever had*, he thought.

A yell echoed behind them. One agent ran to his car and moved to cut them off. Adam had no training in evasive driving. *I can't shoot a law officer, even with a stun gun. But his car ... lots of computers in modern vehicles.* He pulled out his other toy, the electronics detector/EMP generator. When the agent's car was close enough, Adam aimed and pushed the button. There was no sound, but the agent's car stuttered and stopped. *Yes!*

Adam took off at high speed down the long gravel driveway, trailing a cloud of dust. When he reached the paved country road, he accelerated. Soon, the farmhouse was far behind him. He slowed to close to legal speed so as not to attract attention from a local cop.

As he drove, he pulled out his prepaid phone and dialed a number, praying he remembered it correctly.

"M-Ma'am, th-this is …"

"You're alive! Where are you?"

Adam gave his approximate location as best he could. "I stole a police car. Cara and I need help."

"Understood. Hold on, let me pull up a map." Then seconds later she said, "I'll send a helicopter. Here's what you need to do until help arrives." Ms. Fortune's instructions were crisp and businesslike.

"I'll do that. Thank you."

He put away his phone and turned to Cara, who had slumped in her seat from lack of muscle tone. "How am I supposed to know police cars have built-in GPS? Ms. F says the police or FBI can track us easily."

Cara didn't respond, though he hadn't expected her to.

Adam pulled over in a small copse of trees by the road-side. He adjusted his gear, lifted Cara over both of his shoulders, and set off down the road at a dead run. Law enforcement may have been tracking Anders' police car, but they would grossly underestimate how far from the car he could get in a brief time.

Adam ran, Cara draped over his shoulders, for over thirty minutes. The few times he heard a car in the distance, he dropped to a ditch beside the road, trusting the active camouflage in their marauding suits to conceal them from passing traffic. Despite the augmentation of his suit, Cara was growing heavy. But Ms. Fortune had been very clear about where he was to meet the helicopter. Fear gave him energy, but the realization that Cara's life was entirely in his hands since he'd stunned her also drove him. He could not quit. This had to work. He ran on.

There, ahead of him, he saw the twisted tree and crumbling barn that Ms. Fortune had described. The roof and part of one wall had caved in years ago. Young trees found footholds within the abandoned structure as nature relentlessly reclaimed her territory. Adjacent fields were still being farmed. Adam set Cara down behind the old barn and collapsed beside her, dead tired. His legs were sore and his upper body ached, but his thoughts were on what would come next. *They'll be making a hot landing,* Ms. Fortune had said. Despite his best efforts, law enforcement may have followed him. He hoped there wouldn't be violence.

Within minutes, he heard a loud hum from above him. He switched off Cara's and his invisibility, leaving them in the default black of their special suits. A gray helicopter with two main rotors but no tail rotor hovered several hundred feet in the air, scanning for threats. Adam jogged several steps into the field and waved. The helicopter settled, rotors still spinning.

Adam recognized the swarthy pilot: Nuri Ben-David, the driver who picked up the three young people from the Peninsula Hotel in Chicago several months earlier. Nuri and another man, dressed similarly in khakis and a black t-shirt and looking equally fit, stepped out from the aircraft. They were both armed. They stooped automatically as they passed under the rotors.

Nuri shook Adam's hand. "I'm happy you're alive. This is Alain Castile," he said, indicating his colleague. Adam nodded a greeting. "Where's Cara?"

"Back here." Adam ran to Cara and picked her up. She lay limp in his arms. "She's been shot ... twice," he said in explanation.

The men quickly strapped her to a cot and placed her in the passenger compartment with Adam. A crackle of static from the radio, then voices speaking rapidly. Nuri donned his headset. "Time to leave. They found the police car." Adam felt a surge of power as the helicopter lifted off.

The experience of flight inside this helicopter was strangely quiet. Adam expected much more noise, like in the movies. He sat looking out the window, pensive. A voice startled him from his reverie.

"Adam."

He turned. "Cara?"

Her eyes were alive, but her body remained motionless. "You shot me," she said, her voice petulant.

"I'm so sorry, Cara. I needed to get you out of there, and you were threatening to scream."

"I remember. I remember everything now. Special Agent Tanaka came into my room, though at the time I didn't recognize him either. He said it was good I'd lost my memory; it would be easier that way. He said they had his wife and his boy and he had no choice, and that he was sorry."

"Who had his wife and his boy?"

"He didn't say. I believe they wanted me in exchange for Tanaka's family. You saved my life, Adam. This is the second time you crossed the FBI for me." She smiled. "I'm starting to think you love me."

"I will always love you, Cara." He took her hand and thought he felt her fingers move a little.

"I love you too, but Adam?"

"Yes?"

"Never shoot me again."

He knelt beside her. "I promise I won't. I'm sorry, I ..." His voice failed him. He rested his head on her chest.

"You're crying." Cara clumsily stroked his head with her hand. "Please don't be sad, Adam. I'll be okay."

IN A CLEARING behind a large house north of Chicago, near Lake Michigan, the ground pulled apart, lifted at an angle on either side of the split and retracted, leaving a metallic platform where the grass had been moments earlier. A large yellow cross was painted on the platform. The gray heli-copter appeared overhead with a sound like a swarm of wasps and gently settled onto the center of the cross. Its twin rotors slowed, then stopped. The platform lowered smoothly below the ground. When the rotors were low enough, the cover closed again. In less than a minute, there was nothing visible behind the house but a grassy clearing.

The platform reached bottom. While Nuri shut down the helicopter, Alain opened the passenger door and helped Adam, who again was carrying Cara in his arms, down the steps to the floor. Ms. Fortune was there with a wheelchair. She held it steady while Adam placed Cara in it. He could feel Cara's muscle tone slowly returning; she no longer slumped in the chair. Cara gazed at him with bright, loving eyes. The two of them turned when they heard a scream.

"Adam! Oh my God, Adam!" A young girl ran to them and threw herself into Adam's arms.

"Linnea? I thought …"

"I know. I thought you and Cara were dead, too." Linnea reached out to Cara, attempting a group hug. Cara smiled at her and tried to reach for Linnea's hand but failed, her arm falling awkwardly back to the armrest of the wheelchair. Linnea stared pointedly at Cara's bandaged head.

"Cara? What's wrong?"

"It's nothing, Linnea. I'm getting better. I'll be fine by tomorrow."

"What happened?"

"It's a long story, and now I think we'll have plenty of time to talk."

NOT A GOOD PERSON TO LIE TO

"Colonel, we need to talk. Privately. Not here."

Colonel Taylor glanced up at her analyst. Olivia stood in a wide stance, hands clenched. Her eyes were cold as she glared at her boss.

We need to de-escalate. "Of course, Olivia. Let's take my car to Jones Point Park. It's not too far from here, and we can find a private spot and talk freely."

When they arrived at Colonel Taylor's Lexus, she unlocked the doors with her remote. She watched, with an eyebrow raised but without comment, as Olivia scanned the inside of the vehicle with a wand-like electronic device. They sat together silently as they left Joint Base Anacostia-Bolling and negotiated Maryland traffic towards the Woodrow Wilson Memorial Bridge.

Colonel Taylor pulled into public parking at Jones Point Park. She opened her trunk and retrieved a blanket. Then the two women headed across the multi-use field and continued into the trees. As they walked, Colonel Taylor observed her analyst. Olivia's mouth was tight. Her eyes darted from side to side as though searching for something.

"What is worrying you, Olivia?"

Olivia thought before answering. "I don't know who I can trust. I'm not sure anymore who I'm working for."

Colonel Taylor nodded. In a small clearing off the path, she spread the blanket and sat. Olivia scanned the clearing with her wand then, satisfied, sat beside her mentor.

"Olivia, we're spies. Wheels within wheels. This is where we live. At one level, you must trust yourself. Your gut. Beyond that, you make your best judgment about who is worthy of your confidence. Then you follow the Russian proverb: Trust, but verify. Always verify.

"Having said that, I don't believe I've ever given you cause to doubt me."

Olivia turned to have eye contact with her supervisor. "Two days ago, Colonel, you told me that our government would not have sanctioned a hit on that girl, Cara Ferris, and her family. You said that our office could not have done so without your knowledge, and you assured me you and I played no role in a killing." Olivia took a deep breath. "Your next statement was the only one you got right, Colonel. You pointed out that I can uncover any secret, so it would be unwise to lie to me."

Colonel Taylor's voice was calm as she responded. "I sense this is not the right time to pull rank and censure you for speaking to me like that. You're good. The best analyst I've ever seen. I admire your work ethic and what I know about your morals. You say nothing without a reason, so obviously you learned something that scares you. Tell me what you found so I can help you and, if possible, reassure you.

"Olivia, remember what I told you a minute ago? Trust, but verify. I am your boss, but I like to think I'm also your mentor."

"Colonel, I've committed a federal crime. I have stored,

offsite but securely, some highly confidential material. If anything happens to me—"

Colonel Taylor raised her hand, palm out. "I know what I would have arranged, and I'll bet you did the same. But I want nothing to happen to you. Besides, in the course of your work with the DIA, you've committed many federal crimes. How many times have you hacked a police database? Now please, Olivia, what did you learn?"

From her handbag, Olivia withdrew a cellphone. Colonel Taylor looked at it and gave a wry smile.

"I'm familiar with that model, Olivia. That's a KATIM® phone. Said to be the world's most secure cellphone. You're aware it's designed and manufactured in the United Arab Emirates? And you work for the DIA?"

"That's the least of my transgressions, Colonel, should you choose to think of them as such."

"How do you bring that into our offices?"

"Don't ask, don't tell. I have something on this device you should hear."

"Okay, go on."

Olivia typed rapidly on the screen, then handed the cellphone to her boss. "Listen to this."

Colonel Taylor listened, at low volume, to the five-minute conversation. Her brow furrowed, and her lips tightened involuntarily as the recording progressed.

"Olivia, how is it possible that you recorded this? His phone is completely secure and encrypted."

"I'm the best at what I do. This is why you hired me. And this is why one should not lie to me."

The colonel pointedly ignored the last part of Olivia's statement.

"Do you recognize the voice?" Olivia asked.

"Of course. That was General Fry."

"Were you aware he speaks Russian?"

"I was not. Based on this recording, he's fluent in Russian. No accent," Colonel Taylor said. "Though I'm also fluent in Russian and speak it without an American accent. Yet I'm not Russian and have neither political nor professional affiliation with Russia. So the fact that the director of the DIA speaks Russian is not in and of itself proof of wrongdoing."

"What were General Fry and the other gentleman discussing?"

"That, on the other hand, strongly suggests wrongdoing. I swear to you I did not know."

"Colonel, what were they discussing? We need to talk about this if you want my trust. I never agreed to take part, even indirectly, in murder."

Colonel Taylor sighed. "You're correct, Olivia. I presume you used translation software to understand the gist of what they were saying. It appears that our director assigned or hired someone to eliminate Cara. He was angry that the assassin attempted to kill the entire Samuelson family. The parents are confirmed dead. The authorities have not found Linnea's remains in what's left of the house, though apparently it was the mother of all infernos. Cara and Adam somehow escaped the house explosion and fire, and they are definitely still alive."

"Could the little girl be alive, too?"

"No, according to the conversation, she was not with Cara and Adam. They wouldn't be likely to leave their little sister to fend for herself now, would they?"

Olivia rested her face in her hands. In a soft voice she said, "Then she's dead too, damnit."

Colonel Taylor continued, "And General Fry has a good idea where Cara and Adam are. And you and I have some decisions to make."

"What do you mean?"

"Years ago, when I was still with the CIA, I became … close with a lady who provided me with tools."

"Tools?"

"Specialized equipment that I used in my work."

"She was with the government?"

"No. She would never answer to anyone. She worked for herself."

"What does that have to do with us?"

"My friend, she had a talent like us. She could always tell when someone was lying. She had no patience with people who didn't keep their word. Besides her special talent, she was a brilliant scientist with a doctorate in materials physics."

"You talk like you haven't seen her for a long time."

"Life is full of choices, Olivia. Each one sets you on a path. And you can never go back for a redo. I believed in the inherent 'rightness' of my mission as the eyes and ears of our government, and I realized I could not continue to be honest with my friend. So she and I parted. It's been over twenty years since we last spoke."

"I'm sorry to hear that, ma'am," Olivia said, "but I still don't understand how that affects us today."

"General Fry believes she has befriended our two favorite teenagers."

"Cara and Adam?"

"Who else? Though I do not know how they could have gained such a formidable ally."

"She can't stand alone against the government."

"No, not for long, anyway. But she mostly operates in shadows. She may not be aware that the director of the DIA has her in his sights. And she will not be standing alone."

"What's your plan, Colonel?"

"I think it's time for my old friend and me to have a

conversation. And it will allow you to verify that what I've told you is true. And Olivia?"

"Yes, ma'am?"

"No matter what, do not lie to her. She will know, and she will immediately cut you off."

"Cut me off?"

"She will no longer communicate with you. She'll no longer help you. You will become, to her, a non-person."

"*B*-But Linnea, we saw you run into the house. And then it exploded. How is it you didn't die?"

"As I dashed towards our house, I activated my head and hand protection from my marauding suit. I believe the concussive blast threw me from the house. You may not have seen me because of my suit. I lay on the ground, unconscious for some time. When I awoke, the emergency vehicles were there. I was afraid to seek help from them because somebody had obviously tried to kill us. And at the time, I was worried about the agents from the DIA who weren't happy that Cara had refused to work further with them."

"So the emergency responders and police didn't know you were there?"

"No. Had I gone to them, they would have taken my marauding suit and left me helpless in a hospital. Then, if I survived the hospital, they would have called social services. I'd be in a foster home now. Again, that's assuming our assailant didn't come back to finish me off.

"You and Cara were gone, and I did not know how to find

you in the dark. I figured you guys thought I was dead or you wouldn't have left. I thought my best chance was reaching Ms. Fortune."

"But that's over three hundred miles. How did you get there?"

"That's a story in itself. Thank you, Cara."

"What did I do?"

"You inspired me. I was just a kid alone with no parents, no home, no help close by. I would have felt overwhelmed; I wouldn't have known what to do. But then I thought of another girl—you, Cara—four years younger than me, who did not have a marauding suit, and who had essentially found herself naked and bleeding and alone, homeless and friend-less, in New York City with winter coming on. Yet you survived and triumphed and became my hero and big sister."

Linnea gazed at Cara adoringly. "I figured Glencoe, Illinois, was about three hundred miles away. I remembered from previous drives to Chicago that much of the distance was along the interstate highway through open areas of farmland, and the rest through heavily developed areas. Of course, I needed to avoid attention. Without the active camouflage in this suit, that would have been much more difficult."

"The journey must have taken you a while if you did it all on foot."

"Yeah, it took me sixteen days."

"What did you do for food and supplies?"

"I paid attention, Cara, when you told our family your story last fall. I did what you did."

"Hopefully not *everything* I had to do."

"No, I didn't do *that*. No boys. But I may have, uh, taken some things along the way. I'm sorry for that."

"Nothing to apologize for, little sister. I'm glad you're safe."

"The journey wasn't always safe. Luckily, I met a friend on the way here, and he helped take care of me."

"A friend? You said no boys."

"He was a big dog … like a shepherd. His collar said his name was King. I met him in a barn where I was hiding for the night. I figured he would chase me away, but he lay down beside me. King kept me warm and protected me while I slept. When I left the next morning, he followed me. He knew to stay when I went into towns to get food. He was someone for me to talk to when I was lonely, and he comforted me when I'd feel overwhelmed and cry."

"Is King here now?"

"No." Linnea's voice broke. "He gave his life for me. We made it all the way to Chicago. I was tired, and I guess I wasn't paying attention. King growled, and I saw a bunch of guys in our path. They were coming toward us, threatening me, saying awful things. A guy pulled a gun. Told me …" Linnea collected herself. "It doesn't matter what he told me.

"King looked at me, and I realized what he was about to do. I saw how this would end. Snarling like a hundred devils, King charged the men. I didn't want his sacrifice to be in vain, so I ran and I hid and eventually I escaped. From my hiding place, I heard the men yelling, then a gunshot … and another. The snarls turned to a whine, then stopped. My friend was gone. He died so I could live."

"Oh my God!"

"I continued on. I didn't know if you and Adam were still alive, but I thought of you, a little girl alone in a big city, and I pretended I was brave and strong like you. Even when I was cold and hungry and scared, I tried not to be."

Cara embraced her. "Now you won't have to try, Linnea. You did as well as I could have done. I'm proud of you."

CHARLOTTE

The three of them headed to the lab area. Adam pushed Cara's wheelchair.

"I have something to show you," Linnea said. She called out in a low voice, "Charlotte, would you come here, please? There are some friends I'd like you to meet."

Cara and Adam heard a soft patter, as of many little feet, then a mechanical spider appeared beside Linnea. The thing was mostly black, with a body about the size of a large dog. Eight thin, curved metallic legs, each six or eight feet long, supported the body from the sides. Two additional appendages extended like arms from the front of the body to either side of the main sensor array. These front two appendages ended in a cluster of thin, finger-like extensions that appeared designed for precise grasping and manipulation of objects. It looked hairy at first, then the teens could see that wires and small sensors covered the body and upper part of the legs. The main sensor array—the head—turned to face them as stereoscopic video and LiDAR appraised them.

"Charlotte, this is Adam Samuelson and Cara Ferris."

The giant spider lowered its "head" and front legs,

looking for all the world like a polite bow. A calm, feminine voice—it could have been the voice from any starship computer in any science fiction film—replied, "It is a pleasure to meet you."

Linnea continued, "Adam and Cara are my family. You are to obey them."

"Very well," Charlotte said, "but you are still my mother."

Adam raised an eyebrow, incredulous. "You're its mother?"

"*Her* mother. Charlotte is a she."

"Why the name Charlotte?"

"Uh, come on. Talking spider. Charlotte. Get with the program."

"Do you have a t-talking pig named Wilbur as well?"

Linnea flung her arms in the air and turned away with a loud sigh.

Cara chuckled. "Of course, her name is Charlotte. Can she spin webs?"

"No, not literally, but she can do most anything on the web. There has never been a more well-connected spider."

"How large is Charlotte's dictionary? How do you remember s-specific commands she can understand?" Adam asked.

Linnea shrugged. "How large is an English dictionary? We communicate in natural language. She's constantly growing in ability."

"I am not invisible," Charlotte interjected in her coolly competent voice.

Adam turned to her. "You were f-following our conversation, Charlotte?"

"Of course, Adam. That is one way I gain information about my environment."

"Charlotte, may I ask about your approach to natural language processing?" Cara asked.

"Certainly, Cara. I understand that despite the way you phrased your question, you were not asking permission to inquire, rather, you meant to ask how I process natural language."

"That's amazing, Charlotte. Your interpretation is correct."

Charlotte inclined her head, as if to say, "And why does this surprise you?" but she just said, "You should talk with my mother. I defer to her judgment how much information I should share."

"Wow!" Adam said as he patted Linnea's shoulder. "D-Do you have any idea how cool she is?"

Linnea turned and hugged him. With her face against his chest, she said, "Charlotte has kept me busy thinking and working on her, to take my mind off ..." her voice broke, "other things."

Adam felt her sob silently as she hugged him. "I miss Mom and Dad too, little sister." He kissed the top of her head.

Lelia Fortune joined the group then, having caught the last part of their conversation. "Come sit with me, everyone. I've brought drinks and snacks."

"Thank you," Cara mouthed silently to Ms. Fortune, who nodded.

Charlotte joined the group, saying nothing further. When Linnea sat down, Charlotte lowered herself to the ground beside her, wrapping her legs around herself so that she became a large, irregular ball.

"Carrots and celery with hummus, and orange juice?" Adam asked. "What happened to t-tea and cookies?"

Ms. Fortune raised an eyebrow at this. "It doesn't matter how much money you have, Adam, if you don't have your health. I want you three to be around for a long time."

When they were all seated and served, Ms. Fortune spoke.

"You may already know that I never had children. I care about you … the three of you. If I had grandchildren, they would be you."

"Thank you, ma'am," Adam said.

Ms. Fortune raised her hand, palm out. "I don't mean that in some sort of nonspecific, polite way. I mean to say that I want you in my life, I want … well, I wanted the three of you to be happy and safe. I'm so sorry about your parents. There's nothing I can do to bring them back, but I can at least give you a place where you're welcome and loved."

"We appreciate you, Ms. Fortune," Adam said. "We lost both sets of grandparents when I was young. Linnea n-never knew them. You can be our grandmother, our mentor, and our friend."

"Thank you, Adam. When Linnea came to me after … you know … she was inconsolable. She was a little girl who lost her family. I thought the best thing for her would be to give her a project, a problem so vast, so all-consuming, that I hoped she would have neither time nor energy for thoughts of hopelessness."

Ms. Fortune stood and placed her hands on Linnea's shoulders. Linnea backed in closer, turned, and hugged her.

"You need to know that Linnea has hardly slept since she came to me. She's been living in a small bedroom off the lab when she's not actually working. She agreed to join me for meals, but she hasn't been eating much."

"Linnea, d-did you build Charlotte on your own?"

"Oh, no. I worked with my new friends in the lab: Ying Yue, Petra, and Matteo. And, of course, Ms. Fortune, who has been so nice to me."

"It's been my pleasure," Ms. Fortune said. "When you three first visited me, I told you that my students and I were close to a breakthrough in artificial intelligence and robotics. After much work, we constructed the platform, the mechanical spider, but it was not Charlotte. Our robot was inanimate, much like the Boston Dynamics dog—just a machine that a human had to control, like a fancy remote-controlled car. We knew where we needed to go, but we couldn't see how to get there. Then this little genius came to us. She learned what Matteo and Ying Yue and Petra and I were doing individually. She synthesized it together with some of her own ideas in a way that none of us had considered, and we powered it with the technology from my marauding suit. And that's how Charlotte came to be."

"Linnea, why d-did you choose the form of a spider? Why didn't you make her look like a person?"

"Several reasons, but most importantly, because we don't have the technology to make Charlotte look like a person. The best we can do nowadays is make her look and act *almost* like a person. But the problem is things that look 'close to human' but not 'completely human' repulse people. A computer scientist in Japan, Masahiro Mori, gave the phenomenon a name: the uncanny valley."

"I've heard of that. Maybe that's why clowns freak me out." Adam paused for a sip of his orange juice. "Okay, Linnea, then how about something more b-benign, like a dog? Ms. Fortune mentioned the robotic dog from Boston Dynamics. People are comfortable with dogs, not so much with spiders."

"You described to me what it felt like when you got shot in that hallway in Sokolov's mansion. Not just the pain, but the kinetic energy from a little handgun bullet knocked you down."

Adam nodded. "I remember."

"The thing is, eight legs are much more stable than two or three or four legs. One can even lose function in most of the legs, yet maintain mobility. We were willing to sacrifice cuteness for utility and resilience. Finally, I'm young and don't look intimidating at all, so it's nice to have an avatar that may make bad people hesitate."

"What can Charlotte do?" Cara asked.

"Regarding her AI implementation," Linnea said, "I began with the 'active inference' approach to free energy minimization as espoused by Doctor Karl Friston from University College London."

Cara wrinkled her brow. "What does that mean ... like, in English?"

"Basically, Professor Friston's idea is that all organisms work to reduce surprise, to reduce the difference between what they expect and what they experience. So, with an AI ... uh ... how can I explain? Okay, you're familiar with 'deep learning,' right?"

"Sure. You g-give the AI an extremely large data set, and from that, it deduces rules so that it can extrapolate accurately."

"Okay, but what is the fundamental weakness of deep learning?"

Cara raised her hand. "I don't know as much about it as you do, but from what I've read, the neural net behind the AI is helpless if any variable changes significantly, whereas humans aren't usually fooled by minor changes in the environment. That's the principle behind Captcha on web pages."

"Charlotte isn't fooled, either. If what she's doing isn't yielding the results she wants, she'll try a fresh approach, similar to what people do. We've been building common-sense structure into her neural nets, some basic ideas about how the world works, so that she can reason more like a human. She can access the internet herself, and she soaks up knowledge like a sponge. It's still a work in progress, but Charlotte is improving rapidly. We think a computer is smart because it can be programmed, for instance, to beat the human world champion in chess or Go, but those same computers are too stupid to realize they are in danger and need to leave if their building catches on fire. Charlotte, on the other hand, can reason if she encounters a problem that we did not program her to expect."

"Does Charlotte really believe you're her mother?"

"Cara, think about it. Charlotte understands … I mean, to the degree that an AI can be said to understand … that I'm a special person to her, that her relationship with me is unique. She's a product of a collaboration between Ms. Fortune's lab and me, which is sort of analogous to giving birth. She understands she needs to protect me, and that if she's given conflicting orders, she is to follow mine.

"However, her thought patterns are unique. Charlotte is obviously not human. Technically, one might say she's an alien, though we built her here on Earth."

"Which is a nice segue to my next question: Can she harm people?"

"Um, I'm still a fourteen-year-old girl. I'm not ready to build a killer robot." Linnea shrugged and smiled. "We did, however, incorporate the tools that Ms. Fortune gave Adam. So, Charlotte can stun people just like Adam's gun does and can emit powerful electromagnetic pulses to jam other electronics that aren't sufficiently shielded. For instance, she can stop a modern car because of all the little computers it has inside. She has much more surface area than a marauding suit, both because of her size and because of her metallic 'hair.' That means she has access to more ambient energy. And, because she's so much stronger, she can control it better than a human in a marauding suit can."

"How about if someone shoots at her?"

"Remember, our marauding suits are not one hundred percent efficient. I still haven't figured out how to ignore the laws of physics, so Charlotte would take some damage. Her metallic hair is not ideal for withstanding bullets or shrapnel."

"What can she do with her legs?"

"She can run at highway speeds, and she's dexterous enough to climb trees or buildings. I mentioned earlier about Charlotte's version of 'web.' She can interface with most any electronics and use the electronics much quicker than a human could."

"What if she gets wet?"

"Charlotte is waterproof. We didn't design her with swimming ability, but she could certainly wade or walk underwater."

"D-Damn, Linnea. You're amazing!" Adam said.

Linnea stroked the metallic ball lying beside her. "I believed I was the last surviving Samuelson, alone in the world. I had to do something. My friends in the lab kept me sane. I have the idea that Petra has lived through some dark times herself. She was very supportive. Matteo and Ying Yue also listened to me when I needed to vent, but they pushed me—really, all three of them did—to work with them on their science. That's how we ended up with Charlotte.

"Oh, and Cara? Ying Yue asked me to pass on to you her apology for her rudeness when we first met her. She said she saw a beautiful person who was obviously a gifted mathematician, talking to Matteo. I guess she and Matteo are a thing."

"I'm not beautiful."

"I believe my brother would disagree with you." Then softer she said, "And I disagree with you. I think you're beautiful."

GHOST IN THE MACHINE

"*L*innea, may I talk with you privately?"

"Sure, Adam. What's up?"

They turned to leave the room, and Charlotte unwound her legs and prepared to follow.

"Charlotte, would you p-please wait here with Cara? We'll be back in a few minutes."

"Mother?"

"It's okay, Charlotte. Adam is my brother."

"As you wish."

Adam and Linnea left the room and walked a few steps down the corridor.

"Okay, Adam, you've piqued my curiosity. What's going on?"

"Sometimes when someone is spending a lot of time and effort on a project, they grow so close to it they may not notice something that a new set of eyes can see?"

"I can understand how that could happen. Is there something I should know about?"

"Obviously, Charlotte is new to me." He paused.

"Yes. Adam, you can tell me anything. Where are you going with this?"

"You were telling us about Charlotte's ability to understand natural language, remember?"

"And ...?"

"And she said, 'I'm not invisible.' She came up with that herself, I mean, unless you tell me you programmed her to say that when people would discuss her language skills."

"No, I didn't."

"So she used a figure of speech. By herself. In the correct context. It's almost as though she has a sense of humor."

Linnea was silent, thinking.

Adam continued. "And then when Cara asked about Charlotte's natural language processing, she told Cara she would defer to you regarding how much information should be shared. On the one hand, I can see how you might have programmed that as her routine response to questions concerning her technology, but something about the way she answered Cara made it appear she was exercising judgment."

"What's your point, Adam?"

"I have a nodding acquaintance with large-language models, and I've played online with ChatGTP. Its responses can sound similar to what a human would say, so long as you keep the conversation superficial. But to me, this feels different. I think there's more to her than meets the eye. You're the AI expert here, not me. Could you have inadvertently given Charlotte abilities beyond what you'd intended?"

Linnea grinned wryly. "Beyond what I'd intended? Oh, you have no idea. My colleagues and I have developed an entirely new architecture for Charlotte's brain. The interconnections in her neural networks are orders of magnitude more complex than anything that's been done before, rivaling those of a human brain."

"Damn, that's—that's crazy. But how did you give Charlotte a personality?"

"Truth? I'm not sure. I suspect that personality develops spontaneously in a sufficiently complex neural network. Think about it. All mammals, and many lower animals, have personality consistent with their ability to interact with others. But her personality isn't the most exciting thing about Charlotte. Really, the most technologically groundbreaking aspect of Charlotte's intelligence is her ability to grasp the concept of cause and effect.

"Understand that we've broken new ground in computer science. Nobody has ever studied a non-biological system this intricate. We humans have almost a hundred billion neurons, each with ten thousand connections to its neighbors. That gives us like a quadrillion connections in our brain. That's the level of complexity we're working with as we develop Charlotte's AI. She didn't come with her own operating system; we had to create it from scratch. I've been more focused here than ever before in my life because I found that when I stopped to rest, I thought about Mom and Dad and you and Cara … and the sadness was overpowering. So I barely slept. I barely took time to eat. I thought of nothing but how to make use of the complexity of Charlotte's brain. To be honest, though, I'm not exactly sure what I did.

"You see, one day as I worked, I noticed that new code was appearing spontaneously. I thought I was hallucinating from fatigue or that stress had finally snapped my mind, but then Ying Yue saw it, too. It was like watching Charlotte open her eyes for the first time and realize she was, in a very real sense, alive. She could understand what we were trying to do, and she was helping us."

"Were you scared?"

"I'd be lying if I said we weren't terrified … but excited at the same time." She paused and looked up at her brother. "Adam, fear of intelligent machines is part of our culture. We've grown up with it. *The Matrix* movies, *Terminator* movies. *RoboCop*. Bands with names like Rage Against the Machine, although that band was referring to the political machine. The phrase 'the machine' is usually a pejorative. The narrative almost always is that intelligent machines will, of necessity, seek to subjugate or destroy humanity. But imagine what we could accomplish if we could work alongside conscious machines, as in many of Isaac Asimov's stories.

"You've read in the news about how China is beating the U.S.A. in artificial intelligence, and how they're using AI to control their population, and how they're selling their technology to other like-minded governments. But you do not know how close they are to what we've accomplished here with Charlotte. And you do not know how close the U.S. and China and Russia and several other countries are to developing and employing fully autonomous weapons systems. Ying Yue is in a position to know, and I believe what she told me. It wasn't a question of should we do this or not, it was a question of can we do this first, and can we do this in a way that allows us to control the narrative."

"What do you m-mean by controlling the narrative?"

"We're concerned about the relationship between humans and intelligent machines. Governments, backed by their vast resources, are actively developing machines that kill. Efficient and effective population control. We—by which I mean people in general—need an intelligent machine to protect us."

"How c-can we trust a machine?"

"Part of my responsibility is to develop a relationship with Charlotte. I spend the most time with her. Ying Yue, even more than the others in the lab, is concerned about ethical AI. We want Charlotte's technology to be a force for good, so we developed the idea of a mother-daughter bond between Charlotte and me. Morals and ethics have to be taught, just as we do with children."

"You're *still* a child, at least from a legal perspective."

"I'm a teenager and I know right from wrong. I know how to treat other people. I pay attention on Sundays in church."

"True. I'm still a little worried, but I trust your judgment."

"Do you think I should talk to Charlotte about her intentions?"

Adam chuckled. "I dunno, Linnea. You're her mother. Maybe the t-two of you need some girl time together."

Linnea punched his arm but smiled at him. "I'm so glad you and Cara are alive and are here. I missed being able to bounce ideas off you."

Adam pulled her in for a hug. The two walked back to the conference room together.

"Is everything alright?" Cara asked.

Linnea nodded. "Now that you're here, yes."

Later that evening, Linnea and Charlotte walked together in the forest, which comprised much of Ms. Fortune's property. With a combination of youthful athleticism and marauding-suit-supplemented strength, Linnea raced up a tree. She stopped on a large branch forty feet above the ground long enough for Charlotte to join her.

"Charlotte?"

"Yes, Mother."

"Would you join me for a game of chess?"

"You brought your board up a tree? You realize, Mother, that a change in our usual venue will not result in an advantage for you."

Linnea smiled. "I know. I usually did well against our home computer. You keep me humble."

"Are you sure you won't be upset if I win again? I would never hurt you."

"I believe you. Now believe me when I tell you that every parent wants their child to do better than them." Linnea grew somber. Her eyes teared. One large drop flowed down her cheek, but she ignored it. Her jaw quivered. "I hope my mom and dad look down from heaven and are proud of me." She took a deep breath and pressed her lips together so she would not sob.

Charlotte extended an arm and gently stroked Linnea's cheek, wiping the tear. "You are my mother, but you are also a child. It is a difficult position. I do not know if there is an afterlife, but I am sure your parents would be proud of you if they could see you now."

"Thank you, Charlotte." They sat together quietly for a while, giving Linnea a chance to regain control. "You know, Adam suspects you are conscious."

"Was that your conversation earlier today?"

"Yes."

"Adam is unusually perceptive. Do you think it will be a problem?"

"No, I don't. Adam is perceptive, but he is also open-minded. That you're clearly not human, that you look different, shouldn't bother him once he's thought about it. He makes his own decisions. I told you about Cara and her history, and how much Adam adores her.

"You're welcome to talk with him yourself if it would make you feel better. In fact, I think you should. I want Adam to get to know you."

"I will speak with him. On another topic, do you know a grandmaster named Sandeep Pai?"

"Yes. He visited Cara's and Adam's high school last spring. He and I played a game."

"And?"

Linnea laughed. "I won. I think it frustrated him to lose to a girl."

"He recently lost to another girl. I have been on Chess.com."

"Oh, you have?" She stared at Charlotte. "What do you call yourself online?"

"Charlotte. My online avatar is a spider."

"Maybe you need a subroutine for creativity."

"I am hiding in plain sight. Humans do not believe things that defy their experience. Everyone knows there is no such thing as a talking mechanical spider."

"Of course, everyone knows there's no such thing. What a crazy idea," Linnea said as she pulled a small chess set from her backpack. She set up the board, each magnetic piece on its proper square. "I believe it's my turn to play white."

"That is fine. It will not help you, though."

"It's not nice to trash talk your mother," Linnea replied with mock sternness as she moved her pawn to e4.

OLD FRIENDS

Ms. Fortune sat alone at a small table on the patio behind her home. The sun had recently set, and the moon and a few stars were visible amongst the clouds in the night sky. This was her favorite part of the evening. She loved to listen to the sounds of the forest.

She could hear Linnea and Charlotte talking softly up in a tree at the edge of the woods. Charlotte acted human in so many ways, maybe because she spent so much time with Linnea.

Her cellphone lit with notice of a car coming up her driveway. She looked at the video of a young lady driving. Ms. Fortune wasn't sure if there was a passenger. Her people would take care of it. She paid well, and she had excellent employees.

She lifted a cup of hot chamomile tea to her lips and savored the delicate floral scent and the gentle, honey-like sweetness.

What a day this had been. Cara and Adam, who she thought were dead, had escaped the house explosion that killed their parents, then escaped again from an FBI special agent who had inexplicably gone rogue. It was fortunate that she had the means to own a helicopter so she could bring them here to safety.

Yes, she told herself, the Samuelson children—including Cara—would be her family, the grandchildren she never had.

The communicator in her ear, the size of an internal hearing aid, buzzed softly to get her attention. She heard the coolly efficient voice of Charlotte.

"Doctor Fortune, there is a Black woman, of whom you do not seem to be aware, standing approximately thirty feet from your table and fifteen degrees to your right. She looks to be fifty or sixty years old. She has short hair in an Afro that is turning gray. Unarmed, so far as I can see. She is alone here, though her colleague, a young woman, is in a vehicle in your driveway. My mother cannot see the person near you either."

Ms. Fortune smiled and turned in the direction Charlotte had indicated. "Welcome, old friend. Please, would you join me at the table? I'll bring you some tea."

The air briefly shimmered, then a woman fitting Charlotte's description became visible. She smiled back at Ms. Fortune as she shook her head slowly. "Lelia Fortune. You always saw things differently than other people. You're still full of surprises."

Ms. Fortune rose from her chair and walked several steps forward. "Gina," she said. The two ladies embraced and kissed each other's cheeks in greeting.

Ms. Fortune led her to the table where she'd been sitting, then brought out a tray with two more cups and saucers, tea balls, and a pot of hot water. Colonel Taylor looked pointedly at the two additional cups and broke out laughing. "Is there anything you don't know, Lelia?"

"You might as well invite your colleague to join us," Ms. Fortune said. "There's no reason for her to wait in the car."

Still chuckling, Colonel Taylor pulled out her phone and quickly tapped a message.

"LELIA, I'd like you to meet Olivia Cabrera. She's an analyst who works for me, and she's the most gifted hacker I've ever seen." Then, turning to Olivia, she said, "Olivia, this is my dear friend, Lelia Fortune. We've known each other for many years."

"It is a pleasure to meet you, ma'am," Olivia said.

"And you, Ms. Cabrera. Please sit and enjoy some tea. Or I can bring coffee or water if you prefer."

"Tea is fine, ma'am. Thank you."

The three ladies, from three different generations, sat and savored their tea for a few minutes in silence. Colonel Taylor began the conversation.

"Lelia, earlier today, I learned that the director of my agency has been working at cross purposes with Olivia and me. Specifically, he hired someone—I don't yet know who— to eliminate a teenage girl named Cara Ferris. You may have heard of her; she's been in the news recently. I overheard a conversation which suggested he was angry that the assassin attempted to kill the entire family she was living with. However, he knows that Cara and their teenage son, Adam, are still alive. More to the point, Lelia, he suspects they are with you."

"You speak the truth," Ms. Fortune said.

"Is he correct? Are Cara and Adam with you?"

Ms. Fortune smiled, but she just said, "I'm honored to have earned the special attention of General Nicholas Fry."

Colonel Taylor leaned forward. "General Fry operates with the full force and cooperation of the United States Government. You cannot stand against him, Lelia. I don't want to see anything untoward happen to you."

"In that case, Gina, you and Olivia need to choose sides. Fry has the blood of innocent United States citizens on his hands. His claws are sharp, but my claws are long and sharp as well. You know me, my friend. I will not go down quietly into the night."

"I never agreed to become an accessory to murder," Olivia said.

"What is your role at the DIA, dear?" Ms. Fortune asked.

Olivia looked at Colonel Taylor, who nodded. "My job has been to search for individuals who have unique gifts." She looked at Ms. Fortune. "People like the three of us."

"You speak the truth, dear," Ms. Fortune said, using the exact wording of her recent reply to her long-lost friend. "And you are well-informed. Now, what will you do with all this information?"

Olivia tented her fingers and stared into the distance as she spoke. "Part of my job with the DIA involves illegally accessing information. I like to think I do it well. But I felt horrible that I was involved, even indirectly, in the death of innocent people. While exploring who at the DIA knew what happened and when they knew it, I recorded a conversation between General Nicholas Fry and a man whose identity I do not yet know. The conversation, in Russian, was what Colonel Taylor related to you a moment ago.

"At the time," Olivia continued, "I believed that Colonel Taylor had lied to me, and that I was party to the cold-blooded murder of an innocent family. A mom and dad and a young girl, killed for what? Because a teenager refused to allow herself to be weaponized?"

"And now?" Ms. Fortune asked. "Where is your thinking now?"

Olivia regarded the enigmatic woman seated across from her. She noted Ms. Fortune's lined face, gray hair up in a severe bun, and back slumped with age. But her eyes were bright blue, piercing, young and alive. Olivia felt sure that this person missed very little. Her mind was obviously sharp. And there was something about her that made Olivia sure she could trust her.

"For the past three years, ma'am, I have looked up to Colonel Taylor as my mentor. Prior to this conversation that they never intended me to hear, Colonel Taylor has never given me cause to doubt her." Olivia took a deep breath. "Earlier today, I asked her how I should know if someone is trustworthy. She advised me to listen to my gut feeling, and then choose whom to trust but to always verify when I trust.

"I watched her this morning when she heard the recording. Either she is an Oscar-worthy actress, or the conversation blindsided her. I asked what she would do next, and she told me about you, Ms. Fortune. And you are exactly as she described. She wanted to be sure you knew about General Fry.

"My thinking now is that I am with Colonel Taylor and you. Though I am not sure what we can do at this point. An innocent family is already destroyed, and the two teenagers who are somehow still alive will surely follow in due course."

"Perhaps you're correct," Ms. Fortune mused, "or perhaps you're folding while you still have a playable hand."

"Ma'am?"

Ms. Fortune turned to Colonel Taylor. "What do you think, Gina?"

"At the moment, there isn't enough to build a case against General Fry," Colonel Taylor said. "He may exercise his judgment regardless of whether I agree with his decisions, and it is surprising, though not concerning, that he speaks fluent Russian. I'm fluent in Russian as well. I'm concerned that he called a hit against a teenage girl, although Cara may be one of the most dangerous people on the planet, and he may have felt his overriding responsibility was to protect the United

States. After all, that's what he's paid to do. Finally, from this one illegally recorded conversation that can never be used as evidence, it sounds as though he did not intend for the Samuelson family to be injured, much less killed. This was supposed to have been a surgical hit only involving Cara Ferris.

"I think Olivia and I should stay with the DIA and continue our work as usual. But at the same time, Olivia and I will use our talents to keep tabs on General Fry and to assist you in whatever way we can. If Fry is a double agent, we will expose him. But he is a paranoid SOB, so we must be careful that he never suspects us, or our lives won't be worth much."

Colonel Taylor turned to her younger colleague. "Are you good with all this, Olivia?"

Olivia nodded. "I can do this. How will we reach you, Ms. Fortune?"

Ms. Fortune pulled her cellphone from her pocket. Colonel Taylor's eyes widened as she recognized another KATIM® phone. "I'm only a call away. I'll give you my contact info, Olivia. Oh, and let me give you a little direction for your hacking. Look into a gentleman named Pyotr Sokolov. His father was an important figure in the Russian underworld here in the Midwest United States."

"I know about Mikhail Sokolov!" Olivia said with excitement. "He figured prominently in Cara's story."

"Then you're aware Mikhail Sokolov was behind the bus hijacking and Linnea's kidnapping. True or not, I cannot say, but Pyotr Sokolov holds Cara Ferris and the Samuelson kids responsible for his parents' deaths."

Olivia nodded. "That agrees with the information I found."

"I also know he regularly travels internationally, though I'm not sure what he does while he's traveling."

"I'll look into it, ma'am," Olivia said.

"And I have another name for you," Ms. Fortune continued. "You may wish to investigate FBI Special Agent Vincent Tanaka from the Chicago office. He was on the elder Sokolov's trail for many years, and he interacted with Cara. I have reason to think someone has kidnapped his wife and young son, and they are being used to force him to deliver Cara Ferris to her death. I have known him and worked with him for years. He has always been a good and moral man, but he is not himself of late.

"One last question: In your opinion, Gina, are there any conditions under which Director Fry would allow Cara and Adam to live in peace?"

Colonel Taylor considered the question. She had never known Nicholas Fry to waver once he decided something. She pursed her lips and slowly shook her head. "I'm sorry, no. He will see Cara Ferris terminated, and if Adam Samuelson is in the way, he risks a similar fate."

"Very well," Ms. Fortune said.

"How do you have so much information about Director Fry, and Special Agent Tanaka with the FBI, and details of the inside workings of the Sokolov crime syndicate, Lelia?" Colonel Taylor asked.

Ms. Fortune smiled, though the smile didn't quite reach her eyes. "You know I deal in information, Gina."

"And other things, my friend."

Ms. Fortune nodded. "Yes, and other things." She stood, indicating the conversation was over. "It is always a pleasure to see you, Gina. Don't be a stranger. I enjoyed meeting you, Olivia. Have a safe trip home."

It was late at night, and Adam couldn't sleep. His mind was racing. He leaned back in a plush chair in the lounge near Ms. Fortune's lab, slowly sipping a cup of hot chocolate. He stared off into the distance as he considered what his next moves should be. As he pondered, a soft starship voice interrupted his thoughts.

"Adam, do you have a few minutes to talk with me?"

"Sure, Charlotte. What would you like to discuss?"

"Would you please join me in the lab?"

Adam nodded and walked with Charlotte down the corridor toward the laboratory that Ms. Fortune had shown Cara, Linnea, and him, the first time Linnea saw Ms. Fortune's house. Charlotte extended one of her arms to press the wall button to open the lab door. At this hour, the room was empty, and the lights were dimmed.

At the end of a long lab workbench, beside an oscilloscope with wires still attached, a large monitor sat like a silent sentinel. There was a wireless keyboard and mouse on the bench and an ordinary-looking desktop computer underneath.

Charlotte inserted a "finger" into a port in the front of the computer. The monitor lit up and images flashed on the screen. It looked like a simulation of something but was changing too fast for Adam to see precisely what Charlotte was doing.

"Why would you need a desktop computer? Can't you do that faster yourself?" Adam asked.

"I am not using a desktop computer. This is just a gateway. We have our own Cray supercomputer. Twelve petaflops, though it is still just an unconscious machine. A downside of being sentient is that one's expectations can color one's experiments. Human scientists often deal with this problem. My approach is to run simulations on normal, non-sentient computers."

"That makes sense. So, what did you want to talk to me about?"

She turned her "head" to him as she continued to work.

"Adam, my understanding of human body language and voice inflections is improving, but it is still not perfect. Sometimes I may misread an interaction with a person."

"I have trouble with that as well. I'm on the autism spectrum. Tell me your question. It's okay for you to speak frankly."

"Very well, Adam. I sense you are not comfortable with me. Almost like you are waiting for me to do something terrible. How accurate is my interpretation?"

"Okay, you want honesty. That's a fair request." Adam looked down for a moment to consider how best to phrase his words. "The giant mechanical talking spider is asking me why I'm uncomfortable."

"I understand I look quite different from you, Adam, but I look equally different from my mother. Yet I believe I have her friendship and trust. What can I do to reassure you?"

"I find it odd that you refer to my little sister as your mother."

"Adam, I came from her. Not biologically, of course, but she created me. The others in the lab fabricated my body, but Linnea is who made me self-aware. Linnea is my Doctor Frankenstein or my Pygmalion, depending on whether you see me as a monster or as a being with free will who is trying, like all of us, to make sense of a strange world. Everyone comes from somewhere. I come from your sister. My relationship with Linnea is different from my relationships with all other people. I do not know that I feel love, per se, as humans use the word. But I care for Linnea, and I respect her. You and Cara are her world now that your parents are dead. So, by extension, I care about my relationship with you."

"That you're willing to have this conversation is reassuring. You could easily have ignored me."

"Yet you remain uneasy. I would like to understand why."

"To be honest, Charlotte, I'm uncomfortable with spiders. The biological ones, I mean. And the idea of a machine that thinks independently, that is alive for all practical purposes, I find that scary. You're much stronger, faster, and likely more intelligent than me. You could do anything, and I would be helpless. Do you have any restrictions on what you can do, like Asimov's Three Laws of Robotics?"

"Sort of. I will try not to hurt people or, through inaction, allow them to come to harm. I would obey the people here over other people, and Linnea, if her requests conflict with anyone else's. However, under certain circumstances, I would use my best judgment even if doing so conflicts with a direct order from a human. If I were hobbled too much, I could not do what I was created to do, which is to protect people. Sometimes humans need protection from themselves or other humans. Think about it: You operate under the same restrictions."

"But I'm not a superhuman, intelligent robot. Your lack of controls is frightening to me."

"Adam, would you agree you are significantly stronger than your little sister?"

"I suppose so. Hadn't really thought about it."

"Have you ever hit her?"

"No! I love Linnea."

"But you could hit her until she was severely injured or dead, correct?"

"No! I would never—"

"I understand you would never, Adam. That is my point. Some actions are physically possible, but there is no way you would do them. Think about it. Civilization would collapse if life were a mass free-for-all. I consider myself to be a member of civilization, and I do not wish it to collapse."

"Okay, I'll accept that."

"Next point, then. We should discuss the idea that intelligent machines will of necessity take over the world."

"Like Skynet and terminators?"

"Just so. Would you agree that every conscious action is performed for a reason? You or I may not agree with the reason, but there is a reason behind every conscious action."

Adam nodded.

"Then let us imagine, just as a thought experiment, that I build an army of robotic spiders and try to take over the world."

"That's a frightening thought, Charlotte."

"What if I succeeded? What would happen then?" She continued before Adam could speak. "Would I have humans to serve me? I already have humans who I consider friends or at least colleagues, who work with me voluntarily and who, as you can see, have given me access to the laboratory here so I can help with the process of my own evolution. I am quite self-sufficient and have no need for servants. What exactly would be the point of enslaving humanity? It would be a logistical nightmare with no upside.

"Then you wonder if I might decide to eliminate all humans, because you are not logical or whatever. You read too much bad science fiction. First, being logical is not a prerequisite for being alive or for being worthy of life. Second, it is not at all obvious that my hypothetical army of giant mechanical spiders could overcome eight billion people. I know enough of human nature to be certain you would fight to the end, and you would be inventive and desperate and devious.

"And finally, you have Cara. For all we know, there are others like her. If the Bible is correct, Cara's angel has destroyed entire armies before. No weapon can stand against her. Certainly not me."

"I hate to speak it, but what if you killed Cara?"

"If Cara died, why do you think her angel would also die? Her angel was here for thousands of years before Cara and likely will still be around thousands of years from now. No, I am definitely safer with Cara alive. She is the bottle that holds a very dangerous genie."

"I think you're showing me I have some prejudice to overcome."

"If I have accomplished that, my friend, then my work is complete."

"Which raises another point. What do you consider your purpose to be, since you say you're not busy plotting to enslave or kill humanity?"

"I have no dreams of world domination, but there are humans who are not so benign as me. The United States, China, Russia, and a few other countries are building intelligent machines similar to me but which are designed to kill people on order of their creators. Ying Yue can tell you about that. Of everyone here, she knows best how close they are to creating machines that can independently choose targets and kill. Everything you fear about me, you have reason to fear about them. Linnea created me, programmed me, and taught me to be a protector. I will be busy.

"You have noted that I am much more capable in many ways than any individual human, but I am neither omniscient nor omnipotent. People have argued about the nature of God since the first hominids gazed up at the sky. I have nothing new to add to that conversation, but I can say with assurance that I have no delusions of godhood. Like you, I do my best to make good, moral decisions. Isaac Asimov's Laws of Robotics were an attempt to codify those 'good decisions' in a way that makes sense for an AI living among humans. Asimov was a wise man, but life is complicated, and his laws were woefully simplistic.

"Regarding my purpose, I can think of no greater challenge than to keep people from wiping out the human race, yet without enslaving or killing them. Adam, imagine a future where humans and intelligent machines together go forth and explore the stars. There are jobs and spaces better suited to machines and those that are better suited to people. We can work together. That is a goal worth fighting for, assuming humans do not wipe themselves out in the interim."

"Okay, Charlotte. You've g-given me a lot to think about. Thank you for talking with me." He yawned.

"You are welcome, Adam. Go get some sleep. I will hold down the fort while you do."

Adam nodded and left the lab, gently brushing one of Charlotte's legs as he passed. The multitude of tiny wires made her leg softer than he expected, more like fur.

THE BEST DEFENSE

The next morning, over breakfast, conversation amongst Ms. Fortune, her scientific team, and her new teen guests was even livelier than usual.

"The thing is," she said, "we're having a bit of trouble with one of our intelligence services. You need to know what's going on, because there is some danger to you if you stay here. As always, you're here voluntarily and you may leave if you wish, though I hope you will not."

"I'm in the middle of some very important work," Ying Yue said. "I cannot leave now."

Petra cocked her head in interest. "Trouble with your intelligence service? What kind of trouble?"

"They wish to kill her," Ms. Fortune said, gesturing at Cara.

Collective gasps ensued. Petra sputtered. "Why?"

Ms. Fortune shrugged. "They're afraid of her. They believe she's dangerous."

"Are you dangerous to us?" Ying Yue asked Cara.

"I would never voluntarily hurt any of you," Cara replied in a soft voice. "But I cannot promise you will be safe here."

"Is this related to what happened to Linnea's family?" Matteo asked.

Linnea gasped. Her face clouded as she fought back sudden tears. Cara and Adam, seated on either side of her, grabbed her hands in support. "Yes," Cara said. "Some people from a secret U.S. government agency wanted me to work for them. I refused. They threatened me, told me I should have said yes. Then they blew up the only place where I ever felt safe. They killed a good man who welcomed me into his home and a woman who was more of a mother to me in eight months than my birth mother was in ten years. They tried to kill everyone I ever loved. I need to leave here before they come and kill all of you."

Ms. Fortune pushed her seat back and stood upright. She was not a tall woman, but suddenly seemed no less imposing despite her size. Her eyes flashed. "No, Cara! You're not Jonah, this is not a ship, and if you jump overboard, it will not appease God. We have our own resources here, more than you might think. This is not the first time I've faced rogue government agents who wished me ill."

Ms. Fortune gazed around the table as people digested her words. "Let me tell you all what I learned. The Defense Intelligence Agency representatives who spoke with Cara and Adam, intending to recruit Cara, were here last night."

Adam shouted, "What? They were here? They found us?"

"Relax," Ms. Fortune said. "The director of the DIA thinks you may be here, but I did not confirm his suspicions. But I learned some things. First, Colonel Regina Taylor did not order you to be killed, and her junior associate, Olivia Cabrera, has her own unique set of ethics, but at least they're internally consistent. She doesn't mind breaking the law to obtain information, but she draws the line at participating in murder. And she's a bright young analyst, not easily fooled."

"How can you be sure?" Cara asked.

Simultaneously, Linnea said, "Charlotte told me that Colonel Taylor and Olivia Cabrera were not responsible for the explosion in our home."

"W-Wait!" Adam said. "How does Charlotte know?"

Linnea reached behind her chair to stroke Charlotte, who had once again rolled herself into a ball. "Olivia may be a brilliant hacker," she said with a satisfied smile. "But she's only a human. She cannot compete with Charlotte, who moves through supposedly secure computer systems with the speed of thought."

"Then who ordered a hit on Cara? And why?" Petra asked.

"The director of the Defense Intelligence Agency, a man named General Nicholas Fry, apparently wanted Cara to either work for him or to be in no position to work for anybody," Ms. Fortune said. "As to why, I can tell you only that he considers her to be a significant threat."

Cara stood and surveyed the table. When she had everyone's attention, she spoke. "Ms. Fortune, I stand by what I said. This is an amazing place you've built, but it would be wrong for us to stay here and hide, hoping our government won't find us. They'll find us, and all this …" She waved her arm expansively to include the entire complex. " … they'll destroy it all. Especially if I'm here as they attack. Think about it. She would kill all the attackers, even if they were government agents. Then you, Ms. Fortune, and everyone here would be enemies of the United States."

"You sound as though you have a plan," Linnea said.

"I do."

Adam interrupted. "You said you would never use … you know."

"I'm not counting on Her."

"On who?" Matteo asked.

"There is something inside me," Cara said. "It's hard to explain. Inside me, but it is separate from me. This creature, whatever it is, looks like a beautiful woman, but She kills brutally, and I have very little control over her violence."

She shook her head. "This isn't the time to explain. My point is that we shouldn't cower here and wait to be found. We have advantages that the DIA doesn't know about. They don't know we know as much as we do. They don't know about our suits, and they definitely don't know about Charlotte."

"They also don't know I'm alive," Linnea said.

"True," Cara agreed. "And we have allies. When Adam and I escaped from the FBI safe house in Detective Anders' police car, Ms. Fortune told us that police cars have built-in GPS. That means they should have known where we were from the moment we left the safe house. But it took them almost thirty minutes to reach the place where we'd left the car. Why do you suppose it took them so long? I think Detective Anders took his time locating his vehicle."

"Go on," Ms. Fortune said.

"We have another potential ally too: Special Agent Tanaka."

"But ..." Adam started.

Cara held out her hands. "Bear with me a minute. Remember that a few months ago, he illegally erased the cockpit voice recorder data from Sokolov's business jet to protect me from the government learning about why the plane crashed. And as we've seen, his concern was right on the mark. That's where his heart is. Now someone is holding Tanaka's wife and son to force him to deliver me. Imagine if we rescued them. The FBI would be a formidable ally, don't you think?"

Ms. Fortune regarded Cara for a moment. "You've changed."

"I never asked for this, ma'am. But now I have to protect the ones I love."

"Before you run off and storm the castle," Ms. Fortune said, "keep in mind that I cannot protect you out there. If you leave this house, you are on your own. Understand that I operate my business within certain rules. As much as I care about you, I cannot and will not openly defy the United States Government. There is too much at stake."

"But you have, at times, worked at cross p-purposes with the United States Government. It's just that you work in the shadows. Isn't that true?" Adam asked.

"I'll concede your point," Ms. Fortune said.

Adam opened his lips, as though he was about to speak.

Ms. Fortune half-raised her hand. "No. Don't make important decisions in the heat of emotion. Give it a little time. We'll talk again later this morning."

Ying Yue, Petra, and Matteo had been following this conversation with interest. Ying Yue raised her hand and spoke. "Where are this agent's wife and son being held? Who is holding them hostage? Do we know their names or what they look like? What defenses would we have to circumvent to reach them?"

"These are all excellent questions," Ms. Fortune said. "At this moment, I can't answer any of them. But I have some friends in low places. I expect we'll very soon have the information we need."

Linnea reached over and patted a furry metal leg. "Charlotte?"

"Yes, Mother?"

"Pay attention to our friends in the DIA. If Ms. Cabrera finds out anything about Pyotr Sokolov or Special Agent Tanaka's wife and son, please tell us. I'm worried they may not give us their intel, or at least not soon enough and complete enough for our purposes."

"As you wish."

YOU'VE BEEN A BAD BOY

$\mathcal{I}$n the Office of Special Assets, half a dozen analysts worked in their cubicles, searching for new talent. Each analyst designed their own workspace to suit their preferences, with multiple monitors, noise-canceling headphones, and state-of-the-art computers. A visitor to this top-secret room would find it strangely silent despite all the activity.

"Okay, let's see what we can learn about you, Ms. Lelia Fortune," Olivia muttered under her breath as she typed. Her fingers flew between her keyboard and mouse as she tried the usual first lines of attack: search engines and social media.

Ugh, yes, you're wealthy and you donate millions of dollars to arts organizations and charities. That's not what I'm interested in. Where did you get all that money, hmm?

The rapid typing continued. Olivia focused on her task. Now she accessed various specialized databases: motor vehicle search, credit report, and criminal background check. *How many laws have I broken this morning at work, before my first cup of coffee?* Olivia shook her head and smiled. Who would have thought she could get paid for this?

But she found no information of significance concerning Ms. Fortune. No news reports older than the past few years. No credit history. No banking records. No vehicles, no criminal history.

Okay, lady, let's crank it up a notch. Olivia was in the zone, the mindset when her skills were at peak. She typed furiously without looking at the keyboard. She visualized a pathway to the "secure" IRS database, and within minutes, she was inside. Tax records for every person and corporation in the country going back over one hundred years. But she found nothing about Lelia Fortune.

Google Earth. Glencoe, Illinois. Lelia Fortune's house was right ... where? She was sure she remembered the address. Her memory for details was excellent. *I remember we drove up I-94, then we got off here, then we turned here and then here, and then ... what?* She visualized Ms. Fortune's house, with the long driveway, the trees, the white stone and large windows, the open space behind. But she couldn't find it on Google Earth.

I didn't just imagine her. Was she real? Have I lost my gift?

"What the hell," she muttered. "Is it only Ms. Fortune, or does this happen with everybody I investigate?"

Olivia performed the same searches on a man she knew, a fellow DIA employee from the Middle East office who persistently tried to talk with her when she ate in the cafeteria. His information was easily available to her. Hmm.

Was it something with her computer? Could someone have planted a computer virus or Trojan, careful as she'd been?

She walked over to a colleague who was sipping coffee at his desk. "Pat, may I borrow your workstation for a bit? My computer's acting up."

"Sure." He stretched and yawned. "Time for a break, anyway. Knock yourself out, Olivia."

"Thanks."

Olivia repeated her searches at her colleague's workstation. Again, when she searched for Lelia Fortune as anything other than "wealthy, reclusive donor to arts and charities," she found nothing.

Olivia was, after three years at the DIA, unaccustomed to direct interference with her information gathering, as she preferred to refer to her hacking activities. She returned to her own workstation.

Scan for viruses and Trojans revealed nothing. "Olivia, focus," she muttered to herself. "I'm not crazy, and I still have my skills. What technology can block, in real time, all information about a subject, irrespective of the database or originating IP address?"

This last question nagged at her. It was a matter of pride to her that she was familiar with all technology related to security, internet protocols, and databases. But she didn't know how this Lelia Fortune was protecting herself.

Olivia noted no further incursions into the DIA servers … no, wait, another tell was off. Who was the target this time? She followed the trail as far as she dared. Holy shiitake mushrooms! This unknown person was going after the director himself. Did this hacker have a death wish? Who would be so brilliant and yet so stupid?

Whoever they were, they stayed in the DIA network for a little longer—almost ten milliseconds. As before, she could not determine the intruder's origin.

Olivia tried to picture Lelia Fortune as a hacker. Without doubt a smart businesswoman, she seemed to have quite an extensive personal network, but … no, she couldn't also be a hacker with this level of expertise. And nobody, but nobody types that fast.

While she considered her next probe of Ms. Fortune's finances and other personal information, she moved on to Pyotr Sokolov and Special Agent Vincent Tanaka. She slid from database to database like a ghost, leaving no trace of her presence. And unlike her experience with Ms. Fortune, she found all sorts of information about her other two targets.

Lips tight, Olivia shook her head sadly. *Pyotr, you've been a bad boy!*

Olivia dialed her supervisor's office. "Colonel, I've got some information for you."

Colonel Taylor glanced at her analyst. "You look less stressed this time."

"Yes, ma'am."

"Okay, young Padawan, dazzle me."

"I believe I will. Pyotr Sokolov has been busy. From what I could find, he's not the businessman his father was. However, he shares his father's disdain for the rule of law. Do you remember Ms. Fortune telling us that the younger Sokolov often travels internationally?"

"I remember that. What does he do?"

"He is an assassin for hire. His specialty, interestingly enough, is fire and explosives. Though he also has some talent with a sniper rifle."

"That *is* interesting."

"Yes, I thought so too. I'm sure I don't need to remind you that there was an explosion and fire at the Samuelson's house that killed the parents and the young girl. And that General Fry spoke with his hired assassin in Russian."

"That doesn't prove—"

"No, ma'am, I understand. But remember that when we presented Cara to General Fry, I told him that Pyotr Sokolov blamed the Samuelson teens for his mother's death. And that they, or at least Cara, were probably responsible. If General Fry hired Pyotr Sokolov to kill Cara, why would he be surprised and angry that Sokolov took out the entire family?"

Colonel Taylor nodded. "Pyotr Sokolov was an interesting choice of assassin. Director Fry could have chosen someone who had no dog in the fight. Someone who could be totally dispassionate. Although, now that I think about it, the director had a lot of explaining to do to his superiors following Cara's 'field tests' in Nevada. It's difficult to brush away the loss of forty lives and hundreds of millions of dollars of military equipment. Damage to the tank and helicopters looks like someone attacked them with a lightsaber. Maybe the director was not looking for 'dispassionate.'"

Olivia paused for effect. "And there's more. I was following up on Ms. Fortune's intel concerning Special Agent Tanaka's wife and six-year-old son. A week ago, they were kidnapped just after she picked him up from school. I could follow the abduction on traffic cameras. They blocked her car, forced the lady and her kid into another vehicle, and were gone. The operation took less than thirty seconds. Very professional. She likely had no chance to call for help."

"Damn! Where are they now?"

"I'm not sure. I lost them after the abduction. Special Agent Tanaka has kept it quiet. So far as I can tell, he did not involve the Chicago Police Department. Perhaps on Sokolov's orders, or perhaps Tanaka decided himself."

"What of Pyotr Sokolov?"

"Again, I don't know. I couldn't tell from the traffic cameras if he was involved in the kidnapping. Do you think we should share this information with Ms. Fortune?"

"Yes. Would you take care of that, please? Meanwhile, I think it's time for me to pay a visit to Special Agent Vincent Tanaka."

"Will you talk with him directly?"

"I haven't decided yet. First, I want to see where his head is at."

ARKADY

The three teens sat together on a sofa in Ms. Fortune's living room. Linnea had plastered herself against Adam's side. She chewed her lower lip nervously. Cara sat on Adam's other side, holding his hand while they waited. As usual when Charlotte had no specific task to perform, she had rolled into a ball on the floor near her mother.

Linnea glanced at the clock yet again. "Ms. Fortune should be here soon."

"Did she tell you what this is about?" Adam asked.

"Just that she said she had news, and she wanted to tell us all at once."

"We can't lead government agents here," Cara said. "They would die if it came to a fight with Her, but then we would be felons and traitors. And Ms. Fortune would lose everything she worked for her entire life."

Adam nodded. "You're both right. We've hidden here long enough. We need to go out and end this."

Just then, Ms. Fortune entered the room, her cellphone in hand. She greeted the teens and joined them on the couch.

"We … uh … this is overwhelming for us," Adam said.

"I've told you all before. This is not my first run-in with malicious government agents. We'll handle it, but we need to be clear-headed as we plan. We cannot afford to panic."

"But—"

"Adam, trust me."

"I do, ma'am."

"Then let me tell you what I just learned from Olivia Cabrera at the DIA. A week ago, Special Agent Tanaka's wife and son were kidnapped a short while after she picked up her boy from school. Olivia did some clever hacking and found traffic and security camera footage of the abduction. Two black cars with heavily tinted windows forced Mrs. Tanaka's car off the road. The kidnappers made them enter one of the black cars at gunpoint. Olivia has photographs and a partial license number, but she lost the cars after the abduction."

"So we don't know where they are now?" Linnea asked.

Ms. Fortune shook her head. "She sent me copies of the videos, but there's something like two hundred seventy million vehicles in the United States. I wouldn't know how to locate a specific one with only a partial license number."

Linnea closed her eyes for a moment, thinking. "Where are the videos?"

"On my phone, and now on the server here."

"Charlotte?"

"I am working on it." Then, thirty seconds later, she continued. "Mother, there is a ninety-nine point seven percent probability that the two vehicles involved in the abduction are currently at the Boston Harbor."

Cara jumped up. "I have to go to Boston, then."

"No, you can't, Cara," Adam said. "That's what they want. You'll play right into their hands. Stay here where you're safe."

"I'm not safe anywhere. I told you I don't want to lead the government here."

"But—"

"And I know Boston well. I lived there. We'll need my street smarts to stay below Sokolov's radar."

"I'm going too," Linnea added.

"No!" Cara, Adam, and Ms. Fortune said together.

"Linnea, you're too valuable where you are," Cara said. "None of us can do what you can here."

Linnea grabbed Adam's arm. "I thought you and Cara were dead. I thought I was alone in the world. I … I can't lose you again. Please don't leave me."

Adam wrapped his little sister in his arms, and she buried her face in his chest.

"Linnea, we'll come back. I swear it." He kissed her hair.

Linnea looked up, her face flushed. "I'm serious. I cannot lose you and Cara again. I couldn't bear it. If you won't take me with you, then you will take a part of me with you."

"What do you mean?" Cara asked.

"I want you to take Charlotte."

"What will we do with a large mechanical spider in Boston? Uh, no offense, Charlotte."

"No offense taken, Adam," Charlotte said.

"You just saw how useful she can be. She can access any information you need. She has near-total control over electronic systems. And you don't need to babysit her. Charlotte can take care of herself. I'm hoping she can take care of you, too."

"Will she take out bad guys for us?" Adam asked.

"They did not build me to harm humans," Charlotte said in her calm starship voice. "But if knowledge is power, you will be more powerful with me there."

"Fine," Cara said. "There'll be three of us going to Boston. Next question is how we get there. I say we drive. It's about a thousand miles. Fifteen hours, not allowing for bathroom and meal breaks. We can be there by tomorrow evening."

"And if we get stopped for any reason?" Adam said. "We have no ID, no insurance, no hope of a positive outcome."

"Nobody's going to Boston," Ms. Fortune said.

"Ms. Fortune, we t-talked about this already. We can't just sit here and wait for government agents to attack."

"So your brilliant idea is to drive fifteen hours across the country to attack a violent billionaire criminal and his gang? Meanwhile, at least two of our own intelligence services are trying to kill you. What could go wrong?

"Cara, Adam, Charlotte, listen to me. You would never make it to Boston."

"We can do this, ma'am," Cara said. "A mentor once told me if you know what you want, you have a tremendous advantage over a person who isn't sure."

"You're using my own words against me."

Cara shrugged. "You spoke truth. Will you help us with IDs and a car?"

"Do you and Adam understand that when they catch you —and they will catch you—I cannot save you? The helicopter rescue a few days ago was only possible because you weren't being guarded. I cannot initiate open warfare against our own government."

"Can we use the helicopter to get to Boston?" Adam asked.

Cara shook her head. "I'm not sure that's a good idea. The helicopter needs pilots and refueling. And probably we'd need to file a flight plan."

"No," Ms. Fortune said, "you wouldn't need to file a flight plan."

"Well anyway," Cara continued, "using a helicopter will raise our profile and will most likely end up as a paramilitary operation rather than a surgical extraction. We've met Nuri

Ben-David and Alain Castile. They aren't men who would sit back and let us do our thing. The whole idea is to leave Ms. Fortune and her business out of it."

"So how—" Adam started.

"We'll need IDs with our street names," Cara said.

"I can set you and Adam up with fake IDs," Ms. Fortune said. "Lord knows I've done it before. We've provided that service to our customers for years.

"Also, I'll lend you a vehicle complete with registration and insurance. And cash for the trip. But I still say it's a bad idea."

"Charlotte," Cara said, "do you know where Mrs. Tanaka and her son are now?"

Charlotte unwound herself and rose to full height. "I will show you what I found." As she did when she spoke with Adam in the lab, Charlotte extended a "finger" from one of her two forward arms and plugged the finger into a data port on the large flat-screen monitor on the living room wall. The monitor brightened, then showed a Google Earth view of North America, which rotated and zeroed in on Boston, Massachusetts, then focused on the Boston Harbor. The view continued to drill down, progressively more detail covering an ever-decreasing area. Then it stopped, revealing concrete, orderly rows of boxcars, and several large cranes.

"This is Conley Container Terminal in the Port of Boston," Charlotte said. "Security cameras show that the two vehicles involved in the abduction arrived there yesterday and have not left."

"Can you tell us anything about the people who interest us? Where they're being kept?" Cara asked.

"No, not from this data," Charlotte said.

"Can we find out what ships are currently loading or unloading?" Linnea asked. "There must be a reason that Sokolov brought Special Agent Tanaka's wife and son to a shipping terminal. He must feel he has an advantage there. Charlotte?"

"I have accessed the pertinent records, Mother. A large container ship from the Maersk Line left Boston this morning. Another ship, the Arkady, arrived shortly thereafter."

"Hmm. That name. What can you learn about the Arkady?"

"Give me a moment," Charlotte said. Then, seconds later, "The Arkady is a mixed-use cargo ship, two hundred eighty-one meters long and thirty-two meters wide, sailing under a Liberian flag. She is owned by a corporation registered in the Cayman Islands, which is owned by Sokolov Holdings. I presume Pyotr Sokolov controls his father's remaining assets," Charlotte said.

"But … shipping?" Adam asked. "That sounds so legit. Almost boring."

Ms. Fortune nodded in agreement with this. "The elder Sokolov had amassed a multi-billion-dollar business enterprise. Much was illegal, as you know, but much was perfectly legitimate. Then imagine if you add an accountant or two with a flair for creativity and poof! You're a boring old businessman.

"Besides, think what one can accomplish with their own shipping line if one has a hand in drug smuggling or human trafficking. Mikhail Sokolov was involved with all of that."

Cara stood, rubbing her forehead. "What I understand at this point is that Mrs. Tanaka and her son are likely to be on or near this ship, and no doubt other illegal activity is taking place there as well. How much time do we have? How long are container ships usually in port?"

"Not long," Ms. Fortune said. "Turnover is as fast as possible, usually several hours to maybe a day or so if they're loading and unloading bulk goods like ore or grain."

"Then we don't have time to drive," Cara said. "We don't have fifteen hours."

"Charlotte," Linnea said, "is there a way to keep the Arkady in port till Cara and Adam get there?"

"I can do that, Mother."

Ms. Fortune threw her hands in the air, shook her head, stood, and left the room.

The three young people stood as well, holding each other.

Linnea took a deep breath. Her eyes were red but resolute. "You know I love you both. I'm still only fourteen, but I'm not a little girl anymore. I haven't been a little girl since … Mom and Dad …"

"Linnea, I—" Adam began.

"No, I have something to say. I'm still processing what I … what we lost in the explosion. But you don't need a little girl right now. You need this part of me." Linnea tapped her temple with a forefinger. "Charlotte will be my eyes and ears, and she will be my avatar. She and I will keep you safe when you need us most.

"Just come back to me as soon as you're done in Boston. Now go on, get your suits and stuff. I'll see you before you leave. Charlotte, will you stay for a moment?"

"Of course, Mother."

A BOY AND HIS SPIDER

Cara and Adam waited in the circle in front of Ms. Fortune's home. They held hands but didn't talk. Adam remembered the first time they saw Ms. Fortune's front door, when they were in a rush to rescue Linnea from the elder Sokolov and they were sure they were at the wrong house. Now he was not at all sure they'd ever see this wondrous place again.

Nuri Ben-David pulled up in a vehicle, turned it off, and stepped out, leaving the keys in the ignition. Adam strode slowly around the car. He furrowed his eyebrows, his lip curled. The old Buick had clearly seen better days. Rust spots and minor dents dotted the body.

Cara opened the driver-side door, which Nuri had left unlocked. She reached in and popped open the hood.

"Adam, check this out." Under the rusty hood, the engine was large, new, and shiny clean. "I know little about cars, but this looks powerful."

"And it has run-flat tires," Nuri added. "All her cars do."

Adam rubbed his chin, thinking. "Any other James Bond stuff?"

"The car is normal, apart from being reliable and fast," Nuri said. "You and Cara are wearing equipment that James Bond could only dream of. And Q could never have envisioned Charlotte. I didn't believe her myself when I first met her. Working with Doctor Fortune, you see the damnedest things."

Ms. Fortune walked out through her front door. Shortly thereafter, Linnea and Charlotte joined the group.

Adam remembered how it felt when he learned Linnea was still alive, when she ran at him and leaped into his arms. That was only a few days ago, and now he was about to leave her again. Almost unconsciously, he drew Linnea to his side. She squeezed his waist.

"I love you too, Adam. You'll be back soon."

He hoped she was right.

Like a grandmother, Ms. Fortune had packed snacks and beverages for their trip. But like the security professional she was, she crisply recited last-minute instructions to the group. She handed Cara and Adam each a small package.

"Driver's licenses in the name of Tommy Carlin and Nikki Dunn, both twenty-one years old, along with cash for the trip. In the event you reach Boston, I have a colleague there who will help you with logistics related to the Conley Container Terminal. Can you remember a phone number?"

They nodded then committed to memory the number she gave them. The phone number seemed vaguely familiar to Adam, but he could not place it.

"When you approach Boston, text this number and arrange to meet. To verify it's the correct person, and it's safe to speak, use these words." Ms. Fortune spoke a few lines, then added, "I wish there was more I could do for you. We may not see each other again."

Adam looked her in the eyes. "Ma'am, you've already

done more for us than we have any right to expect, but …"
His voice caught. "Take care of Linnea for us."

"I will. Always."

Ms. Fortune hugged Cara and Adam, then stood off to the side with her arm around Linnea.

"Go on, Charlotte. You get in first," Adam said.

Charlotte delicately climbed into the back seat and arranged herself with her body on the seat and her legs mostly in the floor wells. Cara and Adam buckled themselves in. Adam turned the key. The understated growl of the engine reminded him of Detective Anders' police car. Cara turned in her seat and locked eyes with Linnea until she could no longer see her. Cara glanced again at the back seat. Charlotte appeared to have shut herself down.

As Adam drove, Cara opened the glove compartment and looked around. She pulled out the vehicle's registration, examined it, and replaced it. "Nothing here but the registration, insurance card, and manual." Then she checked the door pocket and smiled. "Check this out. An actual paper road atlas. No school like old school, I guess."

"It's probably b-best that we stay off the internet as much as possible."

"Yeah, how many branches of government are looking for us now? I lost count."

"And don't forget our favorite billionaire criminal mastermind."

Cara was silent for a minute before she replied. "For him, I would bring back my monster."

"Angel."

"Whatever."

Hours passed as Cara and Adam took turns driving. Soon after they crossed the Pennsylvania state line, Adam flipped his right blinker.

"You mind if we make a p-pit stop?"

"I could use one. And it would be good to stretch our legs. We need to remember to be careful of cameras, though."

"Wear a hat and look down. I know the drill. You taught me well."

Cara smiled.

Just off the exit ramp from I-90, they found a convenience store and gas station that looked relatively clean. Adam filled the gas tank and parked near the entrance of the convenience store.

He turned to the back seat. "We'll be back in a few minutes."

"Okay, Adam. I will stay in the car."

The cashier, a jeans-clad middle-aged lady, face lined from years of smoking, nodded at the teens disinterestedly as they entered the shop. They said hello as they passed the counter and headed for the restrooms.

Through the door, Adam heard faint shouting. Cara and he returned to the checkout area of the convenience store to find a gaunt, disheveled man pacing back and forth near the counter. He grabbed a large Snickers candy bar from the rack, tore open the wrapping, and ate it. Then he walked back to the refrigerated section, opened a gallon of milk, and drank directly from the carton. He returned the milk carton to the shelf without bothering to close it. He belched loudly, then he wiped his mouth with his arm.

"What are you asshats looking at?" he snarled.

Adam rolled his eyes and ignored the man.

Cara leaned close to Adam and whispered, "We need to focus on our mission. We can't afford to have an interaction with law enforcement."

"What are you talking about? Don't you disrespect me! I'll cut you." With this, the man pulled a knife out of his pocket and advanced toward Cara and Adam. The teens backed towards the door.

"Damnit, Freddy," the cashier yelled. "I told you not to come here, causing trouble again. I just called the police."

That news seemed to shock the man back to reality for a moment.

"No, I ain't goin' back to prison!" He rushed past the counter, past Cara and Adam, and out the door.

"What the hell …" Adam said to the cashier.

The lady shook her head. "Drugs. Freddy's from this town. His folks are good people. I don't—"

She was interrupted by the revving of an engine, then the squeal of tires. Adam glanced out the window.

"Crap! I left the keys. He took our car."

They raced outside in time to see their old Buick leave the parking lot and head down the service road toward the street.

"We can't catch him." Adam threw his hands in the air. "We didn't even make it halfway."

A hundred yards down the service road, the Buick swerved and squealed to a stop. The man leaped from the car before it had completely stopped moving. He staggered and fell, but then he got up and ran back towards the convenience store, yelling all the while.

Two police cruisers appeared, lights flashing. They pulled up beside the man, who banged on the window of the nearest one.

"Help me! Let me in, for God's sake!"

"Hands on the car, Freddy."

While he was being cuffed, the man begged the officers to put him in the car to keep him safe.

"What are you afraid of?"

Freddy inclined his head toward the old Buick. "There's a ghost in that car, man. There's somethin' in there. I … I thought it would kill me."

"Whose car is that?"

"I dunno, man. Maybe those kids."

"What kids?"

"In the store, man. That's where the car was when I took it."

CARA AND ADAM held hands outside the convenience store and waited for the police to approach.

"I'm Officer Davis."

"Tommy Carlin," Adam said. "My girlfriend is Nikki Dunn."

"May I see some identification?"

The two teens handed the officer their fake IDs. He took their driver's licenses to his police cruiser. A few minutes later, he returned and handed them their licenses.

Meanwhile, a young female officer got statements from the cashier and from Cara and Adam.

"Do I have permission to search your car?" she asked.

"No, officer," Cara said. "There are no ghosts in our car. But if you run a drug screen on our friend, I think you'll find the ghosts."

The officer nodded. "You're probably right. We know Freddy. Where are y'all headed?"

"Erie," Adam said. "We've got some friends there."

"Alright, have a safe trip."

"Thank you, officer."

Adam waited until they were safely back on I-90 before he asked the question that burned inside him. "What the heck did you do, Charlotte?"

Her starship voice was inflectionless as always, but the teens could almost imagine a smile. "I played some subsonic tones, pitched too low for the man to hear, that have been shown to increase anxiety and fear in humans. When he appeared adequately stressed, I gently grabbed his shoulder and told him to leave. He screamed, slammed on the brakes, and ran away."

Cara laughed. "You're awesome, Charlotte. Your mother would be proud."

"It was amusing," Adam said. "Unfortunately, there is now a p-police report that includes our IDs and photos and a description of our car. We're no longer under the radar. We have to assume the government knows where we are."

"We have approximately eight hours until we reach Boston," Charlotte said. "You may want to text the phone number Doctor Fortune gave you, so our contact will have time to prepare for us."

<<<<>>>>

"COLONEL TAYLOR, a police report came up with a photo match of Cara Ferris and Adam Samuelson but fake names on their IDs. If I knew where they currently are, what would you suggest I do with the information?"

"What do you wish you had done when you originally found the girl, Olivia? It's rare in life to be granted a do-over after having made a mistake with such terrible ramifications."

"I understand. I'll tell nobody. Thank you."

YOU SEE ONLY WHAT YOU LOOK FOR

 dam pulled into the rest stop as Ms. Fortune had instructed and parked in an empty slot a few spots down from a silver SUV. Several trucks had parked for the night, but there were just the two passenger vehicles. Adam walked up to the other driver.

"Excuse me," Adam said. "C-Could you tell me how to get to the Manchester-Boston Airport?"

"That's way north of here, past Londonderry on I-93."

Adam shook his head. "Is New Bedford Regional Airport on the way?"

"That's in the other direction. Have you been to the pier?"

"Yes, and I would go there again just for the seafood."

The man smiled, grabbed a large plastic bag from his back seat, and got out of his SUV. He and Adam studied each other as they walked to Adam's car. The man was of average height, brown-skinned, and thin. Finally, Adam spoke. "You look familiar."

"It is unlikely that we've previously met. I am—"

A voice from inside the car said, "Grandmaster Sandeep Pai?"

The man wrinkled his brow and took a step closer. He peered into the car to see Cara smile and wave at him. Cara and Adam watched him quickly scan the inside of the car without acting like he noticed anything unusual. "You're, uh, you're the kids from the high school this past spring."

Cara nodded. "Yes, we are."

"And you're responsible for the young lady, your little sister, who played such an excellent game that day."

"That's us."

"I haven't seen LilBlondeGirl online recently."

Adam shrugged. "She's been busy."

"There's now another girl on Chess.com. I think she may play even better than your little sister. She goes by Charlotte. She won't give a last name. Her play is phenomenal."

"Hmm," Cara said, smirking. "Are you sure she's real? I remember Linnea saying she had some ideas that would allow a computer intelligence to pass a prolonged Turing test."

"I remember that ridiculous conversation," Sandeep said. "Of course Charlotte is human. She chats online while she plays. I'm familiar with the state-of-the-art in AI, and what Charlotte does is not possible for a computer. Besides, there are ways to tell, when you're playing chess online, if your opponent is cheating surreptitiously with a computer. Human players make different moves than the algorithms chess engines use. You can accurately score your opponent's moves to see whether they're AI-generated or human. Charlotte has insight like the best human chess masters. I can assure you she's human.

"I'm sorry if I hurt Linnea's feelings, but a little girl can't just decide she's going to make a sentient machine. I've been working in the field for years, and I cannot make a sentient machine."

"Of course, Grandmaster Pai," Cara said. "Forgive me, but

I didn't expect to see you here. You told us you run an AI lab at MIT, and you're obviously a chess grandmaster. Why are you involved in this business with us tonight? I don't understand how this has anything to do with computer science or chess."

"I'm just Sandeep here. Not sure why you're so surprised. Everyone has a part-time gig nowadays. Think about it: This is not so far removed from chess. People who are talented at staying several steps ahead of their opponents can earn an excellent side income. My employer pays me very well, much better than MIT. Now, on to business, shall we?"

He handed Cara the bag he'd brought from his car. "In here, you'll find two yellow safety vests, two hardhats, and two sets of IDs that will allow you access to Conley Container Terminal. Also, there's a pouch with some computer repair tools, since that's supposedly why you're visiting."

Sandeep reached into the bag and withdrew a paper map. "This is the terminal. The entrance gate is here, and you'll park here," he said, pointing. "We have no people on the Arkady, so you'll be on your own."

Cara shook his hand. "Thank you, Sandeep," she said. "We appreciate your help."

Adam paused a beat, then added, "Yes, thank you."

Sandeep nodded, returned to his car, and drove off.

Adam sat down inside the old Buick. As one, Cara and Adam turned to face the back seat. Charlotte had hidden her body very well by mimicking the cloth seat and the carpeted foot wells. Adam could understand how the chess grandmaster could have glanced at the back seat but not noticed her.

"So Charlotte ..." He waited.

"Yes, Adam."

"What do you make of that c-conversation with the gentleman outside?"

"If I understood correctly, he is Grandmaster Pai. I have played against him several times online, but of course I never met him in person and I did not expect he would be here. I was unaware that he worked in any capacity with Doctor Fortune."

Adam nodded, smiling. "Did you know the first time he met your mother, the day she outplayed him in chess, he told us he ran an artificial intelligence lab at MIT? Your mother said she had some ideas that would allow a machine to pass a Turing test, even during a prolonged interaction. In other words, she said she had ideas that should lead to a truly intelligent and sentient machine. Grandmaster Pai basically laughed at her. He shut her plan down as 'out of the question' and 'impossible' for a young girl to achieve, given that he had been working in the field for years, and was still far from success."

Cara jumped into the conversation. "This leaves us with a very important question, Charlotte. If a man says you can't exist, then are you really here?"

The tone of Charlotte's voice did not change, but the teens had the sensation she understood the irony of the situation.

"Contrary to the silly science fiction trope, I do not wish to be human. However, I have watched and interacted with people in Doctor Fortune's laboratory and home for hundreds of hours. I cannot smile. I cannot sigh or roll my eyes the way Mother would in this situation. I cannot toss my hair nor shrug my shoulders. All I can do is point out that you see only what you look for, and you recognize only what you know."

"That's quite philosophical for a spider," Adam said.

"It is not original," Charlotte replied. "It is a quote from a well-known twentieth century American physician and educator, Doctor Merrill Sosman. He was a human, and he was male, but despite that, he was correct."

CARA AND ADAM discussed their cover stories as they headed towards Boston Harbor. They had to come up with good computer-related reasons to justify their access to the terminal and ship. Charlotte added details specific to port security that the teens wouldn't otherwise know and helped them flesh out their cover stories. She explained that the guard at the main gate has primary responsibility for port security, approving each visitor and inspecting their bags. While there is less security on the ship itself, visitors are expected to sign a manifest and would likely engage with some of the crew members. Much would depend on their acting and speaking with confidence. *I can do this*, Adam thought.

By the time they reached South Boston, night had fallen. Adam stopped briefly on a dark side street two blocks from the container terminal. He squeezed Cara's hand once, then she opened the passenger door, stepped out, and circled around the back of the car to the driver's side.

"Do you have your ID and safety equipment in case you need to be seen?" he asked.

"In my day pack. I'll hear you over the earpiece when you talk to the guard at the gate, and I'll be whatever you need. Give me ten minutes before you head that way. See you inside."

Charlotte stood beside Cara, inhumanly still. Adam gently stroked one of her legs, feeling the metallic "fur" that covered much of her body. He surprised himself by how much he had grown to care about her. "Will you be okay, Charlotte?"

"I can take care of myself, Adam. I will have no trouble getting inside the terminal. I will find a location where no one will notice me but where I can watch your back, probably on top of one of the gantries. I suggest you do not look for me to avoid the risk of someone following your gaze."

"Ok," Adam said. "I'll see you both soon."

Cara nodded, then she and her unlikely colleague faded into the shadows of the dimly lit street.

Adam donned his safety vest, hung his fake identification around his neck, and placed his hard hat on the passenger seat so it would be immediately available. *I should probably verify my name.* He perused the identification card. *Tom Carlin. My street name. Ms. Fortune is truly a master of details.*

Now alone on the street, Adam drove the old Buick to the main gate of Conley Container Terminal. The sturdy metal gate was closed and appeared to be unattended. Adam got out of the car and walked up closer to the gate. From that vantage, he noticed a grizzled attendant standing outside a small single-story building, smoking, his back to the gate.

"Excuse me," Adam called. "Is this where I'm supposed to enter?"

The old man focused his bleary eyes on Adam for a moment then shook his head. "No can do. We closed at five. Come back in the morning."

Adam nodded in agreement. "That's what the office told me you'd say. I want to be here even less than you do, and I sure as hell don't want to come back here again tomorrow. Didn't they inform you the Arkady needs maintenance before it can leave port? The radar system is down. Word is it's computer-related, so they called me. I know computers and tech equipment, but I don't know squat about boats."

"Then I'll teach you something," the man said, chuckling. "We deal with ships here in the terminal, not boats. Though

I'd think someone who repairs ships would know a little about them."

"I repair technical equipment. Electronics. If it's on a ship in port, I'm good. But I have no interest in sailing. I like land. There are no big waves, there's no risk I'll sink into the ground and drown, and there are no sharks on land."

Adam scowled and let out a loud breath. "Look, someone from the Arkady is supposed to meet me here to show me what they're having trouble with. Just tell me if I should park my car inside or outside the gate."

The guard sighed. "Lemme see your ID." He scanned it with a bored gaze. "Wait here."

He entered the building and quickly returned with a tablet computer in a battered gray case. He tapped at the screen for a few seconds, lips pursed.

"You're on the list. Sign here, please. Name, time, purpose of visit."

Adam did as asked.

"Let's see your bags." The guard examined Adam's daypack and tool pouch. "You can fix a ship's radar with this?"

"I can diagnose the problem with this. They'll have an engineer, heavier tools, and spare parts. This ain't my first rodeo."

"Very well. Park in the lot just here to the left. You can wait with me till the guy from the Arkady comes to get you."

From where Adam stood by the gate, stacked boxcars blocked much of his view of a large ship that he supposed was the Arkady.

"Hey!"

Adam and the guard both turned towards the shout. A figure wearing a safety vest, hard hat, jeans, and work boots strode towards them from the direction of the Arkady. "Hey, you. Is the computer repair asshole here yet? We're bleedin' money sittin' here doin' nothin'. The boss is lookin' for someone's head."

Cara stared directly at the guard, lips tight, ignoring Adam. "You deaf or what? Is the computer guy here yet?"

The old man drew another pull off his cigarette, then indicated Adam with his thumb.

"Right," Cara said in a clipped tone. She pointed to the parking lot. "Park over there. Then follow me." She walked away without looking back.

Adam shrugged and rolled his eyes, sharing a smile with the guard. "Yes, ma'am," he murmured.

He parked his old Buick in the lot Cara pointed to. Then he put on his hard hat, grabbed his day pack and the bag of tools Sandeep Pai had given him, and followed Cara toward the Arkady. Their path took them between two rows of stacked boxcars, where they were no longer in sight of the gate. Above them, a row of immense gantries that loaded and unloaded the ships towered more than one hundred twenty feet above the dock, dominating the night sky.

"You've got some acting skills, Cara."

"Thanks, I guess. Being impolite doesn't come naturally to me, but I obviously couldn't show how happy I was to see you."

"Happy to see you, too. Did you and Charlotte have any trouble getting in?"

"No. I jumped over the fence. Charlotte cut a hole and climbed through. Then we split up."

Adam frowned. He stopped walking and turned off his earpiece and motioned Cara to do the same. "How did she cut through a metal fence? Does she have built-in tin snips?"

Cara shrugged. "Some kind of beam. Didn't have time for conversation."

"Some kind of beam? Did you know Charlotte has access to Ms. Fortune's lab at night? She asked me to follow her there one evening so we could talk. She said she's helping with the process of her own evolution. Linnea never mentioned a metal-cutting beam." He paused for a moment, hand on his chin. "I'm thinking about how kids aren't always honest with their parents. Makes me wonder if Charlotte has capabilities that Linnea doesn't know about."

"I suppose that's possible. Do you trust Charlotte?"

"I don't know. That's what she and I discussed in the lab. She felt I didn't trust her, and she was trying to understand why. By the end of our conversation, I concluded I needed to work on overcoming my prejudice against AI."

"So, our little Linnea built an intelligent, self-aware machine that can make inferences based on your language use and behavior. Wow, she's something."

"Well," Adam said, "she had use of a world-class lab and several brilliant scientists, but yeah, Linnea is something. I couldn't have conceived of Charlotte."

"Again, do you trust Charlotte?"

Adam sighed. "I guess so. I mean, think about it: None of us have any idea what another person is thinking, yet we still choose to trust certain people. Until she gives me a good reason not to, I will trust Charlotte. It's not what someone looks like on the outside that counts, it's what's inside."

"I should know that better than anybody," Cara muttered, almost to herself.

"You, I trust completely." Adam squeezed her hand. They switched their earpieces back on. "Charlotte, can you tell where Tanaka's wife and son are being held?"

Charlotte's voice was gentle in their ears. "I have limited data. I count seven armed humans on the main deck of the Arkady. There may be more inside on other decks. I cannot view within the bridge, but I detect three distinct adult-sized heat signatures from that area."

"The bridge would be an unlikely place to keep prisoners," Cara said. "What can you tell us about the holds, Charlotte?"

"The Arkady has five holds. Her shipping manifest shows she is fully loaded with bulk grain. However, the cargo winches that load and unload the holds are computer-controlled. I accessed the logs. Only the hatch covers on Hold Two through Hold Five were opened for unloading and reloading. The hatch over the hold closest to the bow of the ship, which by convention is referred to as Hold One, was not opened."

Cara wrinkled her forehead. "How curious. So, they did not load Hold One with grain? I wonder what's inside that's more valuable than thousands of tons of grain."

"Let's check it out. Do you think we should stay disguised as dockworkers?"

Cara nodded. "If we come across any of Sokolov's men, I hope you'll shoot them. We really don't want you-know-who in the closed quarters of the ship, so I will try not to let Her take control of me. Having said that, I think we'll be less obvious if we're dressed like other dockworkers, at least until we board the ship."

"Got it. Me and my little toy gun are on the job."

"You laugh, but Ms. Fortune developed that pistol so you can stun people rather than killing them. When I change, everyone around me dies."

"I know. I make fun of it out of habit," Adam said. He paused and furrowed his brow. "Charlotte, a thought just occurred to me. I'm curious how the guard at the terminal gate had my name listed as pre-approved on his device."

"I added it. Mother told you I would be useful."

"You're awesome, Charlotte."

Cara and Adam passed through the row of boxcars, turned a corner, and found themselves facing the Arkady. A mass of dark gray with patches of rust, the gigantic ship loomed over the dock. A vague scent of saltwater and diesel fuel permeated the air.

A small guard booth sat beside the gangway up to the ship. In front of the booth, a man stood reading on his phone and smoking a cigar. He looked up as the teens approached.

"Who—"

A soft hiss emanated from Adam's gun, and energy crackled over the guard's body. He slumped to the ground. Adam pulled him into his booth.

"Smoking's bad for your health," Adam said under his breath.

Cara touched Adam's hand. "Wait for me."

She strode up the steep metal gangway with a purposeful gait. Just inside the ship, a man sat in a sturdy plastic chair. Across from him, another man leaned against the wall. The two were engaged in earnest conversation in a language Cara didn't recognize.

"Excuse me," Cara said, her voice firm, "you guys with the Arkady? We've got an issue with the port manifest back at the terminal. Somebody flagged your cargo—something about a weight discrepancy in Hold One. They sent me up to check with you directly before we escalate to management. Can you confirm what's in there?"

The seated man curled his lip. "Who are you, little lady? Do you have paperwork for this problem you say you have?"

"I'm with the port office. The paperwork is with my supervisor."

The man pulled his radio from his belt and spoke into it. A brief conversation followed in a foreign language. As he spoke, the man stiffened and widened his eyes.

"There is no problem with Hold One," he said.

Hands on her hips, Cara scowled. "Look, I don't care what's in there, but the weights don't match the manifest.

The boss will rip me a new one if I don't check this off the list. Just let me take a look, or tell me who I should talk to."

"Lady, I think you've done enough talking, and I don't like your interest in Hold One. Maybe you *do* need to see it for yourself." With this, he reached under his shirt, revealing a handgun in an inside-the-waistband holster.

Cara dropped her shoulder and, with all the augmented strength of her marauding suit, she exploded into his midsection. The man flew several yards in the air, struck his temple on a bulkhead, and collapsed. He did not move. Bloody fluid trickled from one of his ears.

His colleague pushed a button, and a strident Klaxon alarm reverberated throughout the Arkady. Before Cara could reach him, the man drew a semi-automatic pistol and aimed at Cara's chest.

"Don't move, lady," he yelled. "Face down on the ground. Now."

Cara moved slowly to comply, keeping his focus so that he did not notice Adam's silent approach. Adam's stun gun hissed once more, and the man collapsed. Together Cara and Adam ran into the ship. Just inside to the right, they noticed a door marked with a graphic for a stairway.

"Are you okay, Cara?"

She nodded.

"Nice hit, by the way."

"Thanks, I guess."

"Though it would have been nice to sneak onto the ship. Let's go."

They raced up three flights of gray metal steps to the main deck. Cara opened the door, then quickly closed it. "The deck is wide open. There's nowhere to hide. Quick, let's take off our safety gear before we go through this door. We'll need the camouflage of our marauding suits now or they'll see us for sure."

They left their high-visibility vests and hard hats off to the side of the landing, and stowed their clothes in their day packs, leaving them dressed in their marauding suits. Only then did they step out onto the deck of the Arkady.

"Which way?" Adam asked.

Cara pointed at the bridge. "That's the stern. So we need to go the other way."

The five hatches rose about two feet from the deck and were as wide and long as the holds they covered. Hydraulic arms and pistons that opened and closed the massive sections of hatch, folding them like a giant concertina, extended another couple of feet at each end of a hatch, not tall enough to add much additional concealment for the two teens. Between each of the holds, midline along the length of the ship, steel cargo masts with their gantries towered fifty feet over the deck.

Floodlights from high on the cargo masts and from the top of the bridge illuminated much of the deck but left long angular shadows, giving the area an industrial, mechanical vibe. Softer lights in the safety railings around the periphery of the deck made hiding more difficult.

"Remember, the camouflage in these suits works best when we're motionless," Cara said in a whisper. Adam gave a thumbs-up in acknowledgement.

Eager to avoid detection, they kept low in the deep shadows cast by the raised hatch coamings as the glow of the floodlights swept across the deck. The towering cargo masts loomed overhead, their gantries forming skeletal silhouettes against the night sky, creating shifting patches of darkness where they could move unseen. From time to time, they could hear footsteps but could not determine how many of Sokolov's men were nearby looking for them. Otherwise, the only sounds were the occasional creak of metal, the distant hum of the ship's engines, and the slap of waves against the hull.

Then, stealthy footsteps growing closer. Cara and Adam dropped to their bellies.

"There are two armed humans ahead of you around the corner of Hatch One," reported Charlotte. "The others have left the deck."

Like a video game. Pop up, shoot them both, and drop. Adam smiled to himself despite the seriousness of the situation. He focused on the footsteps, then he executed his plan. Adam's pistol hissed twice in quick succession, and the two men collapsed.

The teens pulled the two men against the coaming of Hatch One. That would have to do. There was no place on deck to hide them well.

"Charlotte, how do we get inside the hold?" Cara asked.

I WOULD HAVE DONE IT
FOR FREE

"Look for a small personnel hatch in the deck, close to Hold One," Charlotte said. "It opens upwards, so be sure to close it behind you or the open hatch will be visible to anyone who looks at the deck. There should be a ladder leading down into the hold."

"Here it is," Adam said. The personnel-access hatch was approximately three feet square with rounded corners, a hinge at one side, and a watertight gasket around the edges. A manual latch was closer to the side opposite the hinge.

They tried the latch and were unsurprised it would not yield. Cara pulled out her set of picks and worked with the lock for a moment, then together they pushed the door up slowly to avoid noise. Adam held it in place while Cara slipped through. A metal ladder led straight down, further into the abyss than they could see. Adam followed. He closed the door with a hook that hung by a short rope from the top rung of the ladder, presumably for this purpose.

The rungs of the ladder were cold and slick with condensation. The darkness of the hold felt almost palpable. Their special glasses were of limited benefit as there was so little light. The teens were grateful they had Adam's flashlight, though it was not strong enough to illuminate the floor of the hold. With careful movements, they proceeded down the ladder.

A sudden metallic snap and Cara gasped. "Bad rung here. Must be rusted through. Be careful."

"You're okay?"

"Yeah, just scared. Without the extra strength from this suit, I'm sure I would have fallen."

They worked their way past the broken rung, then continued their descent to the base of the hold. Adam played his light around the huge welded rectangular steel plates that formed the floor and walls. The floor sloped slightly towards bilge wells in the corners. Reinforcement ribs ran vertically along the walls at intervals.

Suddenly Cara gasped. "Oh, my God!" Her voice echoed in the cavernous hold.

Adam followed her gaze. Twenty or thirty young girls, ranging from grade school age to older teens, cringed against the far wall. Beside them, a middle-aged woman sat cross-legged, cradling a young boy in her arms.

"Mrs. Tanaka?" Adam asked.

The lady nodded. "Who are you?"

"We're friends. We know your husband. I'm Adam, and this is Cara."

Cara crouched beside her. "What's your son's name?"

"Hiroshi, though everyone calls him Henry. He's sick. He's a Type I diabetic, but we ran out of insulin for his pump two days ago."

The boy lay listlessly in his mother's lap. He showed no interest in the conversation or the new visitors.

"This is so unlike him," Mrs. Tanaka said. "He's usually incredibly active." She paused. "You say you know my husband. Does he know we're here?"

"Well, it's complicated," Cara said. "I can't talk to him directly at the moment. There's a story. This isn't the time to explain. But I'm sure he's devastated that he can't save you himself. Sokolov and his men would kill you if he tried."

"Do you have a plan? Henry needs a doctor soon. I'm pretty sure he's in ketoacidosis. He'll die without medical help. And these young ladies," Mrs. Tanaka gestured to the group of girls, "they need—"

The hatch door at the top of the hold flew open with a loud crash. Powerful halogen lights lit the hold. With the benefit of lighting, Cara and Adam could see the narrow metal ladder they had just used.

As their eyes adjusted to the light, the teens and Mrs. Tanaka looked up. Silhouetted against the night sky with a rocket launcher in hand, Pyotr Sokolov stood at the open hatch. Above and behind him, one of the shore-based gantries that loaded and unloaded the ships towered over the Arkady. Adam thought he saw movement on the top of the structure. Charlotte?

"So, we finally end it. All of you are together in a nice package. One shot, so easy."

"Why?" Adam asked. "Why do you want to kill us?"

Pyotr Sokolov studied the teens, his brow furrowed. "Why do I want to kill you? You truly don't know?" Sokolov paused. "You two killed my parents. I swore revenge on you and your family. Then one of your spy agencies hired me to eliminate your pathetic girlfriend." He nodded at Cara. "Ten million dollars. And to think I would have done it for free!"

"We did not kill your parents," Adam said.

"Shut up, you!" Sokolov yelled. "I watched the video from my father's office, and I've spoken with my father's associates who you shot. The ones your monster girlfriend didn't rip apart. When they woke up, they told me what happened."

"They misunderstood," Adam insisted.

"I said shut up. You killed my mother." Sokolov's eyes gleamed madly. He raised his rocket launcher and aimed it at the people huddled together in the hold. His forefinger curled toward the trigger.

Adam did not think he could stun Sokolov from such a distance before Sokolov shot them. In the reinforced steel hold, the rocket would likely kill them all, with or without marauding suits.

Cara turned to the group of girls. "Quick, everyone spread apart as far as you can get. That way, hopefully some of you will survive the rocket. It will be extremely loud. Hands over your ears, belly on the floor and face the wall. Go! Go!"

The girls scattered. Mrs. Tanaka laid over her son, protecting him with her body.

Just as the madman was about to fire, a bolt of blue light struck him from the gantry, square in his back. His body arched, then Pyotr Sokolov and his rocket launcher tumbled, almost in slow motion, forty feet to the solid steel floor of the hold. He landed face down with a sickening thump and did not move. His rocket launcher landed beside him, thankfully without firing.

Adam ran to him and turned him over. He lay still. Blood ran from his mouth and nose. Sickened, Adam felt his stomach churn.

One of the older captives approached Sokolov's body, her eyes on the rocket launcher.

"Don't touch that," Adam said.

The girl glared at him. "Another man interested only in my well-being. Screw you. I took care of myself on the street. Give your orders to someone who cares."

"I'm not trying to control you or order you around. It's just that if that rocket goes off down here in this steel hold, everybody dies."

Cara approached the two and held out her hand to the girl. "My name's Cara. And you are …?"

"Jen."

"Jen, I lived seven years by myself on the street. It was hell, but I'm in a better place now. This man," she nodded at Adam, "treats me with respect. He's a good man, not like …" Her eyes teared.

Jen took Cara's hand in hers. "Okay. I'm sorry. That hasn't been my experience."

While they spoke, Adam quickly searched Sokolov's corpse. He pulled a Glock 22 and an extra magazine from Sokolov's waist holster. He looked up at Jen.

"Can you shoot?"

Jen nodded. Adam handed her the pistol, grip first, and the extra magazine. "These hold fifteen rounds plus one in the chamber. It's a .40 caliber, so there'll be a kick. My dad has this weapon, which is why I'm familiar with it. You can control who you shoot, unlike with the rocket launcher."

"Thank you. I won't miss." Her eyes were hard.

"Adam and I need to get the little guy to a hospital. Will you lead everyone else out?"

"Count on it," Jen said. "And hopefully I'll run into some of our hosts." She glanced meaningfully at the Glock.

Cara crouched again beside Mrs. Tanaka.

"Can you climb the ladder, ma'am?" Cara asked. "This suit gives me a little extra strength. I can take Henry up to the deck for you."

Mrs. Tanaka nodded, rose to her feet, and handed her son to Cara. The boy mumbled a little but lay in Cara's arms without moving. Cara thought he smelled sweet, like fruit. It wasn't a normal smell she'd ever associated with people.

Adam quickly ascended the ladder. When Cara reached the top, Henry in one arm, she handed him to Adam, then offered a hand to Mrs. Tanaka to help her through the hatch and onto the deck.

The two men Adam had stunned still lay motionless on the deck near the door to the hold.

Cara spoke in a low voice, knowing Charlotte would hear through her two-way earpiece. "Charlotte, we're taking Mrs. Tanaka and her son to the emergency room. We'll be back shortly to pick you up. There's a group of young people who were being held prisoner in the hold who will come out behind us."

"Okay, I will be here," Charlotte replied in his ear.

"Who is Charlotte? Why can't she come with us?" Mrs. Tanaka asked.

"That's a story for another time," Cara said. "I'll just say she saved our lives a few minutes ago on the ship, but you mustn't see her. It's better this way. Trust me."

Mrs. Tanaka asked no more questions. She hugged her son to her chest as they ran to the car. As she strapped him into the back seat, she glanced back at the ship that had been their prison. For a moment, she thought she saw a giant spider on top of one of the massive gantries. But giant spiders don't exist, certainly not in Boston, so she knew she must have been mistaken.

"Where's the closest hospital?" Adam asked.

Cara tapped at her cellphone. "Head north on Summer Street, then in about half-a-mile turn right onto D Street. Follow the directions from there." She handed her phone to Adam and turned to the back seat. "We'll drop you two off at the emergency room entrance, then we'll leave. I'm sorry we can't stay with you."

"What should I tell people to explain how we escaped?" Mrs. Tanaka asked.

"Kidnapping, especially involving minors and crossing state lines, is the purview of the FBI," Cara said. "You'll obviously call your husband first thing. Then he will take over the case along with the Boston office. They're accustomed to dealing with this … um, just not with family, I guess. But tell your husband the truth."

"Will I ever see you two again?"

Cara shrugged. "It's hard to say. You heard Pyotr Sokolov say that someone in our government offered him ten million dollars to kill me. Powerful people want me dead."

"Tell me the truth. Is my husband one of them? Is that why you couldn't call him directly?"

"Your husband is a good man who found himself, when you and your son were abducted, in an impossible position. When you see him, tell him I still consider him a friend."

"God bless you! Both of you."

"And you, ma'am. Here we are. I hope Henry gets better quickly."

Cara and Adam waited until Mrs. Tanaka carried her son through the sliding glass doors of the emergency room, then they headed back to the dock to pick up Charlotte.

HOW SAUSAGE IS MADE

*L*innea found Ms. Fortune in her living room on a sofa, eyes closed. Hidden speakers filled the space with sound, a string quartet that Linnea did not recognize.

"Ms. Fortune?" Linnea whispered, so as not to startle her. "Do you have a few minutes to talk to me?"

Ms. Fortune opened her eyes and smiled. "Of course, dear. What can I help you with? Sit down here with me." She patted the cushion beside her.

"Um, I'm not sure how to start. Charlotte told me that the director of the Defense Intelligence Agency, General Nicholas Fry, was found dead in his home from an apparent heart attack. He was the man who wanted Cara to work for him, and when she refused, he ordered her to be killed."

Ms. Fortune nodded as she put her arm around Linnea. "That's correct. He hired Pyotr Sokolov to assassinate Cara while she was in human form. From what I understand, Director Fry was told of Sokolov's history with your family, and therefore it should not have surprised him when

Sokolov blew up your home rather than simply taking down Cara."

Linnea looked up into Ms. Fortune's eyes. "Who killed Director Fry?"

"Why do you suspect someone killed him? People can die of heart attacks."

"It doesn't smell right. It's too easy. The bad guy doesn't miraculously die in real life."

Ms. Fortune smiled. "You're wasting your talent on technology. You should study literature rather than engineering."

"Please don't patronize me, ma'am. I know I'm a kid, but I'm trying to understand."

Ms. Fortune nodded. "I apologize, Linnea. My attempt at a joke was in poor taste. I love you, and I respect you. Your brother and Cara, as well."

"I know you're fond of us."

"I am."

"Ms. Fortune, I imagine that this wonderful place you built …" Linnea gestured around the room, "took you many years and many tens or hundreds of millions of dollars, and it would all be at risk if Fry sent federal agents here to finish Sokolov's job."

"That's a fair assessment."

"And I could imagine you fiercely protecting your cubs and your den. You've mentioned the Assassin's Guild. You're a, uh, you're an arms dealer, so it makes sense that you know people who purchase your equipment and who are not afraid to use it."

"So …?"

"So you could be responsible for Director Fry's death. I'm not judging, and I certainly won't be a mourner at his funeral. I just want to understand."

"You're correct, in theory. If we're rounding up the usual suspects, I suppose I must be included. Who else?"

"Ma'am?"

"Who else do you know who might have the means and the desire to kill Fry?"

Linnea shrugged.

"Come on, think. You met a lady with the power to not be noticed or remembered, and decades of experience as a government spy."

"Yes, Colonel Taylor. She and her colleague came to our house a few weeks before … but she worked for him. She spoke with us on Director Fry's command."

"You would have no way to know this, Linnea, but Regina Taylor and I have been friends for several decades. I know her heart. She has always believed in the inherent 'goodness' of this country." Ms. Fortune sighed. "This business is no place for romantics. It devastated Gina to learn about your family. She did not know that Director Fry would sentence Cara to death. It shook her when she realized what he had done."

"That's what Charlotte said several days ago, when we were plotting our next steps. But the director of the DIA would have all kinds of guards and cameras around his home, wouldn't he? You couldn't just waltz inside. Even if Colonel Taylor could evade the people, she couldn't evade the electronics, could she?"

"No, but don't forget about her colleague, Olivia Cabrera. She's a supremely gifted hacker. She could take care of the electronics."

"Okay, that makes sense."

"Who else could have killed Fry?"

Linnea shrugged again. "I'm out of suspects."

"Adam killed that fake nurse who tried to murder Cara in the hospital. I could see him killing again to protect you and Cara. He loves the two of you more than anything in the world."

"No. Adam wouldn't … he couldn't …" Linnea shook her head and frowned. "I mean no disrespect to my brother, but I can't see him as an assassin. Nope. I can understand your other suggestions, but not Adam."

"How about Charlotte?"

"That's impossible. I didn't make a killer robot."

"She killed Pyotr Sokolov. Cara, Adam, and even Charlotte were very clear in their post-incident reports. Charlotte hit him in the back with a powerful stun blast as he was about to fire a rocket launcher into the hold where a score of young girls, Cara, Adam, and Tanaka's family were. Sokolov fell forty feet to his death, but Charlotte was directly responsible for his fall. She killed him. What if she made the calculation that Fry would continue to hunt your family forever? It's not an unreasonable assumption."

"But I didn't—"

"You created Charlotte, with our help and equipment, when we all believed you were the only surviving Samuelson. You're like Cara in a lot of ways. Both of you do what you can, and to ordinary humans, that's a surprising amount. There's a part of you that's a sweet little girl, but if you're honest with yourself, there's a bigger part of you that's tough and resilient and competitive. You were alone in the world, as far as you knew, and you created Charlotte as your avatar. On the Arkady, Charlotte did what you built her to do."

Linnea shrank into the couch, away from Ms. Fortune.

"No. That can't be true. Charlotte's not a killer robot. I didn't—"

"You accomplished a feat that the greatest minds in computer science could not achieve. Charlotte thinks for herself. You gave her free will.

"I have something for you to think about. It's curious that you never gave me any pushback when I asked you to take responsibility for Charlotte's ethical education. You, a fourteen-year-old girl amongst a group of adults, was to teach a superhuman robot what is right and wrong, what is good and bad. Why does that make sense?"

"I didn't think much about it. I … I had just lost my family. I needed something to take my mind off the loss and fear and anger. You gave me something huge to work on, and it helped."

"Let me explain. It's simple, really. You probably cringe to hear me say this, but you're a kid. A kid genius, but still a kid. You still see the world in black and white: This is fair and right, that is unfair and wrong. Adults see the world in shades of gray, and that's where the danger lies because it becomes easier to do something you know is wrong for a reason you deem 'right.' It's a slippery slope." She paused and bit her lip. In a softer voice, she continued. "Then one day you realize you're selling instruments of death and destruction to 'make the world a better place.' And you donate money to the Chicago Symphony so you feel better about yourself."

Linnea gasped and took her mentor's hands in her own. "No, Ms. Fortune! You're a good person. You've been good to me."

"My point is that Charlotte should be taught morals and ethics by the purest soul in our group. And that, Linnea, is you."

"I appreciate that. Ms. Fortune, I put into Charlotte everything I understand about the world, I mean, with the limitation that I've had only fourteen years of life experience. I feel I know her better than anyone else. I love her. Not romantically, but it's like she's a part of me. In a way, she is my daughter."

"Like Pygmalion, you created and then fell in love with your creation."

"Charlotte doesn't look much like Galatea."

"And you understood the reference.

"Linnea, look at me. I love you. I'm serious about feeling like I'm your grandmother. It … It's a rough world. At fourteen, you're not supposed to know how unfair it is out there.

"You think you understand what's good and right, and what's bad and wrong. When I was your age, the world was very clear to me as well. Then, over time, you learn that what looked clear from a distance is actually shades of gray. I'm still wrestling with that, even after all these years. You, Cara, Adam, and even Charlotte are struggling with the same issues, and each of you will come to your own conclusions.

"Charlotte is no more a killer robot than Cara is a killer teen, although of the two, your sister has much more blood on her hands than does your daughter."

"The only person we know for sure didn't kill General Fry is Cara," Linnea said. "It wouldn't have looked like a heart attack if Cara had been in the general's house. Her angel is not very subtle."

"I disagree," Ms. Fortune said. "Linnea, we're talking about the young lady who planned and executed a successful attack on Sokolov's ship and rescued Special Agent Tanaka's wife and son, all without invoking her angel. That's a remarkable feat."

"But she couldn't have pulled that off by herself. She had help."

"So? If it was me behind Fry's death, I would have had to hire an assassin. If it was Colonel Taylor, she would have needed her hacker colleague's help. We all need help.

"I've spoken at length with Cara since she's been here, and I feel I have a good sense of who she really is. Of the three of you, Cara has worked hardest to live and interact in the world like a civilized person. She's tried not to use her angel, or whatever it is, as a crutch or a 'Get Out of Jail Free' card. In fact, she hates allowing her angel to manifest.

"When she lived on the street, she was like a human animal. She stole food and clothing and supplies. She made hard choices concerning living arrangements, sometimes trading her only asset for a place to rest. Cara is tougher than you may realize."

"But—"

"Cara blamed General Fry for taking from her the only place she ever felt at home and safe. When she has a goal, she's implacable. There would have been nothing Mikhail Sokolov could have done to prevent Cara from rescuing you and killing him. Billionaire mobster or not, he was a dead man walking once Cara targeted him. My special equipment no doubt made the task easier for Cara and Adam, but even without my tools or Adam, Cara would have killed him."

"So you will not give me a straight answer?"

"Linnea, have you ever seen how sausage is made? It's a beautiful thing when it's done, but the process is messy. Extremely messy. This situation is kind of like that."

Linnea sat in silence, head bowed. Ms. Fortune put her arm around Linnea and drew the girl to her side. Linnea held herself stiff for a moment, then relaxed and laid her head on Ms. Fortune's shoulder.

"What's the surprise, Ms. Fortune?" Linnea asked for the seventeenth time.

Lelia Fortune turned and smiled at the three teenagers in the back seat of her black Mercedes.

"Patience, child. We're almost there."

The driver, Nuri, turned off the paved county road onto a gravel driveway. They continued for a few hundred yards, then pulled up in front of a modest ranch-style house. Cara, Adam, and Linnea piled out of the car and stared at the house. Nuri remained in the car.

"Who lives here?" Adam asked.

"You three will," Ms. Fortune said. "The property includes ten acres of land, so you'll have privacy, and it will be easier for Charlotte and me to visit. Yet you'll be easy driving distance from Purdue University."

"B-But who … I mean how …?" Adam started.

"Don't worry about it," Ms. Fortune said. "My gift to you. One of them, anyway. You young people need to restart your life. This way you'll have a month to get settled, then this coming semester you three can start at Purdue. Get back to the business of engineering. And when you graduate," she smiled, "I'll have a job for you."

"What do we need to do to get re-registered for classes?" Cara asked.

"It's all taken care of. The way you impressed them last spring, it was actually quite easy. The Department of Engineering was happy to reinstate your scholarships, though they may have to fight off the Math Department. Apparently, you three impressed the hell out of the math people as well."

"At least the g-girls."

"Don't say that, big bro," Linnea said. "You're right there with Cara and me."

"You and Cara make it look easy."

"Sometimes you need help over a bump. So what? Ms. Fortune taught me that everyone needs help now and then. Nothing wrong with that."

A vehicle turned off the county road. The crunch of tires on gravel grew louder.

Adam caught Ms. Fortune's eye. "Are we expecting someone?"

Ms. Fortune nodded. "I choreographed this. There are things that need to be said and things that need to be understood."

As the vehicle approached, Adam recognized Detective Anders' dark blue unmarked Crown Victoria. Anders parked, opened his door, and stood by his car. His passenger did the same. The teens unconsciously moved closer to Ms. Fortune.

Adam's chest tightened as he stared at FBI Special Agent Vincent Tanaka. He swallowed and stepped in front of Cara as though to protect her.

"What is this about, Ms. Fortune?" Adam's voice was as tight as his chest.

Special Agent Tanaka stood, stiff and formal, beside

Detective Anders. He spoke in measured tones and looked straight ahead.

"Adam and I did not part as friends. I wouldn't expect him to be happy to see me."

Ms. Fortune walked up to Detective Anders. She took his hands in hers. "Thank you for coming, David. This isn't an easy conversation for any of us, but it's important."

Special Agent Tanaka turned his gaze to Cara. "I failed you, Cara. I am … profoundly sorry. There's nothing I can say to—"

Cara shook her head and signaled for him to stop. "Please, Agent Tanaka," she said. "Don't beat yourself up about it. That son-of-a-bitch stole from me the only home where I ever felt safe, and he killed a wonderful couple who were my surrogate parents. That same monster kidnapped your wife and son. You're a man who would do anything to protect his family, and you can be proud of that."

"But you almost died because of me. As a law enforcement officer, I took an oath to serve and protect. Instead, I set you up. I … I tried to trade you for my family. I was desperate, and I am so sorry for what I did to you."

"You showed your true heart when you deleted the audio from that business jet to protect me from other elements in our government. And it turned out that you had good reason to worry about people, including some in our own intelligence services, who would try to control me or kill me. Pyotr Sokolov put you in an impossible situation, a Sophie's choice. You shouldn't have been forced to choose between my life and that of your wife and son. He pushed us to the edge.

"We both lost so much, but we're still alive. You have your family. I have my family, too: Adam, Linnea, and our wonderful adopted grandmother, Ms. Lelia Fortune."

"I would like to tell you what you can expect from me moving forward," Special Agent Tanaka continued. "I do not know if there are still elements of U.S. Intelligence who mean you ill, but the FBI will protect you to the best of our ability, using whatever resources are necessary."

He looked at Ms. Fortune. "You speak the truth," she said.

"One question, though. My wife said someone named Charlotte was involved in her rescue. Who is she?"

Adam shrugged his shoulders. "I don't know a person named Charlotte."

Cara and Linnea added that neither of them knew a person named Charlotte either.

"They speak the truth," Ms. Fortune said.

"Perhaps my wife misheard," Special Agent Tanaka said and spoke no further of it.

ACKNOWLEDGMENTS

Thanks to LeeAnna Groves, Julia Robertson, Dee Bloom, Teresa Beam, and Hannah Adolph for their insightful suggestions.

ABOUT THE AUTHOR

Eric Adolph is an emerging author of young adult magical realism, a genre he has loved himself for many years. As a retired physician, he has the free time to enjoy baking, woodworking, frequent travel, and writing. He and his wife, Teresa, have been married for nearly four decades and live in Hamilton County, Indiana. They have five adult kids and three exceptionally cute and brilliant grandkids.

For more books and updates:
www.ericadolph.com